Thomas Bernhard

THE LIME WORKS

Thomas Bernhard was born in Holland in 1931 and grew up in Austria. He studied music at the Akademie Mozarteum in Salzburg. In 1957 he began a second career as a playwright, poet, and novelist. The winner of the three most distinguished and coveted literary prizes awarded in Germany, he has become one of the most widely translated and admired writers of his generation. He published nine novels, an autobiography, one volume of poetry, four collections of short stories, and six volumes of plays. Thomas Bernhard died in Austria in 1989.

INTERNATIONAL

ALSO BY THOMAS BERNHARD

THE LIME WORKS

THE LIME WORKS

Thomas Bernhard

TRANSLATED FROM THE GERMAN BY SOPHIE WILKINS

VINTAGE INTERNATIONAL
Vintage Books
A Division of Random House, Inc.
New York

FIRST VINTAGE INTERNATIONAL EDITION, MARCH 2010

Translation copyright © 1973 by Alfred A. Knopf, Inc.

All rights reserved. Published in the United States by Vintage Books,
a division of Random House, Inc., New York, and in Canada by
Random House of Canada Limited, Toronto. Originally published in
Germany as *Das Kalkwerk* by Suhrkamp Verlag, Frankfurt am Main, in 1970.
Copyright © 1970 by Thomas Bernhard. This translation originally
published in hardcover in the United States by Alfred A. Knopf,
a division of Random House, Inc., New York, in 1973.

Vintage is a registered trademark and Vintage International and
colophon are trademarks of Random House, Inc.

The Cataloging-in-Publication Data for *The Lime Works* is on file
at the Library of Congress.

Vintage **ISBN**: 978-1-4000-7758-8

www.vintagebooks.com

But instead of thinking about my book and how to write it, as I go pacing the floor, I fall to counting my footsteps until I feel about to go mad.

THE LIME WORKS

. . . when Konrad bought the lime works, about five and a half years ago, the first thing he moved in was a piano he set up in his room on the first floor, according to the gossip at the Laska tavern, not because of any artistic leanings, says Wieser, the manager of the Mussner estate, but for relaxation, to ease the nervous strain caused by decades of unremitting brain work, says Fro, the man in charge of the Trattner estate, agreeing that Konrad's piano playing had nothing to do with art, which Konrad hates, but was just improvisation, as Wieser says, for an hour first thing early in the morning and another late at night, every day, spent at the keyboard, with the metronome ticking away, the windows open . . .

. . . next, Konrad bought a lot of guns, partly from fear but also because he had a passion for firearms, second-hand rifles mostly but in prime working order, from the estate of Forestry Commissioner Ulrich who died last year, well-known makes like the Mannlicher etc., which Konrad, an extremely shy man (Wieser), full of apprehension that tended to grow into panic ever since the landowners Mussner and Trattner were mysteriously murdered not so long ago, felt he needed to protect the lime works against burglars and in general against what he called *outsiders* . . .

. . . Konrad's wife, whose maiden name was Zryd, a woman almost totally crippled by decades of taking the wrong medications, and who had consequently spent half her lifetime hunched over in her custom-built French invalid chair, but who is now, as Wieser puts it, out of her misery, was taught by Konrad how to use a Mannlicher carbine, a weapon the otherwise defenseless woman kept out of sight but always within reach, with the safety off, behind her chair, and it was with this gun that Konrad killed her on the night of December 24–25, with two shots in the back of the head (Fro); two shots in the temple (Wieser); abruptly (Fro) putting an end to their marital hell (Wieser). Konrad had always been quick to fire at anything within range of the house, they say at Laska's, and as everyone knows he did shoot the woodcutter and game keeper Koller who was passing by on his way home from work one evening about four and a half years ago; quite soon after Konrad had moved in, carrying his knapsack and a hoe, and catching it in the left shoulder because Konrad mistook him for a burglar; for which shooting Konrad was in due course sentenced to nine and a half months at hard labor. The incident brought to light about fifteen previous convictions of Konrad's, mostly for libel and aggravated assault, they say at Laska's. Konrad served his time in the Wels district prison, where he is being held again right now . . .

. . . apart from the exceptional few who found his eccentric though quite inconspicuous personality interesting, people began little by little to cut him dead; even those who wanted his money preferred to have nothing to do with him. When I myself ran into him a few times on the road to Lambach, or Kirchham, and a couple of times walking through the high timber forest, he'd nail me every time by starting to talk without let-up on some topic of a medical or political or scientific kind, or a mixture of all three; more about that later . . .

. . . at Lanner's the word is that Konrad killed his wife with *two shots;* at the Stiegler place, with *a single shot;* at The Inglenook, with *three;* and at Laska's with *several* shots. Obviously nobody really knows except, presumably, the police experts, how many times Konrad pulled that trigger . . .

. . . but the trial, set for the 15th, should cast some light— even if only in the legal sense, as Wieser says—on the mystery of this shooting, a mystery that only gets darker as time goes on . . .

. . . despite what most people thought even as recently as last January—that Konrad gave himself up right after the alleged bloody deed—it is now known that he did nothing of the kind. At Laska's, where I managed yesterday to sell no less than three new life insurance policies, they are saying that it took the police two whole days to find him at long last in the frozen manure pit behind the lime works. The story is that the police were called by the so-called handyman, Hoeller, because of the strange prolonged silence in the house, and when they broke in they found the murdered woman slumped in her chair but no trace of her husband, whom the evidence promptly led them to identify as the killer. They combed the whole building from top to bottom several times, then they searched the annex where Hoeller lives, and all the other structures on the grounds, the nearby woods, everything, without success. Not until the next day, when it occurred to Reserve Officer Moritz to lift up the rotting planks covering the manure pit, was Konrad discovered, cowering half-frozen underneath; he was arrested and taken without the least resistance on his part, exhausted as he understandably was, straight to the room at the lime works where the murder had occurred and where at this point an old straw mattress dragged down from the attic was doing duty for the corpse in the chair. Even though the police let Konrad change before starting to grill him, they kept rushing him in their anxiety to get him to Wels as quickly as possible, I am told. Only after Konrad showed them some full bottles of liquor he had in the room and encouraged them to drink it all, did they suddenly relax and begin to take their time. The drinks were just what they needed after all the bother of looking for Konrad, and those men reputedly emptied the four or five or maybe even six bottles of schnapps in the patrol wagon, though to gain the necessary time they chose a detour of about sixty or seventy miles, crossing the Krems River right after they passed Sicking, so that it took them two and a half hours from Sicking to Wels, a distance that ordinarily takes less than half an hour—two and a half hours! And when they finally got there, Konrad actually came tumbling out of the wagon head first; with his handcuffs on he could not hold on to anything and maybe one of the officers pushed him a little, and him without any shoes on, all he had on his feet was a pair of felt socks, they say, because the police were in too big a hurry to give him a chance to put on a pair of clean shoes; as for the shoes he had on when they dragged him from the manure pit, they were so bloated with liquid manure that once he'd dragged them off his feet he couldn't possibly have gotten into them again, and they wouldn't give him time to get a fresh pair from his own room; it was, Wieser said, inhuman. And Fro says that Konrad should never have been taken on that ride in the freezing cold without something to cover his head, Konrad being of an age when the slightest chill can have the most devastating effect; why, a draft to the back of the head has been known to cause death! but, on the other hand, considering the monstrous crime he committed, and more particularly that he survived two days and even the grueling night-time cold in that manure pit without coming to serious harm, it would be absurd to make a fuss over such trivia as the missing shoes, when he was at least back in dry, relatively warm clothing. They do say that Konrad asked for his long leather pants that he said were the best protection he had against catching cold, but Reservist Moritz who went to Konrad's room for his things paid no attention and reappeared with an ordinary pair of dark gray loden pants, also a loden jacket, which he tossed on the floor at Konrad's feet along with some underwear, a shirt, the aforementioned felt socks, and a handkerchief, ordering him to dress and be quick about it. Officer Halbeis who meanwhile was using his rifle butt to keep Konrad pinned in the corner near the desk, Fro says, as if the totally defenseless and wholly apathetic prisoner was likely to offer any resistance, is reported to have said "murderer" repeatedly to Konrad, whereupon the county magistrate, who, on entering the room, heard Halbeis using the word *murderer* is said to have pointed out that it was not for the police to call Konrad a *murderer* at this stage of the proceedings. Nevertheless the police disregarded what Wieser calls the magistrate's highly proper instructions and continued to call Konrad a *murderer* in the presence of the magistrate who, it seems, did not notice that the policemen went on calling Konrad a *murderer* despite his explicit warning. Reservist Moritz, incidentally, is said to have acted quite against regulations when he pulled the Konrad woman's body upright in the chair where it lay slumped forward, with her head all ripped to pieces from the shot or shots from that carbine; he did it, supposedly, after Police Inspector Neuner had briefly left the room in order, Wieser guessed, to find out some detail from Hoeller, the man who knew the lime works better than anyone else and who happened to be in the downstairs vestibule just then; it must have been right after the body was discovered, and the reason Moritz straightened it out was that he was afraid its own shifting weight would send it suddenly slipping from the chair onto the wooden floor. But the magistrate, referring to this in passing, called Moritz a bungling amateur, Fro says. Editor Lanik of the local paper, one of the rottenest characters around, is said to have been refused admittance to the lime works altogether. Wieser also mentions the shattered wrist on the corpse, proof that she had her hands up in front of her face when the shot fell. Fro keeps using the word *unrecognizable,* over and over again he says *streaming with blood* . . .

. . . at Laska's they say that Konrad had tried at first to drag the corpse out to the upstairs vestibule, which has a window overlooking the water; like every man who has just killed someone, Konrad thought, says Wieser, that he could get rid of the victim, and the first thing that naturally occurred to him was to drag the body to that window and then, after weighting it with some good-sized object of iron or stone, as Fro thinks, simply drop it out the window where there happened to be, right under the sill, two marble blocks intended as door posts but left unused by Hoerhager, Konrad's cousin and the former owner of the lime works, who had decided to use tuffstone instead; Fro feels sure that those two marble blocks will play a part in the course of the trial. Anyway Konrad soon realized that he could not drag the body to the window overlooking the water, because he simply did not have the strength, besides which it may have dawned on him that it would not make sense to throw the body into the water that way, because even a medium-bright flatfoot would soon have seen through so clumsy a way to dispose of the victim, as Wieser says; malefactors always began by thinking up the craziest ways to cover their tracks, and what could have been crazier in this case than to toss the Konrad woman out the window. So when Konrad had dragged her about midway he gave up the idea, possibly he decided at that point not to get rid of the body at all is Fro's guess, but in any case he dragged it right back, the blood pouring from it harder all the time, dragged it all the way back to her room and somehow he mustered the strength to prop her up in her chair again, as the police reconstructed what happened; they say Konrad admitted that his dead wife kept slipping through his arms to the wooden floor as he tried to get her back into the chair, it took him over an hour to get the heavy, lifeless woman's body that kept slipping down on him back into that chair. When he finally made it he was so exhausted that he broke down beside the chair . . .

. . . immediately after the murder, he is alleged to have told them, he began to run around inside the lime works as if he had gone completely crazy, he ran around from top to bottom and back again, and it was when he finally stopped to lean on the window seat overlooking the water in the upstairs vestibule, that it occurred to him to throw the dead woman out that window into the water. In fact there were blood tracks throughout the lime works that show exactly where and how Konrad ran all over the place, his statements, easy enough to check, were true, and Fro believes that Konrad had no reason not to tell the truth, actually it was characteristic of Konrad to be a fanatic about telling the truth, and still is. At The Inglenook they were saying that Konrad shot the woman in cold blood from behind, made sure she was dead, and then instantly went to give himself up. At Laska's the word was that the woman's head was shattered by a bullet fired into her left temple. When they're discussing which temple it was, some keep saying it was the left temple and others that it was the right temple. At Lanner's there were some who said that Konrad had killed his wife with an ax and then shot her with the carbine only after she was already dead, plain evidence of insanity. At Laska's they said that Konrad held the muzzle of the gun to the back of his wife's head and did not pull the trigger for a minute or two, so she knew when she felt the gun at her head that he was going to do her in this time, but made no move to defend herself. Probably he shot her at her own request, they say at the Stiegler, her life was hell and getting more agonizing every day, and it was just as well that the poor soul—which is the way people almost always referred to her everywhere—was out of it. Still, they do say that Konrad should have shot himself after shooting his wife, because all he had to look forward to now was the inescapable horror of prison or else the madhouse for life . . .

. . . but a man who kills someone close to him, says Fro, is hardly likely to act in a logical manner afterward . . .

. . . the magistrate is supposed to have said to the policemen around him that the woman's brains on the floor reminded him in texture and color of Emmentaler cheese, says Wieser. Hoeller confirms this statement. About Konrad the magistrate is supposed to have said that he had Schridde's hair syndrome, a symptom of stomach cancer . . .

. . . Konrad had actually kept an ax hidden in his wife's room for some weeks, a common wood ax, but Hoeller says that Konrad did not kill his wife with the ax, which lay on the window seat behind the invalid chair for weeks gathering dust, but that he shot her with the gun. The time of the killing is supposed to have been three A.M., but other possibilities are being discussed; at Lanner's they insist that Konrad killed his wife at four A.M., at Laska's they make it one A.M., at Stiegler's, *five* in the morning, at The Inglenook, it's two A.M. Nobody, not even Hoeller, heard a shot. Even while Konrad himself was still insisting that the lime works at Sicking was the only place in the world where it was possible for him to live and do his scientific work, Wieser says, he had actually come to feel that Sicking threatened him with a kind of doom, increasingly so during the last two years, says Fro; he knew, though he could not admit it, that he felt totally depressed and defeated here, that it was, as Wieser puts it quite pathetically in his way, a tragedy. Konrad had begun a long time ago to move heaven and earth for possession of the lime works, which had always been owned by the Konrad family, but had been parlayed into the hands of Konrad's nephew, Hoerhager, as Konrad once confided to Fro, by means of all kinds of testamentary chicanery, between the two world wars; the idea of buying the lime works had been Konrad's dream for three of four decades, though as time went on the dream seemed less likely ever to materialize, said Fro, but then suddenly, or as Wieser says, overnight, it became realizable. Even as a child Konrad had fixed his mind on the idea of settling in the lime works one day, Fro thinks; he had planned to move in and live there ever since he could remember; planned to take possession of the old stonework labyrinth and spend the rest of his life in it, in what he once described to Fro as the total isolation of Sicking, to live intensely to the end as he needed to live, specifically by using his head intensively, his head over which he still had perfect control; but the way his nephew Hoerhager kept raising the price and changing his mind about selling or not selling, one day he would sell and the next day he wouldn't sell, downright sadistic it was, Konrad felt, the way his nephew would agree to sell the lime works one minute and the next minute he would deny he had ever made such a promise, or else he would threaten Konrad with selling it, but not to Konrad, then again promise to sell it to Konrad only and no one else, all of this continual wanting-to-sell then not wanting-to-sell, the incessant and absolutely unjustified raising of the purchase price (Fro), it nearly destroyed Konrad, but he wouldn't have been Konrad if he hadn't, in the end, despite the monstrous obstacles put in his way, succeeded in getting possession and finally moving into the lime works. Though it is certainly true, as Wieser says, that Konrad left no stone unturned for decades to get possession of the lime works, pushing and pursuing his plan more and more ruthlessly until the day he actually realized it, his wife—whom no one ever laid eyes on because of her crippled and paralyzed condition, no one that is except Hoeller, and the baker, the chimney sweep, her hairdresser, the local doctor, and the Stoerschneider woman, and about whom they say that though crippled she was a great beauty— the Konrad woman had made every effort and done all she could to keep from having to move into the lime works; while her husband, as Wieser says, had naturally thought only about his scientific work, for the completion of which the lime works had always seemed to him to be the ideal retreat, she began to dread it even before she started to take his ideas about the lime works seriously, and as he kept bringing these ideas up with a more and more passionate insistence, she would say later on, she became increasingly terrified of what her life, sad as it was already, was bound to turn into there, as her husband's intention to move into the lime works neared fulfillment, and as we know now, her fears were certainly realized; what she wanted was to go back to Toblach, her home town, and her parents' house, but going back to Toblach meant to him nothing less than giving up his life's work, his aim in life, and therefore hers as well; his wife was after all his half sister, and her dependence upon him was absolute, says Wieser, the most absolute imaginable, so moving back to Toblach would have been equivalent to suicide for both of them, willful suicide, because it is in any case deadly to return, in the helpless despair of a final effort to survive, and therefore in a redoubled helplessness and despair, knowing of no other way and knowing that there is no other way, that there can be no other way, it is deadly to return in the end to one's parents' house in one's home town, one's home land, one's so-called final refuge. Actually his wife had always thought of Toblach as the ideal refuge, in her mind the idyllic Toblach was incessantly juxtaposed to the terrifying Sicking, which she dreaded. But it was Sicking, of all places, where they both went, says Fro, because the husband's will prevailed; she had ways hated the lime works, she had always done all she could to make him give up the idea, first keeping after Konrad's nephew Hoerhager not to sell, or at least not to sell the lime works to Konrad, then she tried to bribe the nephew,

Fro says she offered him a sum in six figures to sell the lime
works to someone other than Konrad, finally she took to
threatening him, she would alternately warn him and threaten
him and blackmail him, but to no avail, says Fro, it was
Konrad who finally prevailed as always and in every instance,
Fro says. The five and a half years the Konrads spent in
Sicking had convinced Konrad, according to Wieser's statement, that his decision, his ruthless determination to move into
the lime works, away from the world which for decades he
had regarded as worthless, offering no attraction whatsoever,
a world he had always regarded as anti-historical, a world
that was merely marking time, out of which he chose to move
into the lime works for the sake of his scientific task, which
meant his survival. The place had to be his legally purchased
property, not merely a rented home. Hoerhager had of course
offered to rent Konrad the place in the normal way, on a
twelve-year or even a twenty-four-year lease, but Konrad had
always firmly refused the offer, as Wieser says, because to live
in a rented lime works would have gone against his grain, and
Konrad felt that his decision and his ruthless determination
had been the correct decision and the correct ruthlessness.
From time to time, Konrad told Fro, the word and the idea
Toblach had surfaced in his wife's head during their first
years in Sicking, this childhood notion of hers would spook
around in her head for hours and then in her room and finally
in the entire lime works, but as time went on it came up less
often, Konrad is said to have told Fro. At the so-called Cold
Food Market only a year ago Konrad is supposed to have told
Wieser that it seemed to him as though Toblach was no longer
surfacing, suddenly the idea of Toblach had ceased to matter,
his wife had given it up, in giving up Toblach it was as though

she had given herself up, he noticed. She had always opposed
Sicking, Konrad said to Fro, always opposed the lime works,
always pitted herself against him, Konrad, against his work,
which meant of course against herself as well. She had
brought Toblach into the debate against Sicking from the
first moment the question of Sicking arose. In the end her
opposition to the lime works, to his work, had become a habit,
so that her struggle against his research for his definitive book
on the sense of hearing, had become instinctive, as it were.
Suddenly Toblach had ceased to exist, Konrad is supposed
to have said, and: you must understand that my wife has never
had anything apart from Toblach, even now she has nothing
in the world apart from Toblach. Sicking was of course a
dungeon, Konrad said to Fro, even at first glance it gave the
impression of being just that, a workhouse, a penal institution, a prison; an impression disguised for centuries, according to Konrad, concealed behind a veneer of bad taste, he
alone had ruthlessly stripped away this cheap mask to let the
underlying reality emerge into the light again. This reality
was made manifest, to begin with, by the barred windows he
had installed in those thick walls immediately after acquiring
ownership; functional iron bars, as Konrad put it, I ripped out
the ornamental ironwork and installed functional iron bars,
he has been quoted as saying, those thick walls and the iron
bars sunk into them instantly show that this is a prison. The
ornamental wrought iron with which the lime works had been
decorated before Konrad's time, relics of two centuries of poor
taste, were removed at Konrad's orders, he said to Wieser,
they all had to go at once, he had torn most of them out of
and off the walls with his own hands, he broke them off,
knocked them off, broke them down, knocked them down,

tore them down, ripped them out, and never replaced a single
one of these knocked down and broken up and ripped off
squiggles with any new squiggles. The lime works were now
totally bare of ornamentation, Konrad is reported to have told
Fro, even the paths leading up to the lime works, though in
fact there was only a single stony path leading up to the lime
works as anyone could see at once, had been loosely paved
with coarse gravel. Everything was simplified. He aimed to
restore the lime works to their original condition, regardless
of what anyone thought. Tall hedges, yes, but no ornamental
bushes whatsoever. To Wieser: he, Konrad, had never been a
so-called nature freak, after all; he was no nature fanatic, no
nature masochist, absolutely no wilderness freak of any kind,
in fact; external nature tended to inspire Konrad with horror
at his own nature, never with joyful amazement; the so-called
sense of wonder in contemplating nature was a mere perver-
sion, he said. Nor did he love mankind, and if not mankind,
then certainly not animals, he did not love animals even
though he was incessantly, even exclusively preoccupied with
nature, you might say, he was nevertheless no friend of nature,
quite the contrary, particularly *because* of his incessant preoccupation with nature. His wife naturally thought it weird
how passionately he hated nature and, as a logical consequence, all the creatures. To Fro: bare walls, functionalism,
strategy for self-injury. Catastrophicephaleconomy. To Wieser:
firmly locked, firmly bolted doors, closely barred windows,
everything locked up, bolted, barred. Do you realize that the
lime works doors used to be fastened by simple latches! Konrad is supposed to have cried, imagine, simple latches! Nowadays the doors were all secured by heavy bolts of dressed
timber set deep in the walls. Set deep into those thick walls,

Konrad is said to have told Wieser, bolts that have to be pushed in or pulled out by force, what with the constant humidity here it was of course always necessary to use a good deal of force. The security factor was the most important one by far. First of all, Konrad had said to his wife according to Wieser, they had to secure themselves against intrusion from the outside world from which they had at last succeeded in escaping, so all the windows had to be barred at once, and all the doors had to be bolted, and that was what in fact they did, right after moving in, Konrad told Wieser, the very day after paying an unheard of, actually an incredibly high purchase price for the lime works, the Konrads moved in and instantly had all the windows barred and all the doors bolted, they had bolts attached even to the inside doors, heavy bolts, and heavy bars on the windows, in fact, the blacksmith at first refused to make bars that heavy, Konrad said, but he finally gave in because Konrad would not yield an inch and also promised to pay quite a lot, and the carpenter made him those heavy wooden bolts, actually the blacksmith who made those heavy bars and the carpenter who made those heavy bolts are said to have shaken their heads over Konrad, but in the end his arguments are said to have convinced both the blacksmith and the carpenter, and now the blacksmith and the carpenter are both proud of their handiwork, the blacksmith is proud of his heavy bars which he shaped with extreme precision in accordance with Konrad's strict instructions, and the carpenter is proud of the heavy bolts he made just as exactly in accordance with Konrad's precise instructions. And to stop the curiosity seekers who kept passing the lime works, unwanted and unbidden, as is their way, from eyeing the building, Konrad is said to have told Wieser, Konrad and his wife needed high thickets, as Konrad said to his wife, we need high thickets around the lime works, the tallest-growing shrubs there are, and they had immediately ordered the tallest shrubs from Switzerland brought to Sicking where they were planted by experts. Today the lime works is totally hidden from view, Konrad is supposed to have told Wieser two years ago, completely unnoticeable, unseen, and even if it should be noticed and seen, Wieser remembers Konrad saying, there is absolutely no way to get inside. The thickets have grown so high, my dear Wieser, that no one can get a glimpse of the lime works, there is no way to see the lime works, in fact, unless you are standing right in front of it (Konrad to Wieser), that is, standing a yard or half a yard from the building, which is not to see it, after all, there's no seeing it that close up. Remember that the lime works is accessible only from the east, it's a strange fact that the lime works is accessible only from the east, but then again it is not so strange, Konrad is supposed to have said to Wieser, on the one hand it was strange, on the other hand not so strange after all, everything is strange on the one hand and not at all strange on the other hand (Wieser specifically recalls that bit about strange-yet-not-strange); to the north and to the west, the lime works is surrounded by water, ideally one might say, and to the south it is bounded ideally by ramparts of rock. Even access from the east is often barred in winter, because the lime works is no longer a lime works and so the snow plow no longer comes as far as the lime works, obviously no snow plow is going to come this far out to a dead, abandoned lime works, Konrad is said to have told Wieser, no workmen, no lime production, no snow plow, he said; for the sake of an individual good-for-nothing Konrad and his wife, an equally good-for-nothing

Konrad, no snow plow comes in, it was economically waste-
ful to have the snow plow come in just for their sake, consequently the snow plow had not come that far for years, as it
suddenly struck Konrad, not since his nephew Hoerhager was
no longer at the lime works had the snow plow come any
farther than the tavern, for Hoerhager had served in various
ways as a town official, a man in public office could count on
the snow plow coming all the way to his door, while I, Konrad is supposed to have said, I serve no public function, I
serve no function whatsoever, certainly not a public function,
he even hated the word *function,* there was nothing he hated
more bitterly than the word *functionary,* a word it nauseated
him even to hear, because nowadays everybody was a functionary, all of them were functionaries now, they all func-
tioned, there are no human beings left, Wieser, nothing but
functionaries, that's why I can't stand the expression *functionary,* the word *functionary* makes me retch, but my nephew
Hoerhager was a functionary by nature, a town functionary,
and to a functionary, especially a town functionary, the snow
plow comes, it will always come to a functionary! Konrad
is supposed to have exclaimed to Wieser, while for an old
fool like me and a crippled old fool of a woman like my wife
the snow plow will not come, even though it would be so
easy for the snow plow to make a turn at the lime works, but
it simply does not come as far as the lime works anymore. A
winter harassment! Konrad is supposed to have shouted, over
and over: A winter harassment! Wieser says that for over an
hour Konrad kept calling it a farce that the public snow plow
comes only as far as the tavern but no longer as far as the
lime works. In Sicking everything was a farce, whatever you
looked at in Sicking was a farce, no matter what you looked

at, from whatever point of view, you were looking at a farce. However, it was also to the Konrads' advantage that the snow plow no longer went on past the tavern to the lime works, Konrad insisted: not a soul comes stomping through that deep snow all the way to us. To be so cut off from everything and isolated naturally meant that they enjoyed absolute quiet. Wieser thinks that the absolute quiet at the lime works in winter was precisely what had so enthralled Konrad at first about the lime works. The thought haunted him, the thought that in winter there was absolute quiet at the lime works gave Konrad no peace for years on end. He nearly drove himself crazy brooding about it. To the lime works! he kept thinking, to the lime works! only the lime works! again and again, even while his wife was thinking of nothing but: Toblach, back to Toblach! but his wife was obedient to a fault. The rock spur even shielded them from the sawmill noises on the other side of it, Konrad is supposed to have said over and over, but if he was to be frank about it, Konrad conceded, sawmill noises bothered him not at all, they never had bothered him, no more than his own breathing bothered him, because like his own breathing they had always been there; he had never thought: there, that's a noise from the sawmill, I can't hear myself think because of it! because he had always lived and done his thinking next door to sawmills, no matter where he had lived it had somehow always been in the vicinity of one or even several sawmills, his family, all his people, even all their relatives, had always owned at least one sawmill. As to the tavern, Wieser reports Konrad saying, it stood far enough from the lime works so that Konrad never heard any-thing from there. Just as the rock spur keeps the sawmill noises out, no sounds come from the tavern either, even at its

noisiest, here at the lime works he heard none of it. Sometimes you could hear an avalanche, Konrad is supposed to
have said, or a rock slide, ice, water, birds, the sound of wild
animals, wind, all that, yes. Because one heard hardly any
sounds at the lime works, one's hearing tended to grow remarkably acute here, especially with as hypersensitive an ear
as he had. This gave him a natural advantage in the research,
for his book dealing, not quite coincidentally, with the sense
of hearing, after all it would bear the title *The Sense of Hearing*. That the Konrads lived where they did (Konrad to
Wieser) was of course the result of a calculated move for the
benefit of his work on *Hearing*. All of it, everything having
to do with the lime works, my dear Wieser, is calculated,
Konrad is supposed to have said. It's all been carefully thought
through beforehand, though much of it may seem to be pure
chance, even pure nonsense, nevertheless it was all thought
out well ahead of time. Sensitivity in a state of immunity to
surprise was sensitivity perfected, deadly in fact, Konrad is
supposed to have said. Fro reports Konrad saying to him as
follows: when he, Konrad, was in his room working on his
book, he could hear his wife breathing upstairs in her
room, believe it or not, it was a fact. Of course his wife's
breathing in her room, one flight up from his, was not
normally audible in his room; he had tested it out time and
again; nevertheless *he* did in fact hear his wife breathing in
her room while he was in his room. But of course he, Konrad,
was chronically in a state of the greatest possible attentiveness.
He could even hear human voices across the lake, even though
it was normally impossible to hear human voices across the
lake from the lime works. Those people on the opposite shore
would be heard by him, Konrad, not when they broke into a

loud laugh or anything like that, all they had to do was talk normally to each other, Konrad is supposed to have said to Fro. How often I hear a sound, an actual sound, and the person I have been talking with will not have heard it, though I did. I hear people talking across the lake, and I get up and walk to the window where I can hear them even better although I can't see them, he said, but my test cases hear and see nothing, Konrad is said to have told Fro, the problem of living with other people had always consisted in the fact that he was always hearing and seeing things while the others heard and saw nothing, and it was impossible to train them, no matter who they were, in hearing and seeing. A person either hears and sees, or else a person hears, or a person sees, or else he doesn't hear or see and you cannot teach a person to hear and to see, but a person who hears and sees can perfect his hearing and his seeing, above all perfect his hearing, because it is more important for a person to hear than to see. But as for my wife, Konrad is supposed to have said, his efforts to perfect her hearing and seeing had failed midway: suddenly, as long as ten or fifteen years ago, he had been forced to realize that it was pointless to continue to teach her to hear and to see any better, he soon gave up trying, it was in a woman's nature to give up a disciplined mental effort, a mental effort of the will, midway, in fact she would do it every time at the moment of highest concentration and also always at the moment when success seemed assured. The Urbanchich method he had been using, especially since they moved into the lime works, in the ruthless training of his wife, he was now keeping up for his own purposes only, he had dropped it from her program altogether. As regards my hearing of conversations between all sorts of people on the opposite shore, Konrad is supposed to have said to Fro, I could often hear words, even difficult words, and sometimes the most complicated sentences, too, with truly exciting clarity, inside the lime works. Suddenly he said: my test cases, my wife for instance, Hoeller for instance, Wieser for instance, have never yet heard what I was hearing with the utmost clarity from the opposite shore, while I hear everything too clearly, Konrad is supposed to have said, though the others never hear a thing, and in fact you yourself never hear anything from the opposite shore, Konrad said. It was a triumph, after all, to hear absolutely everything, in consequence of his rigorous training in the course of decades of study, but at the same time it was terrible. Still, there was nothing like perfect, or nearly perfect hearing, for the greatest possible clarification. To revert to the subject of the lime works, Konrad is supposed to have said to Fro that everyone seeing it for the first time was instantly dumbfounded by it. Every decade saw a new addition, a superstructure tacked on, some part of it torn down, and think of the vast number of subcellars, I always say to the public works inspector, Konrad said to Fro. Here, where the water is deepest, actually the deepest spot in the lake, he, Konrad, was looking out of the window. But anyone stepping suddenly from behind the surrounding thicket to confront the lime works could not possibly have any conception of its vastness, such as was reserved only for the man who lived inside, inhabited the place head and soul, as he phrased it, and therefore able to sense all of its true extent. Not grasp it, exactly, but get the measure of it, Konrad is supposed to have said. An onlooker would be irritated, a visitor offended; while the onlooker would be both attracted and repelled by the lime works, a visitor was bound to suffer immediately every kind of disappointment. Whoever sees the place will turn around and take to his heels, whoever enters or visits will leave it and take to his heels. How often Konrad had observed a man come out from behind the thicket, look alarmed and turn back, it was always the same reaction, Konrad is supposed to have said; people step out of the thicket and instantly turn back, or else they step inside the lime works and immediately come running out again. They always have a feeling of being watched, approaching a structure like the lime works one always has a feeling of being watched, watched from all sides, soon one feels unnerved, Konrad is supposed to have said; starting out with an exceptional alertness, a high tension of all the senses, there is a gradual ebbing away of strength, everyone entering the environs of the lime works tends to succumb suddenly to deep exhaustion. One could hardly help being struck by the way one look at the lime works would make people turn back, as if suddenly deserted by the courage to knock on the door and enter. If the mere sight of the lime works does not frighten them, Konrad is supposed to have said, then they give a start when they knock at the door, though very few go so far as to knock, knocking makes a terrible noise. Every architectural detail of the lime works is the result of a thousand years of calculations. For instance, stepping through the thicket, at first glance one would assume that inside the lime works one would have very little freedom to move around, very little elbow room, but in fact there was lots of elbow room inside the lime works. But then, every preconception, as well as every preconception of a preconception, was likely to be wrong, humiliatingly so, every time. Anybody who thought at all was bound to know that. The actuality always turned out to be, actually, something else, quite the opposite, always, of the given actuality, in fact. That our very existence is pure self-deception and nothing else cannot be stated unconditionally. In the lime works, Konrad said to Wieser, as in no other building I know of, and I know the largest and the handsomest and in general every possible kind of building, stone or brickwork structures of all kinds, you can walk forward and backward and on and on in every direction as much as you want without having to go the same way twice, you can progress in the most progressive way there. The construction as a whole aimed at total deceptiveness, so that the superficial onlooker would fall into the trap every time. The moment you enter the vestibule, Konrad said to Wieser, you see at once that you have been made a fool of, because the vestibule alone is three times the size of the annex, to take only one example, and of course the upstairs and the downstairs vestibules are the same size; the lime works, designed as a lordly manor, had for Konrad all the advantages of a kind of voluntary self-imprisonment at hard labor. (The vestibule leads through to the courtyard, which is paved with cobblestones, they tell me at Laska's. Inside the lime works Konrad could walk about for hours without going crazy, he is supposed to have said to Wieser, even though the same kind of pacing the floor he did here, back and forth, this way and that, in buildings as large or even larger, possibly, would drive him crazy in a matter of minutes. His head, Konrad is supposed to have said to Wieser, felt at home in just such a building as the lime works, he believed; his body, too. While his wife, oriented toward Toblach as she was, felt uneasy in such a building as the lime works, found herself constantly depressed by it, Konrad himself breathed freely and existed fully only in such buildings as the lime works that were naturally responsive to the highest claims of absolute originality, what he needed were rooms where you could take at least fifteen or twenty steps forward or backward without running into any obstacles, Konrad said to Wieser, by which I mean, you realize, long steps, the kind of strides I take when concentrating on my work, brain work, while, as you know, most of the rooms you enter, most of the rooms we have to live in, time and time again, to spend the night or simply to exist in, you can barely take eight or nine steps without running your head against a wall; it has always mattered enormously to me to be able to take those fifteen steps back and forth freely, Konrad said to Wieser, the moment he entered a house, he said to Wieser, he tried it out, to see whether he could take those fifteen or twenty steps in one direction. I immediately take my first steps in one direction without regard to anything else, and I count those steps; let's see now, I ask myself, can I take fifteen or twenty steps this way and fifteen or twenty steps back again, and I check out the situation only to discover, more often than not, that, as I told you, I cannot even take eight or nine steps in a straight line, whereas here at the lime works, Konrad said, I can easily take my twenty or thirty steps right off, in every room, wherever I want to, without running my head into a wall. In large rooms like these I can breathe again, of course, Konrad said. But his wife found large rooms oppressive. I feel depressed in small rooms, she feels depressed in large rooms. My wife is of course conditioned by the cramped rooms in Toblach, she grew up in those small, cramped Toblach rooms, in the general constrictedness of Toblach, everything in Toblach is uptight, everywhere in Toblach one always has the feeling that one is suffocating, Konrad said, and anyway in small rooms he always feels he is suffocating, the same feeling he has in mountain glens and so he has it in Toblach every time, while his sister, who is accustomed to Toblach, feels crushed by the size of a large room, in a vast landscape she feels crushed by the vastness of the landscape, under an enormous sky she feels crushed by the enormousness of the sky, with a man of stature she feels crushed by the man's stature. By the same token Konrad always felt he was about to suffocate when he was inside the annex, which is why he so seldom visited Hoeller who lives in the annex, Konrad went to see Hoeller in the annex only as a last resort, after a few minutes inside the annex he felt as if he were running out of oxygen and rapidly suffocating: some people simply preferred small cramped rooms and others preferred big spacious rooms, Konrad is supposed to have said, a conversation of any extent with Hoeller in the annex had gradually come to be impossible, even though Hoeller was a man toward whom Konrad felt the most protective love of which he, Konrad, was capable, but the cramped space in the annex and his own violent reactions to the constricted feeling of the annex the moment he entered it, made it impossible to visit Hoeller in the annex except for the briefest possible time, Konrad is said to have told Wieser. When they moved into the lime works it was immediately obvious that his wife would move into the smallest of the rooms. But even in her room, which actually is the smallest room in the lime works, Konrad was still able, as he said to Wieser, to take easily fifteen steps forward and fifteen steps back. From the first it had been clear that his wife would move straight up to the second floor, they had both decided on this as far back as Mannheim where they were staying just before they moved to the lime works, because the second floor was the most salubrious, a judgment confirmed every time by the expert opinions of every kind of specialist, they never gave a moment's consideration to putting her on the first floor or on the ground floor or on the third floor, Konrad said. Strange as it seems, people are always saying that the second floor is the best for a person's health, everybody chooses the second floor if possible, they all prefer it. Myself, I moved straight into my room here on the first floor, Konrad is supposed to have said. From the first they had agreed upon this, here is where I go, into this room on the first floor, and this is where she goes, into this second-floor room. Here in the lime works he had almost all the right conditions, conditions that could not be bettered, for getting on with his work, he said, and at first he did not ask himself what it meant for his wife to be moved suddenly into the lime works, even though he knew what it meant to her, he did not keep thinking about it, one simply can't keep thinking about a lot of things that one is aware of. That he had a window overlooking the lake where the water was deepest was an additional advantage for his work, even if he could not or would not say what kind of an advantage. It was also advantageous that his wife, too, had a window overlooking the water, though not the deepest part as in his case, because, as he said to Wieser, she must on no account have her window where the water was deepest. At first his wife had wanted a window facing on the courtyard (her usual preference for that enclosed feeling!) or even a window giving onto the rockface, but she had let him talk her into realizing the advantageousness of having a window overlooking the water instead, and in time she did in fact come to spend hours, what was he saying? whole days on end, staring into the water, Konrad said. As for himself, Konrad said, a room facing the courtyard would have been bad for his work; a room looking out at the rockface would have been impossible, out of the question. To move into a room facing the courtyard or the rockface would have been a deliberate invitation to total despair, something he was prone to fall into anyway. When it came to furnishing the house, as Konrad once explained to Fro: though we did our own rooms completely the first day, once and for all, putting in only the most indispensable things, the bare necessities, you understand, we did nothing at all about the rest of the building. Since we moved in during the winter, we had to use the barge, it took two trips by barge across the lake, Konrad said to Fro, two full loads of those hundreds of thousands of household effects we still owned even after all our travels all over the world during all those decades, Fro; it was incredible how much furniture and household stuff we still had when we moved into the lime works, despite two world wars and all those catastrophic unheavals! it was fantastic, Fro, considering that we never lifted a finger to hold on to all these furnishings and household goods, quite the contrary, neither my wife nor I ever gave a moment's thought to the stuff, and of course all these hundreds upon thousands of furnishings and household goods represent only a fraction of what we used to have, because my wife, after all, brought a great deal of property into the marriage and I also contributed a good deal, and what with a few deaths in the family, war casualties you know, we acquired quite a bit more, though we lost much of it in the cities, we never lost anything in the country, most of it was stored in the country. Imagine, two huge barges loaded to the limit with furniture

and household effects! Luckily the lake was not frozen over,
though it freezes over every winter, in January it is usually
frozen hard, but the year we moved into the lime works the
lake had not frozen over. No one would dare to cross the
frozen lake by car or truck ever again, not after that wedding
party, several Konrads among them, Konrad is supposed to
have said, broke through the crust about twenty years ago. For
centuries people drove over that frozen lake with impunity,
and then suddenly that wedding party had to break through;
since that date no one would risk it. Three huge barge loads
of household stuff, Konrad said to Fro, and you know how
much one of these barges will hold. The chances are that
barge is no longer fit for use, these days, Konrad said, not a
soul has given it any attention in years, such a barge had to
be oiled and painted every year at least, but nobody has ever
oiled or painted that barge. Eaten up with rust and rot as it is,
the barge was doubtless quite unfit for use by now, and
Konrad is supposed to have said: the way everything around
the lime works is eaten up with rust and rot, when you think
how much there is, lying around the lime works and eaten
up with rust and rot. As I was saying, he said to Fro, for
years nothing at all was done to make the lime works
habitable, and when we got here we gave less than an hour to
fixing up our two rooms. Of course he and his wife, Konrad
said, were the most unassuming people in the world. He had
gotten by all his life using only the most indispensable articles
of furniture, always the same ones. Nevertheless they had
somehow, despite their tendency to concentrate only on what
was absolutely necessary, managed to have two full barge
loads of movables to bring to the lime works. Mrs. Konrad
is alleged to have said repeatedly that she could never have

found enough room for all those furnishings and effects in Toblach. In Toblach not even half of the stuff would have got inside, she said. There was absolutely nothing, Konrad said to Fro, that she couldn't somehow connect with Toblach, just to drag in Toblach somehow. The problem in moving, Konrad said to Fro, was primarily to begin with the pieces intended for the first or the second or the third floor and to avoid dragging pieces meant for the third floor to the second floor, as had happened again and again, for example, or dragging first floor pieces to the second floor or third floor pieces to the first, and so forth. By the time they had finished, almost every piece of furniture etc. was standing in the wrong place, so that the end result, as he expressed himself, was one of hopeless confusion. As you know, Konrad is supposed to have said to Wieser, I sold quite a lot of the furnishings and stuff right after we moved in, and by now I have converted most of these wooden absurdities into cash. And to Fro, a year ago: my wife hasn't the faintest idea that I have sold nearly all the furniture and household things; but that's another subject. Behind her back I sold nearly all the furniture and fixtures, Konrad is supposed to have said (his own words) almost all the rooms in the lime works are completely empty now because I had to convert everything to cash these last few years, considering especially the high cost of litigation. The lawyers swallowed up most of it! He had naturally had to hire a number of hands, what with Hoeller being bedridden at the time they moved in, he was down with pleurisy, and as everyone knew it was hard even in Sicking, even if one was ready to pay dear for it, to find men for such unskilled occasional work as moving furniture, Konrad had in fact lent a hand himself, while his wife, exhausted by the hardships of moving, slumped in her invalid chair that was the first thing to be set up in its permanent place in her room; Konrad helped move the furniture and fixtures into the lime works side by side with the hired help, he is supposed to have told Fro, though of course as long as one had hired help one was obliged to get as much work as possible out of them, so he had ordered the men to work hard and quickly, not with the excruciating languor that had become customary among working men ever since they had become accustomed to being coddled and spoiled in the course of recent history, he asked them to work as quickly as he did, and the men obeyed instantly, says Fro, they suddenly began to move the furnishings and household goods with remarkable speed, and even with extraordinary skill; with zeal, one might say. Konrad evidently had a knack for getting the men to put their backs into it, Fro thinks. For the first few days he had managed to conceal his normally glaring misanthropy, suppress it enough, anyway, so that the hired men, who had heard of him but never seen him face-to-face before, took him to be a thoroughly well-meaning, kindly gentleman, whom they could look forward to using for their own purposes, such as extracting from him high pay for little work, high pay for sloppy work, etc. etc., in fact their yielding to Konrad's orders to work fast and efficiently too was pure cunning on their part. Konrad of course realized that he had to put his best foot forward with the men, what with the terrible fix he was in, having those huge barge loads of stuff at the lime works with not a helping hand in sight. It would take months, Konrad is supposed to have said to Fro, to bring some order into all this furniture chaos, but in fact no order has been brought into all this furniture chaos to this very day, he said to Fro, but then, by this time, there is only a fraction of the original number of pieces etc. here in the lime works, everything else has been sold, so there's not much point in arranging the remnants so late in the day. Especially as I intend to convert even these remnants into cash as soon as possible, Konrad is supposed to have said. To his wife he would say over and over, whenever she asked him, that all the rooms were in order, that everything was in its place in every room of the house, that little by little every single object had found its proper place, without a word to let her know that everything had in fact been sold off by then, that Konrad had never once and not for a moment considered putting the furniture in place, but had thought only and always about selling it as quickly as possible, had in fact managed to sell it off gradually at quite good prices, to antiquarians here and there, one of whom in particular had taken almost everything off his hands at a relatively high price, for sale in America, a trade at which the dealer had occasionally made profits of a thousand, even two thousand, percent, as he admitted to Konrad; who said not a word of all this to the sick woman glued to her invalid chair, to whom he went on reiterating his lies about the furnishings being in perfect order. For decades it was by lies and nothing but lies that Konrad and his wife managed to save themselves from total despair, to go on somehow, to stay in touch and endure each other for just a while longer; without lies the two of them would have become totally estranged and lost in despair, Fro thinks. My God, what do I need in a room besides a table, a chair, a wardrobe, and a bed? Konrad is supposed to have exclaimed to Fro once, when they were coming out of the tavern and saying goodbye under the horse chestnuts, as they so often did after playing rummy for four hours at a time; Konrad used to stretch their game for as long as he could so as to put off going home to his waiting wife. Fro: Konrad was afraid of going home to his wife. The lime works are out of earshot, Konrad is supposed to have said quite frequently to Wieser; anyone crying out inside the lime works was not going to be heard. If someone were to break in with criminal intent there would be no point in screaming, as the screamer would not be heard. The sawmill was out of earshot, the tavern was out of earshot, not a soul lived within earshot of the lime works. The wood cutters were out of earshot. That the Mussner property and the Trattner property had been out of earshot, as the two still unsolved murders of the owners Mussner and Trattner proved, was a matter of catastrophic consequence. Even though Konrad appreciated the total seclusion of the lime works as advantageous for his work, it did on the other hand hold a constant threat, indeed an extraordinary threat, because the types that were suddenly coming out of the woodwork everywhere, strangely enough more than ever in the present era of general affluence, came crawling out of all sorts of holes for the sole purpose of committing crimes, primarily crimes of violence and preferably the meanest, most brutal kind of violent crimes, and those types were known to shy away from nothing, from no conceivable horror they could find to commit. Basically Konrad lived, he said, in constant terror of violent criminals, his whole existence could be said to be a state of pauseless dread, as he literally put it, a dread of encountering violent types, and the lime works were virtually predestined to be the scene of violent crimes, the place was by nature a deliberate provocation to violent crime, in fact all the crimes at the lime works so far were chiefly still unsolved murders committed in the course of robbery, all the crimes (violent crimes) committed here in Sicking and environs were ninety-five percent unsolved cases, the hundreds of them committed at the lime works all unsolved just like the cases of the two landowners Mussner and Trattner, whose properties had also been isolated like the lime works and where it was customarily regarded as a miracle, as it was at the lime works, if by December 31 no violent crime had occurred there, as at the lime works alone eleven murders were known to have been committed in about a hundred years, not counting burglaries, robbery, common theft, the kind of crimes so customary no one kept count. Buildings like the lime works, in fact, attracted precisely the sort of character whose entire being was oriented toward the committing of none other than violent crimes, basically it was no use at all to build walls, install locks, etc., and the so-called psychological sciences always theorizing in collaboration with the physiognomists always came up with erroneous conclusions. Nothing was more deceptive than the human face, Konrad is supposed to have said to Wieser. That he himself carried a revolver at all times was generally known, at least since the incident with the woodcutter and game warden Koller, as well as the fact that he had a hidden weapon in readiness at all times in nearly every room of the lime works, a fact publicized in the course of the Koller trial; better to shoot someone occasionally in the shoulder or the leg, Konrad is supposed to have said to Wieser, and get locked up for it, rather than allow oneself to be the victim because of a failure to draw, because one had become intimidated by already having a record of criminal convictions. No period in history had a better right than this period to be designated as a period of violent crime, Konrad is supposed to have said, in no previous period did people have a greater right to expect a violent crime to occur at any moment, and violent crimes not only occurred far more frequently in the country than in the city, but here in the Sicking area, as everyone knew, one had to deal daily and hourly with the most revolting forms of violent crime. The familiar thesis that the typical perpetrator of violent crimes was likely to shy away from no conceivable monstrosity, proved to be the absolute terrible truth in the Sicking area. That even Konrad's wife had a gun within reach behind her invalid chair, as Konrad told Wieser about a year ago, is confirmed by Fro. Both he and his wife could not exist for a moment in the lime works or even in Sicking without the protection of firearms. Inside the lime works a person had to be armed at all times, had at every moment without exception to reckon with the likelihood of a crime against oneself. Only a fool would live unarmed in such a building as the lime works and in such an area as Sicking. Of course he had never sold a single one of his guns, Konrad said to Wieser, on the contrary, while I tried to sell every saleable thing on the premises, I bought up, as you know, nearly all the weapons in the Ulrich estate, you could never have enough guns when you were living in the lime works even though the place was as securely locked up, bolted, and barred as could be, any criminal determined to commit a violent crime would always find a way to get inside and do it. There was actually no way to prevent a criminal, no precautionary measure imaginable that would keep him from committing his crime, or crimes, once he had made up his mind to commit them. Even if the decision did not always originate in the criminal's own brain —the crime or crimes of any given criminal hardly ever originated in the criminal's own brain—the criminal's whole being nevertheless was predisposed to the crime, or crimes, his whole being aimed at the crime, or crimes, until they have been, or it has been, committed. The nature of the criminal was such as to aim incessantly at the crimes to be committed, and once this was done, the criminal's nature tended of course to concentrate on a fresh crime, or crimes, and so forth. You can scream, of course, Konrad is supposed to have said to Wieser, but you will not be heard. The setup inevitably attracts criminals, and that means violent criminals. (Wieser remembers these statements of Konrad's perfectly.) There had also been many accidents at the lime works, accidents which ended lethally for people who lived or worked there, in most cases, because their cries or screams for help had not been heard. Think of the accidental explosion in early '38, Konrad is supposed to have said, seven dead, twenty-four wounded. Yet he had refused to install a telephone in the lime works, though he knew his wife had set her heart on having one, a telephone would unquestionably be a great help to her, but there was his work to be considered, which made the installation of a phone at the lime works a thing quite out of the question. No telephone! No telephone! Konrad had exclaimed time and again, says Wieser. Naturally, if you need a doctor, a doctor must be called! he is supposed to have said. But the installation of a telephone was bound to be the end of his work, that is, it would be the end, period; he knew what he was saying. Implausible as it may seem to you, Konrad is supposed to have said to Wieser, if I had to choose between my wife and my work, I would of course choose my work. Quite apart from the fact that the installation of a phone would by far exceed my financial means, he said, because I have suddenly awakened to the fact that, contrary to my fixed idea that I was well off, we are suddenly totally impoverished. We are penniless, which is why I sold so many of our things, of course, but my wife must not hear of it, he is supposed to have said, her faith in our inexhaustible funds implying our inexhaustible wealth is all she has left, there is nothing else left for her to cling to, but as long as she can believe that there is plenty of money, something she has been able to believe until just two years ago, he said, as Konrad himself had been able to believe too, she could be at peace. If we had a telephone, Konrad is supposed to have said, we would be in the same situation as before we moved into the lime works. What did I move into the lime works for, he asked himself, if we are to have a phone here? Of course even the most absurd kind of building had a phone nowadays, there was no place without a phone anywhere, but the lime works did not yet have a phone. There's a phone at the tavern, there's a phone at the sawmill, but there will be no phone at the lime works, ever. Sometimes he thought of the original purpose for which the lime works was built, and of his own purpose in living there now, the purpose for which he was misusing it, he said. How bitterly all sorts of people had slaved in the place, for instance. He would think what the lime works had once meant to the entire region, and how long it was since it had ceased to mean anything. Even though it was still referred to as the lime works, when it came up, it would after all be truer to speak of a shut-down or deactivated lime works, when referring to the lime works. People are always referring to all kinds of structures or mental complexes, Konrad is supposed to have said, that have long ceased to be the same structures or mental complexes they once were. For twenty years now the lime works had been shut down, dead. One fine day someone realized, Konrad said, that the lime works had become unprofitable, so they let the workers go and shut down the lime works. The manager had written to Hoerhager in Zurich that the lime works had ceased to make a profit and the manager proposed to Hoerhager that he shut it down, Konrad is supposed to have told Wieser; liquidate the lime works, the manager is supposed to have written to Hoerhager, or rather, to have telegraphed, and Hoerhager immediately liquidated the lime works; Hoerhager, who was a bachelor, is said to have instantly liquidated the works without a moment's hesitation, upon receiving the manager's proposal to liquidate, Konrad is supposed to have told Wieser. But the manager was a crook, Konrad said, everything about him was crooked, at least his intentions were. Hoerhager had actually never paid any attention to the lime works, Konrad told Wieser. The manager had been using Hoerhager, managers are by their very nature the exploiters of owners, all the managers in the world are exploiters, they never think of anything else than how to exploit the owners, the principle of exploiting owners has gradually been developed by them to a truly vertiginous science. At the time the lime works were liquidated, Konrad and his wife were living in Augsburg, crammed with all their possessions into a house that, as Konrad told Wieser, was well-suited to Konrad's carrying on his research. Konrad at this time remembered

the lime works, as he had remembered it for decades before and for decades to come, as his first childhood play-
ground, a structure associated in his mind with damp, chill,
darkness, getting hurt, currently owned by his peripatetic
nephew Hoerhager who was then spending his time mostly
in Zurich, caught up in social distractions. Already the lime
works had meant to Konrad a place of eclipse, an ideal
retreat for working on his book, and already in Augsburg he started to think about buying the lime works from
Hoerhager, Konrad reminisced to Wieser, though he did
not know, did not even dream that he would actually one
day buy the lime works from his nephew, even though that
day would not arrive for two decades more. Hoerhager was
then at the point of liquidating the lime works at long distance, from Zurich, and in cold blood. Yet despite the fact
that the nephew never took the slightest interest in the lime
works other than the financial, Hoerhager held off for decades on selling it to Konrad. My nephew probably knew
that I was absolutely determined to buy the lime works,
that my life, my very existence, depended upon my acquiring the lime works, and so he would not sell to me, Konrad
is said to have told Wieser. My wife's health was growing
noticeably worse that time in Augsburg, as I remember,
Konrad said, we kept trying every kind of specialist in nearby
Munich, which was at the time world famous for its outstanding doctors, particularly its specialists for the various
kinds of deformity, for cripples. In Augsburg I used to take
long walks along the Lech River, Konrad recalled, it's a
usable sort of city, actually. The lime works manager was
rumored to have demanded a horrendous sum of compensation from Hoerhager, Konrad told Wieser, which Hoer-

hager instantly agreed to pay, just as Hoerhager always instantly agreed to whatever the manager proposed, simply to avoid being bothered, Konrad supposed. The manager offered to discharge the workmen, turn off the power, lock the gates for good. Lime works like this one in Sicking, i.e., of middling size, no longer had a future, the manager wrote to Hoerhager, so he, the manager, would undertake to wind it all up in orderly fashion; as usual, Hoerhager agreed to everything the manager proposed. The manager could have Hoerhager's power of attorney to do whatever needed to be done, Hoerhager wrote from Zurich to Sicking. I remember his being in Zurich then, Konrad said to Wieser, while we were in Augsburg, he was in Zurich, a city that takes a great interest in the advancement of culture. The lime works were liquidated within a week. All that hardly interested my nephew Hoerhager in Zurich, said Konrad, while I was always interested in anything to do with the lime works, and the liquidation of the lime works aroused my interest in Augsburg all the more, in that a shut-down, abandoned, really dead lime works was more suitable than ever for me and my scientific work, more ideal a place to live and work than ever before. I instantly dispatched a telegram to Zurich: "Buying limeworks" two words just like that, "Buying limeworks," but Hoerhager, my offer in hand, would not sell, Konrad is said to have told Wieser. So began my decades of struggle for possession of the lime works. The harder I kept after him, Konrad said to Wieser, the less inclined Hoerhager seemed to make a deal, though he could certainly have used my money, especially on the eve of World War II, yet he would not sell to me, but on the other hand he did not sell to anyone else, either, so as not to put an end to my efforts to buy the lime works, he needed for me to go on making those desperate efforts, in which he took a sadistic delight, Konrad is said to have told Wieser. As my offer went up, his resistance stiffened. This went on for two decades. In the end, by this time we had moved to Mannheim, I did buy the lime works for a high price, probably by two hundred or three hundred percent too high a price, and probably, Konrad is said to have told Wieser, when it was already too late. Hoeller was to continue staying in the annex, on a pension, as the lime works manager is supposed to have requested and Hoerhager agreed instantly to the pension for Hoeller and to let him stay on at the annex, an additional charge Konrad took over, Hoeller's pension and continued occupancy of the annex, along with the lime works, but he didn't mind, on the contrary, he needed Hoeller. It was necessary to keep someone at the lime works who would be part and parcel of it, the manager wrote to Hoerhager in Zurich, and Konrad is said to have told Wieser that this was correct, a complex like the lime works needed a man like Hoeller. Hoeller had been lime works foreman for thirty years. He would have been incapable of leaving the lime works, besides; the others simply went, most of them took jobs in the brewery, the candle factory, the quarry, and that was that. Workmen simply turn their backs on their place of work, Konrad said to Wieser, their place of work is no more to them than a machine for providing them with money. To Hoeller the lime works was home. Though it must be said that the shut-down, dead state of the lime works depressed Hoeller, Konrad told Wieser, even now. It felt weird to him. Konrad struck him as weird, too, Konrad said, but Konrad for his part regarded Hoeller, quite to the contrary, with increasing warmth as a thoroughly dependable, needed man. Konrad to Fro: he (Konrad) would start by going up to the attic, then down to the third floor, then the second, the first, and finally he would walk through all the rooms on the ground floor, to make sure that there really was not another salable thing in the house except for the Francis Bacon which he had bought in Glasgow. Just looking for something that could be converted into cash, that's all. But he found nothing. Apparently, he thought, he had sold everything already. He did not know the full extent of his indebtedness, but he knew it was enormous. His debts amounted to more than the value of the lime works. Now he had absolutely nothing left, he thought. He might go up to the attic once more, but there really was nothing at all left in the attic. Old suit cases, beer glasses, preserve jars, hat boxes, crutches. He would search every corner, because he could not believe that there could be absolutely nothing salable left in the attic, not even an old icon, nothing at all. Nothing left in the rooms, nothing on the walls, nothing. Only three years ago all these walls had still been full of things, but there was nothing hanging on them now. You could still see how much there had been, the outlines of the pictures were still visible. Now the lime works walls were bare. It had all been taken down and sold. At a ridiculous price, Konrad is said to have told Fro. But though he realized that everything was gone, that there was nothing left because he had gradually sold even the most unsalable items he'd had, he kept going back through all the rooms again, as if to reassure himself for the hundredth or the thousandth time that there was nothing left in those rooms, not one thing. The empty rooms on the ground floor are the most depressing of all, he said, according to Fro. High-ceilinged empty rooms make a terrible impression on first entering a house. He had only just been through all the rooms again, including the annex, he said, according to Fro, and there was no doubt at all that there was nothing salable left even in the annex. He said he had been considering sneaking something out of his wife's room to sell, but that would be the hardest thing to do. In his own room there was nothing left except the Francis Bacon, which he would not sell, he would never part with that painting. I might just possibly succeed in smuggling something salable out of my wife's room without her noticing it, he said. You must remember that I've nothing left in the bank, Fro quoted him saying. They had already told him at the bank that he had exhausted his account. But a man had to have *some* money, even after he had reduced his needs to the absolute minimum. What can we be living on? he was thinking, he told Fro, as he stepped into his wife's room to look around for something salable there, though he thought immediately that there actually was nothing salable in his wife's room at all, the stuff on her walls was nothing but junk, he said to Fro, his wife had always surrounded herself with junk, valuable things always depressed her, a woman who had owned so many things of value, but even when they moved into the lime works she did not want any valuable things in her room, Konrad said to Fro, he remembered this the instant he stepped into her room and noticed again that there really was nothing salable in there. All the things in my wife's room are worthless and tasteless, he is supposed to have said, but I don't want you to think that my wife doesn't have good taste or a sense of value! The total absence of taste revealed on all the four walls of his wife's room had struck him with full force, on this occasion, that whole room was an all-encompassing demonstration of a lack of taste, it was full of tasteless things, he thought, while puffing up her pillow and slipping the ottoman under her feet. The more he looked around in his wife's room the more tasteless it seemed. Except for the sugar bowl, an heirloom from her maternal grandmother, he thought over and over, only the sugar bowl and nothing else, the sugar bowl, the sugar bowl, the sugar bowl, he thought, but to sell her sugar bowl, to take it out of the room under some pretext and to sell it suddenly struck him as absurd, they'll give me next-to-nothing for this sugar bowl, though it actually is a fine object of value, he thought, they'll pay me far too little to make it worth while, he thought, according to Fro. It was ridiculous to think of selling her sugar bowl. Now he felt totally exhausted, certain that there was nothing salable left in the whole lime works, nothing to be cashed in for even a trifling amount of money, and he also remembered that he had broken off his business dealings with even the Voecklabruck antiquarian, the one with access to the American market, long since, after finally catching on to the man's shady practices, and so he sat down, according to Fro, feeling utterly exhausted, knowing that he was through financially, sat down in the chair opposite his wife's invalid chair where she usually sat dozing, half asleep, the way she had been for decades now. Sitting there looking at her he kept saying to himself, I will not sell the Francis Bacon, never the Francis Bacon, absolutely not, I will not sell the Francis Bacon, no I won't, not the Francis Bacon. If the men from the bank come snooping around I shall hide it. I had better hide the Francis Bacon, Konrad kept thinking over and over. And later: eight o'clock, supper time, and time, the whole evening, half the night, has passed us by, the two of us sitting here, a couple facing each other, and we haven't had a bite or taken a sip of anything all day, as happens so often. As a child, Konrad was the one who had been sickly most of the time, while she, as Konrad tells it, was never once sick until her accident. How often he had been forced to stay in bed, feverish, in pain, while his brothers and sisters were laughing, having fun, right under his window in the garden, free to not think about their health at all. The slightest shift in the weather was enough to make Konrad catch cold. Something cold to drink, and Konrad caught cold. Nearly all during his childhood he had suffered from headaches. Later on, when he entered secondary school, his chronic childhood headaches had ceased overnight, says Fro, but Konrad continued to be in poor health all through secondary school, most of the time he was ailing in some way though the doctors never got to the bottom of his ailments; whatever caused them—and they are said to have worsened noticeably between his twenty-second and twenty-eighth year—was never cleared up by any doctor because, as Konrad told Fro, not one of those doctors who collected such exorbitantly high fees from his parents really bothered to look into it. Doctors were always surprised at the manifestations of a disease, any disease new to them, but they never did anything to find the cause of it, even though, as Konrad said to Fro, it was in the nature of a disease to be open to exploration, diseases were there to be investigated, i.e., doctors were in a position to find the causes of disease, but they did nothing about it, they were always and in every case satisfied to be surprised by it, out of indifference and laziness where disease was concerned. Actually, whenever they made any real effort, they could find the causes of disease, and in time they would find the causes of all the diseases, Konrad remarked to Fro, but they would take centuries to do it, and since new diseases kept turning up, the doctors would gradually uncover the causes of one disease after another without ever completely uncovering the cause of all diseases. Konrad took pleasure in making that kind of remark. Everything throughout all his childhood and youth and in fact throughout all of his life, Konrad is supposed to have told Fro, had simply been too much for his strength. While his brothers and sisters went in swimming together and enjoyed themselves in the water, he did not even dare look at the water for fear of catching a chill, the mere sight of the water could give him a chill. What characterized his whole childhood, his whole youth, was timidity without a respite, not fear, timidity. In addition he suffered because his sister and his brother Francis were only one year apart in age, they were practically the same age and inseparable companions in consequence, of course, while he, years older than they, which made him much weaker than they, was separated from them by the difference in age between them and him, a separateness that hurt him to the roots of his being, and so he had grown up in isolation because of the ruinous gap in age between him and them. He had always been alone. As the much older brother, his siblings had always repulsed him, excluded him from everything to do with themselves, they quite naturally drove him out into a loneliness that grew more and more complicated, into a solitude that more and more sapped the roots of his being. The misfortune of being six years older than his sister, seven years older than his brother Francis, as Fro says Konrad told him, led to his life of chronic isolation. For at least three decades, at least until he married his wife, all of his physical and spiritual forces had been focused on nothing other than extricating himself from this unfair isolation. All during his childhood he worried about losing touch with his siblings and his family in general, because of their continuing instinctive rejection of him. He had often thought: if I am not to go out of my mind altogether, I must break out of my nearly total isolation from my brother and sister, my parents, relatives, all my fellow human beings, in fact. Shut in as he was, all he could do was look on as gradually everyone turned against him. Meanwhile his parents, as he told Fro, brought him up along with the other two, if they did bring him up, that is, if you could call it that, in nearly total ignorance. Nature seems to have designed parents to function in such a way, he told Fro, as to induce in the first-born child acute depression and revulsion, so that it ends by pining away, going to seed, perishing. What superhuman energies I would have needed to cope with the unfairness of it! Konrad said. To get myself out from under the weight and swelter of such a wholly mindless upbringing. It was because of this upbringing, which ultimately he could regard as nothing less than unscrupulous, that he could not write his book, though he had been working on it most intently for two decades, more or less; he was always on the brink of writing it down, but unable to start writing it down, and all because of the unscrupulous way he had been brought up, as Fro tells it. Everything from his earliest beginnings conspired against his getting his work down on paper. One appalling phase of life after another, all adding up in the end to a catastrophic effect on his ability to write his book. Perhaps he had no right to say it, but he had a right to think it, that to look into his childhood was to look into a snake pit, into a hell. To open a door into his childhood was to open a door to darkness itself. Nothing but coldness and ruthlessness. In that pitch darkness the indifference and secret heartlessness emanating from his parents still made themselves felt. The loneliness he had learned to endure even in his earliest childhood, the principal lesson of his childhood, he made an incessant study of his loneliness, he said to Fro. At the very moment when he needed the opposite he had been struck down by the most acute loneliness imaginable. He was nearly destroyed through the sheer solitude in which he had to arrive at a decision about his special subject of study and so, yielding to his parents' wishes, he never did embark on any program of studies, never went to a university, never took a state examination, because he simply did not have the energy to assert himself against his parents and study natural science or medicine, as he longed to do though later on when he had reached manhood he had been able to assert himself in every respect, whenever necessary, because as a child or youth he had never been able to assert himself, not even in the most insignificant ways, including of course his desire to study natural science or medicine, both of which had aroused his interest early in life, but his parents had always opposed his going to a university, they would never have let him study natural science, specifically medicine, if anything they might have let him attend agricultural school, like his father before him, they never intended to let him pursue academic

studies, he was to function solely as the heir to their properties, considerable enough even after the so-called upheavals
of the First World War and its attendant chaos, sizable hold-
ings in real estate and other kinds of property; the way they
saw it, and it never occurred to them to see it any other
way, was that he was to come into his huge, far-flung inheri-
tance at the high point of his life, be a man of position, and
spend his life managing his estates. Possibly, Fro says Konrad told him, this parental opposition to his academic plans
had broken his spirit, so that he had become habituated to
living in a state of demoralization and indifference, which
ultimately incapacitated him for writing his book at all, an
incapacity that grew more incurable as his wife's illness grew
worse. Ever since he could remember, whatever he started
out to do had a way of ending in utter exhaustion. Even
here in the lime works, Fro reports Konrad as telling him,
which he had always assumed would be the one place in the
world most favorable to his writing, everything had turned
against it. For his failure to write his book he blamed,
in addition, all sorts of illnesses occurring in and around
Sicking. The fact that nobody grew old in Sicking. Although everybody gave the impression of being old, nevertheless. Wherever you went in Sicking, you would see nothing but old people, he said, even the children; if you looked
at them hard enough, you were struck by the way they
exhibited the repulsive mannerisms of the old. The natives
had a way of catching early in life one of the hundreds of
thousands of chronic diseases that were so hard to classify,
and then they tended to withdraw into their chronic un-
classifiable diseases, encapsulate themselves in their diseases,
and simply wither away. He saw it happening all the time.

All kinds of names were found for these diseases, but they invariably turned out to be all wrong because the men responsible for naming them were hopelessly superficial and loathed making an effort. The entire countryside around the lime works was a constant source of every kind of universally infectious disease, all of these diseases were supposed to be known diseases although in fact absolutely nothing was known about any of these diseases to this very day, he is understood to have said, because medical science is the most dimwitted of all, medical doctors were the most dimwitted, the most unscrupulous, and the sick, left to their diseases, tended gradually to withdraw into themselves in the most self-degrading way, they had no choice, taken in continually by their quacks as they were, all they could do was to die off. He happened to be in an ideal position to observe all this happening in the case of his own wife, to whom such and such a disease was attributed even though it was common knowledge that medical science knew nothing at all about her disease, Konrad is supposed to have said. The doctors talked about it as if it were a lung disease, for instance, Fro says Konrad told him, but in fact the so-called lung disease they talked about was no lung disease at all. Heart disease was also mentioned, but in fact this so-called heart disease was no heart disease. Whatever disease the doctors talked about was in fact something quite different from what they called it, Konrad said. They would say that so-and-so was sick in the head, that he had a head disease with such-and-such a name, when in fact nothing at all was known about that disease, including whether it was or wasn't a head disease. The man limps, they would say, but the cause of his limping is unknown. They would talk about the kidneys and the liver, but the disease the doctors were talking about had nothing whatever to do with the liver or the kidneys of that particular patient. All of these diseases were primarily so-called psychosomatic diseases that masqueraded as organic diseases. Basically there was no such thing as organic disease. All there was were the so-called psychosomatic diseases, Fro recalls Konrad saying, and all these psychosomatic diseases, all diseases in short, that were known, which does not mean that these known diseases were fully researched diseases, but which were in any case always so-called psychosomatic diseases, ultimately became organic diseases because the doctors had no integrity, paid no attention, because of their vacuous arrogance, vacuous depravity, vacuous brutality. It was the doctors who were to blame for so-called organic disease, Konrad is reported to have said, whereas the blame for so-called psychosomatic diseases falls on nature or, if you like, the creation. It all begins in nature, or creation, but ultimately the doctors and only the doctors are to blame. But to speak of so-called psychosomatic diseases is to be on the wrong track entirely, Konrad is supposed to have said, just as much on the wrong track as to speak of organic or so-called organic diseases. Besides, all the cases in the Sicking region, Fro reports Konrad as saying, were invariably cases of premature death, everyone who died here had died prematurely, they all died here sooner than they should normally have died. To blame were the climate and the doctors, demonstrably so, and the causes of the diseases as well as the deaths were in every case something other than the official causes given. To Wieser: at the very moment when Konrad thought he could turn his attention to his work, he would suddenly hear Hoeller chopping wood.

He would get up, go to look out the window, and of course see nothing; but he would hear it. It was always at the precise moment when he felt like starting to write, and everything seemed propitious to getting it all written down quickly, that Hoeller chose to start chopping wood. As though everything were in conspiracy against my writing the thing, Konrad is supposed to have said. Yesterday it was the public works inspector, today it's Hoeller, all sorts of trifles, thousands of them, keep getting in the way of my work. Then there was his wife's earache, probably brought on by his intensified use of her in accordance with the Urbanchich method of hearing tests and exercises, brought on by the progressive ruthlessness with which he had to make her undergo these exercises, which he had resolved to apply in a more complicated, radicalized form, increasingly so, an unshakable resolve which naturally caused growing tension between him and his wife. He couldn't possibly stop experimenting on her now all of a sudden, he told Wieser; he had gone too far to stop. He had been progressively perfecting the Urbanchich method, until it had become a martyrdom for her, as he put it. The essence of every method was after all its total amenability to further development; its absolute pitch, as he called it. The rest could only be a matter of perfecting these experiments of his, and thereby perfecting his book, which already existed in its entirety in his head. Unfortunately the public works inspector ruined everything for me yesterday, Konrad is supposed to have said to Wieser, and today Hoeller started with his wood chopping, and for the time being everything to do with his work had simply been wiped out. When a man had condemned himself to a scientific task such as his, Konrad said to Wieser,

meaning a lifelong sentence at hard labor, it was tantamount
to having surrendered himself as victim to a conspiracy that
would ultimately involve the whole world and even whatever possibilities existed beyond the world. It was all part of
a single conspiracy against a man, that is, against the intellectual labors he must perform. There was nothing one could
do about it, except to be constantly aware of the wasting
away of one's energies, an awareness that all by itself and
unaided would have to fuel the intensification of a humanly
almost impossible effort on behalf of his intellectual labors,
to bridge all the gaps simultaneously each moment, he
thought, ultimately a high art to be mastered only by brain
automatism, an art that was the only enduring refuge, the
only purpose of one's existence one might hope for and find
and, ultimately, invent. But the world, especially the part of
it that constituted one's immediate environment, regarded
every intellectual, scientific undertaking as an enormity di-
rected in every case against the world, against the environment; such an undertaking, though possible only for the
individual, was considered to belong by right to the mass,
and the individual was always exposed to the mass's radical
opposition, which was in effect the criminality of the mass,
a criminality that ended by empowering the individual to
think and master and perfect precisely all the thought and
action which the mass forbade and denied him all his life
long. The mass denied to the individual what was possible
only to the individual and not to the mass, the individual
denied to the mass what was possible only to the mass, but
the individual did not concern himself with the mass, ultimately he concerned himself only with himself to the advantage of the mass, just as the mass ultimately did not

concern itself with the individual to the individual's advantage, the mass recognized the individual's achievement only after the destruction of the individual, as the individual recognized the achievement of the mass only after the destruction of the mass and so forth. If it wasn't the public works inspector then it was the forestry commissioner, or Hoeller, or the baker, or the chimney sweep, or Wieser, or myself, or his wife, it was everyone. It then occurred to him that he did not really have to put up with all that, and he would go down and forbid Hoeller to chop wood. When he, Konrad, was working, then Hoeller did not have to chop wood at the same time, and vice versa, when Hoeller was chopping wood, Konrad could not think or write, Hoeller would have to do his wood chopping when Konrad gave him leave to get on with it, and so forth. Hoeller instantly stopped chopping wood and went inside the annex, Konrad calling after him to do something noiseless, like repairing those torn, frazzled waste baskets Konrad had personally brought to the annex for that purpose three days ago. Unfortunately he said this in loud, accusatory tones, Konrad is supposed to have told Wieser, and no sooner had Hoeller disappeared inside the annex than Konrad felt remorseful about taking that tone with a man he had always been so careful to address in the gentlest possible way, and he spent hours brooding over the reasons why he might have been so loud, rough, and impatient with Hoeller, why he had suddenly lost control over his voice, i.e., over himself, especially toward Hoeller of all people; and to Wieser Konrad is supposed to have said that it was possible to speak too sharply to a person while irritated about something quite unconnected with that individual, who could only feel taken aback and often terrified by the unprovoked attack upon himself, and in this way one would have suddenly damaged a relationship with a person one happened to be warmly attached to, as Konrad was to Hoeller. However, going back to his room, he had decided that he had not really spoken too sharply to Hoeller, he told Wieser. Absolute quiet had now been restored and Konrad was able to get back to work, he said; he sat down at his desk and thought: here is the first sentence, and he wrote down his first sentence. A few more such sentences, he thought, and the book will be on its way to being written at last. But he had thought so hundreds if not thousands of times, Konrad said to Wieser, that if he could only get a few sentences down on paper, the rest of the book would gradually write itself, all at once, he had thought thousands of times, and yet he would break off after getting a few sentences down on paper, as long ago as Augsburg he had believed he would be able to get the whole thing on paper in one continuous flow, once he had gotten a few sentences down, it was the same in Augsburg and in Innsbruck and in Paris and in Aschaffenburg and in Schweinfurt and in Bolzano and in Merano and in Rome and in London and in Vienna and in Florence and in Copenhagen and in Hamburg and in Frankfurt and in Cologne and in Brussels and in Ravenna and in Rattenberg and in Toblach and in Neulengbach and in Korneuburg and in Gaenserndorf and in Calais and in Kufstein and in Munich and in Prien and in Muerzzuschlag and in Thalgau and in Pforzheim and in Mannheim. All those beginnings and ideas, lost time and again and forever. Suddenly there is a knock at the front door, downstairs, Konrad said to Wieser. At first I ignore it, he said, but one cannot ignore it indefinitely, the knocking doesn't stop, so I finally have to get up and go down to answer it. By the time he has reached the vestibule, he has lost the connection between those beginning sentences. He opens the door, and there stands the public works inspector. Well, what is it? he asks, and then he says, Ah, it's you! thinking that the inspector always shows up at the most inopportune times, and then Konrad said: Do come in! quite against his will, as he told Wieser, Do come in, and the works inspector came in, and then they sat down in the room to the right of the entrance, the so-called wood-paneled room. This room at the time still contained a set of chairs usually described as Viennese baroque; incidentally most comfortable to sit in. Do sit down, Konrad said to the works inspector, though it is rather cold in this so-called wood-paneled room, but if you keep your coat on you can sit here quite comfortably. I myself am quite hardened to the cold, Konrad is supposed to have said to the works inspector, of course Konrad took the works inspector into the ice-cold room deliberately, says Wieser, hoping literally to freeze his guest out, but even though Konrad remarked that the temperature in the so-called wood-paneled room was only three degrees above zero, the inspector did not leave, on the contrary, he seemed to be quite at ease and apparently found the so-called wood-paneled room not at all too cold, but settled back in a Viennese baroque chair for quite a while. We can't go to my room, Konrad said to the works inspector, my desk is piled high with papers, I am working on my book, as you know. Then Konrad brought his guest something to drink, even though he had absolutely no wish to talk with him, longing as he did to get back to his desk and his work, but "no, no" he (Konrad) said when the inspector asked whether he was interrupting Konrad in his work, *your writing* is what he is supposed to have said. Oh no, Konrad lied, thinking that the lie was about the only means of contact with another human being. Let us attend to whatever needs our attention, Konrad is supposed to have said, and the works inspector said something about grading the road and Konrad, without being asked, as he admitted, said, as you know, I am working on that book I have so often told you about. I am so entirely caught up in it, you know, he said, it's a mania I'm afraid, I seem to be possessed by it, all there is of me, as you know it is in the nature of a mania that a man will give his entire life to it and destroy himself entirely by his obsession alone and nothing else. It's a study of the sense of hearing, Konrad is supposed to have said to the works inspector. As you know, Konrad said, so much has been written about the brain, but virtually nothing, at least nothing of any consequence, has been done on the auditory sense. He had been working on it for about twenty years, Konrad is supposed to have told the inspector; I started by exhausting myself, he said, slowly but with gradually increasing intensity, with these experiments, then I summed it all up, did more experiments, summed up again, and again, etc., Konrad said, then I went back to experimenting, completed the experiments, wrote a summation and another summation, etc. I constantly experiment, and a series of experiments is always followed by another series of experiments, Wieser reports Konrad as saying. Then it all fell apart, at the very peak of concentration it all fell to pieces again. But now Konrad said he had the whole thing complete in his head, all the details together and in place, the most incredible material you can imagine, he said, everything to do with the auditory sense. But no sooner have I reached my peak of concentration than it all falls apart again, Konrad said. *Now I have it,* I think, but at that very moment it has all collapsed. But when one has had it all in one's head for so long, completely in one's head for all those years, he said to the works inspector, one is bound to assume that it is only a question of time, that the auspicious moment must come sooner or later when one will suddenly be able to set it all down on paper. This was the moment he had been waiting for, it had come, as he also said several times to Wieser, the moment was here, now, as he said to Fro too, as I know, and Konrad actually said this to the inspector, the moment came every day, indeed there was not a day without such a moment when he believed the time to begin had come, and that he would now finish writing his book, but every time it came, Konrad said to the works inspector, as soon as he sat down at his desk he would be interrupted, whether, as he said, by the baker or the chimney sweep or on one occasion by Wieser or else by Fro, or by the works inspector, or Hoeller, or his wife, or the forestry commissioner, or a noise, or whatever it was. But it was quite impossible not to go down and open the door when there was a knock at the door, he said to the inspector, to let someone knock incessantly on the door without responding was something impossible for him if only because it would drive him crazy in record time. People never cease their knocking, Konrad said, even when they know they are disturbing me, delaying my work, possibly ruining my book, ruining everything, but they will not stop knocking until I get up, move the papers aside, and go down to open the door. Invariably it is the most ridiculous trifle for the sake of which I am interrupted in my work, Konrad is supposed to have said, some enormous absurdity that threatens to ruin my life's work. To think that he had always dreamed of the lime works as a place where he and his wife would be living in perfect isolation and freedom from interruption by people, that here in the lime works the destructive apparatus of the increasingly disturbed, nervous so-called consumer society, with its chronically irritating and ultimately ruinous effect on everything in the nature of intellectual effort could not touch them, that here they would have escaped all that, but in reality they continued to be irritated by people even here at the lime works, he simply did not have the strength, Konrad said to Wieser, to resist opening the door when someone knocked, he invariably yielded and opened the door, Konrad said, not from considerations of humanity, not from motives of civility about which he couldn't have cared less, he hated every kind of propriety, he had learned to hate propriety in the course of decades of experiencing life, he hated everything to do with social forms, everything implied by civility toward people, and it was purely, as stated, a pitiable lack of personal energy that made him go down and open the door, made him desert his work, what could be more depressing than to desert a task like mine, so laboriously constructed in decades of hard work, to desert it for the sake of a chimney sweep, a baker, a works inspector, how low a man must have sunk to desert his work for the most absurd, the most trifling reason, because his wife upstairs wants her pillow straightened or needs a drink of water or wants to be read to from her favorite romantic poet, or wants the curtains drawn or opened, a piece of bread cut, her hair ribbon tightened, her garter tied, her sugar bowl filled, her spectacles set on her nose, her back rubbed with alcohol, or else because of Hoeller's wood-chopping or Fro, or the man from the sawmill, or on your account, Wieser. Actually, Konrad is supposed to have said to Wieser in a tone of utter weariness, this endless knocking on my door, though quite constant in its actual sound level and intensity, in my head swells to a terrifying, ear-splitting thunderousness and drives me completely crazy. It forced him to get up, drop everything, go down and unlock the door, just to stop the knocking. Having done this, Konrad said, there was no point in being impolite about it, because the damage is done by then, so I am exquisitely polite although of course I ask myself every time I am so exquisitely polite why I am being so exquisitely polite. The whole day is ruined, everything in his head is dissipated beyond recall, there is nothing left but a few polite formulas such as, Do come in, Come in, How are you, Ah yes, or maybe just Yes indeed, or You don't say, suddenly issuing from his lips. This time you have really ruined my work completely, Konrad said to the works inspector, according to Wieser, telling him the truth for the first time. First Hoeller started it with his wood-chopping, Konrad said to the inspector, and I went down and ordered Hoeller to stop it instantly, I ordered him to repair the waste baskets and went back to my room and sat down at my desk feeling that my book was saved, because Hoeller did not actually cause an interruption to the extent of completely dissipating my concept, but now you have come knocking at the door and you've wrecked the whole thing, to be interrupted twice in a row in so complex a mental effort as my book is fatal. While it was still possible to return to my book after Hoeller's relatively superficial disturbance, this second interruption makes it impossible for me to go on with what I was doing. I hope you won't mind, Konrad said to the inspector, according to Wieser, my speaking to you so frankly about it, and went on to say that the first interruption by Hoeller had been possible to overcome, with a little skillful effort, but not the second interruption by the inspector. Besides, it makes a difference, Konrad said, whether an interruption is caused by a man like Hoeller or a man like yourself; a simple man like Hoeller or a complicated man like yourself, after all, so complicated a man, Konrad is said to have exclaimed while offering the inspector some schnapps, but the inspector is said to have declined, at first, that is, but he ended by accepting, one always declines at first but one ends by accepting, Konrad said to the inspector, a type that Konrad felt quite familiar with, the type that always declines at first and then ends by accepting anyway. It's a fact, Konrad said to the works inspector, according to Wieser, no really informative work on hearing exists, the only honest study of the subject that has any value is some three hundred years old, all the rest is botch work. Which is why I have become wholly absorbed in the idea of writing about it, doing a serious book on the subject, on the sense of hearing, has come to be a totally absorbing task for me, not at the beginning, of course, not totally absorbing before my thirtieth year, nor did it absorb me totally as yet even between my thirtieth and fortieth year, but ever since my fortieth year I have been totally absorbed by the idea of studying the sense of hearing, and writing the definitive book on it, I have been relentlessly, more and more exclusively absorbed by it. It was a fact, he said, that all thinkers tended to develop a subject of their own, until their thirtieth

year, that would begin to absorb them completely one day,
some time after their fortieth year, but only a very few surrender themselves wholly to their subjects, most of them flirt
with their subject after the age of twenty-five and develop it
for a time, but after their thirty-fifth or fortieth year they tend
to drop it and drift off into society or quite simply into a life
of bourgeois comfort. In this way, most regrettably, hundreds
of thousands of vital scientific studies are lost to the world,
works needed to bring light into the world's darkness. As
regards hearing, that would tend to be written about, quite
superficially at that, Konrad is supposed to have said to the
works inspector, according to Wieser, by a medical doctor,
the wrong approach entirely, or else by a philosopher, also
the wrong approach. Whatever a medical man wrote about it
was sure to be worthless stuff, and whatever a philosopher
wrote about it was also sure to be worthless. To tackle a subject such as the sense of hearing and write it up, one had to
be more than a mere medical man or a mere philosopher.
To do this it was absolutely necessary to be a mathematician
and a physicist as well, that is to say, one should be a master
of all natural science, as well as a prophet and a superlative
artist. It was simply not enough to be a medical man, or a
philosopher, or a physiognomist, to write the kind of book
that was needed on the sense of hearing. To think that such
specialists could do justice to the subject was a misconception.
What I have in mind is the formulation of a definitive statement on the subject, Konrad is supposed to have said, the
final word on it, though of course the moment you achieved
such finality it ceased to be final, and so forth. The principle
involved was one on which Konrad said he had spoken
to the works inspector before, had indeed familiarized him

with it sufficiently so that he could now proceed from the premise that any final point is a starting point for a further development toward a new final point and so forth, Konrad is supposed to have said to the inspector, according to Wieser. However, it was all much more complicated than that, because basically much simpler than we assume, which is why nothing could be elucidated with any finality, ultimately. A so-called approach to a subject would get you nowhere. Communication was impossible except by means of the work as a whole. Radical changes were to be expected, Konrad is supposed to have said to the inspector, and said again, significantly: radical changes that would be transformations, and despite the fact that the inspector had listened to this remark with particular interest, Wieser reports that Konrad said to the inspector at this point that people tend to turn a deaf ear to the significant point, they just miss hearing it, even you, my dear inspector, miss hearing the significant point, just as everyone tends to miss hearing the most significant, or at least the highly significant remarks addressed to them, they miss them all the time, though apart from that, Konrad is said to have added, there is really no such thing as a really significant remark, not even a highly significant remark, nothing at all has any real significance and so forth, but intentionally or not, listeners tend to miss a great deal that is said to them, so that in effect they miss everything, and so forth; the unintentional is the intentional, the most unintentional the most intentional, and so forth. Whenever I am not working on my book, Konrad is supposed to have said, then it is quiet, the whole lime works is completely encapsulated in the quiet characteristic of the place. No need to describe this quiet to the works inspector, who was sufficiently acquainted with it. It was totally quiet when he, Konrad, was not working, when he was walking up and down, this way and that, turning things over in his mind, because when I am turning things over in my mind, he is supposed to have said, I am not actually working, i.e., of course I am working when I am thinking things over, but basically I do not really begin to do my work proper until after the phase of considerations and reconsiderations is ended, which is when I begin to do the actual work, but by then it's all likely to be all over with the quiet here, what with Hoeller starting to chop wood all of a sudden, or else the baker arrives, or the chimney sweep, or Stoerschneider turns up, or the man from the sawmill, or you arrive, Wieser arrives, Fro arrives, someone comes knocking at the door, or else my wife needs something or other. All in the midst of this enormously demanding task, this medico-musico-metaphysical-mathematical work of mine, which is at all times so totally disruptible! As soon as I dare to sit down and start to think that the moment has come when I might be able to write the whole thing down in one sitting, someone invariably knocks at the front door, or my wife rings for a change of stockings. Even though she happens to be the most considerate person in the world, Konrad is supposed to have said. At Laska's, too, everyone is always saying that Konrad's wife is the most considerate person there is, and at Lanner's it's the same story. The moment someone says, as someone did at the Stiegler, yesterday, for instance, that Konrad is the most inconsiderate person, then someone else instantly counters with the observation that Mrs. Konrad is the most considerate person in the world. Twenty years ago, Konrad said, he had in all secrecy set his mind on writing this book of his, behind his wife's back. And this foolishness, undertaken behind his wife's back, held him in its grip ever since. At first he managed to keep his preoccupation with his work a secret from his wife, fearing that if she should suddenly discover that he was busying himself with a scientific work the results might be catastrophic, since she naturally knew that, as with anything else he did, he would never relinquish the undertaking until he had completed it. For years he had been able to keep it a secret, not only from his wife, of course, but from everyone else as well. She had known nothing about it in Augsburg, as yet, nor had anyone else, nor as yet in Aschaffenburg, nor in Bolzano, Merano, Munich; then suddenly, in Paris, he had revealed to her in the most casual manner that he was at work on a book. I am working on something about the sense of hearing, he is supposed to have said to his wife, about the auditory sense, no one has done anything about it yet. At that instant she realized that he, who had been everything in the world to her always, Konrad is supposed to have said to Wieser, was lost to her—it was then she knew for certain that it was all over. It's a fact, Konrad said to Wieser, the moment I decided to devote myself to my book on hearing, I was lost to my wife, and that was actually four or five or even six years before the moment when she suddenly knew that she had lost him. All sorts of people have already written about all kinds of things, all kinds of excellent disquisitions, dissertations, whatever, Konrad said to the works inspector, but there is no first-rate disquisition, or dissertation, or even one good essay on the sense of hearing. This fact struck me most forcibly, but at the same time I perceived in it a chance, if not the only chance, for me. Especially because the ear is indisputably more basic than the brain, if you take the ear as your point of departure, and as long as you do not take the brain as your point of departure in this context. The works inspector did not understand this point, Wieser is supposed to have said. There were so many inadequate, amateurish doctoral theses about the hearing, Konrad said to the works inspector, according to Wieser, and of course the amateurishness of a doctoral dissertation was the most embarrassing kind of amateurishness. The dilettantism of the specialists was the most embarrassing kind, the most distressing thing about the specialists was their boundless dilettantism, every time. I can tell you, Konrad is supposed to have said, that I sweated through no less than two hundred dissertations on the hearing, and not one of them contained an inkling of what the hearing was all about. None of the authors had any ability to do their own thinking, at all, Konrad said; all they are is professorial ruminants. The salient characteristic of our era is, after all, the fact that the thinkers no longer do any thinking of their own. What we have nowadays is whole armies, numbering in the millions, of apprentice workmen in science and history. But anyone who dares to say so runs the risk of being declared insane. These days, the clairaudiant as well as the clairvoyant is instantly branded as a madman. The keen of ear as well as the keen-eyed are not wanted these days; when a man is keen of ear or keen of eye they simply wipe him out, lock him up, isolate him, destroy him by locking him up and isolating him. Society exercises great vigilance in guarding itself against its geniuses by being vigilantly on guard against its so-called madmen. Society is in favor of the dim, vegetative existence and nothing else. People want to be left in peace, and consequently they hate nothing more deeply than the ear and the brain. The social ideal is the totally deaf and dumb mass, and so society naturally inclines to shoot on sight any ears or brains that crop up; here is a brain, they say, shoot to kill; here is an ear, shoot it down. From the beginning mankind has been waging a war, Konrad said to Wieser, an increasingly costly, monstrous campaign against the ear and the brain; everything else is a lie. History proves that the ear and the brain are always being hunted down, shot to death. Wherever you look, ears and brains are being murdered, Konrad is supposed to have said to Wieser. Wherever there is an ear or a brain, there is hatred; where there is an ear, there is a conspiracy against the ear, where there is a brain, there is a conspiracy against the brain. The rest is lies. The dying birds of Europe are being protected, Konrad is supposed to have said, but not the dying brains, not the dying ears. But all this is ridiculous, whatever one can say is ridiculous, Konrad is supposed to have said, the moment you say something you find you have made an ass of yourself, no matter what it is, we make ourselves ridiculous, whatever we read is ridiculous, whatever we hear, ridiculous, whatever we believe, ridiculous. Open your mouth and a ridiculous statement is sure to come out, some embarrassing absurdity or other, or else an absurd embarrassment, whichever. Then Konrad said to the works inspector, according to Wieser, aren't you cold? Konrad was inclined to believe that his guest might be feeling cold, even though Konrad himself was not cold, he had his fur vest on underneath his jacket, one had to wear fur underneath one's outer garments here in the lime works, this quite apart from the fact that Konrad was by now hardened to the cold. The conditions prevailing in the lime works had hardened him. Everything in the lime works was cold, the cold was everything here. In fact, all of the last twenty years, he said, you might even say all my life long, I have been preoccupied with the sense of hearing. Only for as long as my book remains unwritten in my head, is it a scientific work; it will not be a work of art until after I have written it down. It is hearing that makes everything else possible. But for the uninitiated everything I say is no better than blasphemy. If I could, Konrad is supposed to have said to the inspector, Wieser says, I would make you acquainted, even intimately acquainted, with the most important parts of my book, but it is not possible. The moment he began to explain matters he could see at once that it was absurd to try to explain. Every explanation led inescapably to a totally false outcome, the more things were explained the sicker they got, because the explanations were false in every case, and the outcome of every explanation was invariably the wrong outcome. This book of his was divided into nine parts or sections. The number 9, in fact, played a most important part in this work, everything in it was divisible by 9, everything could be extrapolated from 9; as the inspector might not be aware, the 9 was more important than the 7, and especially with regard to the auditory sense the 9 was of the greatest importance. The first section is an introduction to all the others, the ninth section is an elucidation of all the preceding ones, Konrad is supposed to have said to the inspector, the second section naturally deals with the brain and the ear, the ear and the brain and so forth, the sixth section is entitled "The Sub-auditory Sense," a lengthy treatise primarily on the so-called dysarthria of the ear, the seventh section dealt with hearing and seeing. The hearing is the most philosophical of all the senses, Konrad said to the inspector, as reported by Wieser, but he had all nine sections complete in his head, for decades by now, it was a monstrous strain on a man to keep so complicated an intellectual structure in his head in every detail, carrying it around with him in the constant and continually increasing anxiety that it would fall apart and dissipate itself from one moment to the next, dissolve into nothing, and all because he was constantly missing the right moment for capturing it all on paper. I spent two whole years preparing for the first section of my book, and in the following eighteen years I was able to develop and complete my preparations for the rest, a feat that was enough in itself to make a man suspect, as he had unfortunately found out for himself, enough to bring him under suspicion and into disrepute as a total madman, frankly and obviously a clinical case. Of all those nine parts the fifth was the hardest, in fact he still had no title for it. Nothing could be easier, of course, than to go really insane, Konrad is supposed to have said, but my task is too important to let myself be deterred by the fear of insanity. Nothing would be easier than to go crazy from one minute to the next and thereby be relieved of so monstrous a burden. To be suddenly totally psychotic, without any preceding craziness, a sudden full-fledged psychosis. But as long as he had not gotten it all down on paper it was wasted, and he said so every day to his wife, that all his work was wasted as long as it remained in his head without being set down on paper, and she would say, then why didn't he get it down on paper, she'd been saying this for years in the same tone of voice, Konrad is supposed to have said, because she still had not caught on to the fact that it was possible to carry a book like this around in one's head for years and even for decades without ever being able to get it written down. Women were all alike in this respect, they were simply incapable of understanding peculiarities of this sort, they will not accept them and they can go on refusing to accept them for decades on end. A book a man has in his head but not on paper has no real existence, after all, Konrad said to the works inspector, according to Wieser. I must write it down, simply write it down, he kept thinking, that's all there is to it, to get it written down, sit down and write it, this was the thought that had begun to dominate his every waking moment, not the thought of the book as such, but the thought of writing it, of getting it written down from one moment to the next; but the more obsessed he was by this idea, the more impossible it became for him to write his book down. The problem was not so much that he had something in his head, everybody had the most monstrous things in his head, where they went on without a break to the very end of the man's life, the problem was to get all this monstrousness out of one's head and on to paper. It was possible to have anything in your head, and in fact everybody did have everything in his head, but on paper almost nobody had anything, Konrad is supposed to have said to the inspector, according to Wieser. While the heads of all mankind were crammed with every kind of monstrousness, what they had on paper amounted to only the most lamentable, ridiculous, pitiful stuff. If his book did not turn out to be the most sensitive distillate of the subject conceivable, Konrad is supposed to have said, a sensitive distillate by a hypersensitive brain overstrained to that end for decades . . . It was in the lime works, in the total seclusion of the lime works, that he had always believed he would be able to get it all written down, all at once. A head that was totally secluded, isolated from the outside world, would be able to write this book more easily than one involved with the outside world, with society. But think what an extra effort of concentration it takes, Konrad said to the inspector, according to Wieser, to work up such a book for the first time in such a head as his and hold it there, when this head was not completely sequestered from the world, from society, let us say, because it is linked with a person who is not completely sequestered from society. Head and person, as you know, Konrad said to the inspector, according to Wieser, are inescapably linked together. Body and head are hopelessly interlinked, or, as he often thought, most gruesomely interwedged. Well, who could even begin to describe nature and its machinations, anyway. In the lime works, at any rate, Konrad is supposed to have said, lay the best imaginable chance for his work. But nothing could be accomplished without ruthlessness, you can ask my wife, Konrad is supposed to have said, I know that everyone is saying that she, my wife, is the most considerate person, while I, her husband, am the most ruthless, I am fully aware of it, nor does it upset me, because if it did all these opinions would long since have upset me to death, Konrad is supposed to have said to the inspector, nobody's opinion upsets me any longer, on the contrary, all these opinions, and all of them are against me as a matter of course, take me progressively a step further. To reach one's goal one simply has to accept an enormity, or even a crime against all of so-called mankind or against an individual, as part of the deal. In my case it happens to be a book for the sake of which I am prepared to do anything and everything, and I mean prepared to sacrifice everything, Konrad is supposed to have said to Wieser. Nothing can be accomplished without a measure of ruthlessness, Konrad said, because once you let yourself in for such a piece of work as this, you are letting yourself in for doing it with extreme ruthlessness, usually against the person with whom you are living, sharing your life, and who becomes your chief victim; looking at it this way, my wife is Victim Number One, but I cannot allow myself to be in the least concerned about that. This victim is defenseless, we know that. This horrifying thought is what alone enables a man to make the horrifying mental effort he believes he has to make. Of course he knows that he will be regarded as a madman from beginning to end, precisely because he is the exact opposite of a madman, and he can expect to be incessantly jeered at. He goes through the mill of being incessantly derided. No one goes with him, unless he forces someone to go with him, a woman, for instance, whom he simply forces to come with him, because no one will, otherwise. But even if someone does come with him, Konrad is supposed to have said, he still walks alone, he walks alone into an intensifying solitude. He walks into an intensifying darkness, alone, because the thinking man always moves alone into an intensifying darkness. But back to my work! he said to himself, and: No excuses! Yet even in the lime works, nearly empty as it is, there is continual distraction. No friends, actually, Konrad is supposed to have said, actually no real friends at all, only curiosity seekers, trouble sniffers, enemies only, in fact, and one's bitterest enemy was oneself, of course. Nevertheless progress was being made, despite all the constant impediments of one kind and another, including being negatively impeded, by omission; omission, in fact, is more decisive than its opposite. To do something by not doing it, he is supposed to have said. For example, not to do something that could be done and about which they say (on all sides!) that it must be done, was a kind of progress. It's maddening, he is supposed to have said, but I do not permit myself to go insane. Then: my book is, at first, simply a lone decision, which later turned into being the loneliest of tasks. Virtually nothing coming from the outside. Fragility itself. A man like himself in constant fear that this ultimate in fragility would break up his head, and vice versa. Fear that everything would break in his hands. A man like himself frequently looked around for a way to defend himself, but couldn't find anything, because defenselessness was all there was. Incessantly he was faced with the absolute threatening to destroy him. Whatever point a man like himself reached, arrived at, all he ever reached or arrived at was irritation, further irritation. But all of it is ultimately so comical, it's all more comical than anything, which is why, he is supposed to have said, it is all quite bearable after all, because it is comical. All we have in this world is the very essence of comedy, and do what we will, we can't escape from this comedy, for thousands of years men have tried to turn this comedy into tragedy, but their effort had to fail, in the nature of things. This whole business with the lime works here, Konrad is supposed to have said to the works inspector, as Wieser says, is of course nothing but comedy, too. But to endure this comedy one has to empty one's brain from time to time, sort of like emptying one's bladder, that's all it is, my dear inspector, micturation of the brain, to relieve the brain as one relieves the bladder, very simply, my dear inspector. Or else, think of the brain as a spiritual lung. He poured another glassful for the works inspector, who by this time was completely drunk, saying: probably it's the interruptions that do my book the most good. To Fro: That everything he, Konrad, said, was nonsense; to me: nonsense, all nonsense; to Wieser: it's all nonsense, naturally, Wieser, what else. Fro says that Konrad would open a window and hear the branches of the pine trees, when he opened the window overlooking the water he heard the water. He could hear the pine branches and the water even when there wasn't a breeze stirring, even though the eye perceived no movement at all in the branches, on the water, Konrad heard the trees and the water. He could hear the incessant motion of the air. He could hear the surface of the water moving even when no such motion was perceptible to the eye, or: he could hear the movement in the deeps, the sounds of movements in the depths. He heard movement in the deepest places, he said so over and over, not only to Fro but to Wieser also, under my window the lake is at its deepest, you know, just under my window, it is as though I had always known that the deepest point is just under my window. Naturally only an ear trained to hear movement in the deepest places actually does hear what goes on in the deepest places, no other ear can hear anything coming up from those depths, none of my human guinea pigs ever hear anything there, I can take whoever I want to the window, he is supposed to have said to Fro, and ask him, do you hear anything coming up from the water? and get *no* for an answer, invariably, *no, nothing*. While I myself naturally hear not just one sound, I hear thousands of different sounds and I can distinguish these thousands of sounds from each other; why, I have filled several dozen notebooks solely on the subject of my perceptions of these thousands of sounds coming up from the deepest point in the water right under my window, Konrad is supposed to have said to Fro; Fro is deeply interested in those notebooks, in fact, and hopes one day to get hold of them, if only one knew where they were, and if Konrad would let Fro borrow these notebooks, for his, Fro's own scientific work, of course, said Fro, because it was precisely such observations

of Konrad's as these, on the sounds rising from the depths of
water beneath his window, that interested Fro, so much so
that he had decided against waiting until after Konrad's trial
at the Wels district court, against waiting until Konrad was
convicted, because Fro could have no doubt that it was important for him to see those notebooks of Konrad's as soon as
possible, and so he, Fro, was submitting a petition to the district court at Wels to give him access to Konrad's notebooks
containing observations on the sounds at the deepest point
in the lake right under Konrad's window. Konrad will probably agree at once to let me have the notebooks, says Fro,
but I am interested not only in these particular notebooks but
actually in all of Konrad's notes as well, but most of all in
his manuscript, but then, Konrad has not written his manuscript to this day, says Fro, and as far as anyone can judge
Konrad was not likely to be able to write it, ever, because
whether he is transferred to the prison in Garsten, or to the
mental institution at Niedernhardt, probably for life, he
would be unable to write it in either place because he
couldn't begin to write it down without his heaps of notes
accumulated in several decades of research; the writing of his
book had, ultimately, become impossible for Konrad, who had
short-circuited himself, so to speak, by committing the horrifying murder of his wife. This very day Fro intended to
send off a letter to Konrad asking for the notebooks on
sounds from the depths of the water under his window, he
said. Even a man as intelligent as the late forestry commissioner, a man who was always taking a positive interest in my
experiments, Konrad is supposed to have told Fro, when
asked whether he could hear anything from the depths while
standing with Konrad at the open window overlooking the

water, could hear nothing. A completely untutored person could not even hear any sounds from the surface of the water, not to mention the depths, Konrad had said to Fro as recently as the end of October. My experimental subjects hear nothing, Konrad said. Exactly the same result was obtained when he stationed himself with an experimental subject at the window overlooking the trees. The subject admitted that he saw nothing and therefore heard nothing, either. However, it was not quite that simple, even though it was also impossible to explain the process that made a person observant, on the other hand. And why bother to try explaining it? Konrad is supposed to have said to Fro. He wondered, even though he marveled at the patience of his experimental subjects, the forestry commissioner, the works inspector, Hoeller, Wieser, Fro, the baker, Stoerschneider and the rest, he nevertheless asked himself why he bothered at all, considering how they always ended up by leaving him depressed over their boundless incapacity. His wife and chief experimental subject, as Konrad said himself, Fro reports, had always shown extraordinary patience with him and his researches, his efforts, his experiments and, as Konrad told Fro as recently as late October, she went on performing ever greater miracles of patience in the course of his incredibly radicalized experimentation; by using her he had developed the so-called Urbanchich method to its utmost perfection, in fact his radicalization of the method was such that he would be justified in no longer referring to it as the Urbanchich method at all, but his wife had allowed herself to be driven to a state of total exhaustion by his use of the Urbanchich method on her. Toward evening, if we happened to have started early that morning, or after midnight, if we started in the afternoon, she would be done in. Among other things, for instance, he recited to her a series of sentences with the short *i* sound, such as, "In the Inn district it is still dim," a hundred times slowly, then a hundred times rapidly, and finally about two hundred times as fast as possible in a choppy manner. When he was done he demanded an immediate description of the effect his spoken sentences had on her ear and her brain, Konrad is supposed to have told Fro. Then he commenced his analysis. But after only about two hours of such experimentation she would ask him how much longer it would take, Konrad told Fro, and start complaining about her earache which was steadily worsening, especially in winter; he would tell her, then, how long the experiment would take that day, whether it was to be only a brief three or four hours, or a longer six or seven hours, in any case his experiments in accordance with the Urbanchich method were important to him and he had let not a day pass without experimentation. He might say, for instance, how long is it now since I've experimented with the short *i* sound, or, how long since we've worked on the short *o*? or the short *a*, or the short *u*? He would alternate, for instance, between reciting the sentence, "In the Inn district it is still dim" into her left ear, then into her right ear, then moving from one ear to the other and back again. In one hour of such work he might produce about two pages of notes, but usually he destroyed those notes right away, so that no one could deduce his method from his notes. In the midst of an exercise he might, for instance, suddenly say to his wife, you must distinguish between the hard and the soft *i*. She understood perfectly, and yet she did it all wrong, time and again. So the effort had to be redoubled, which meant that the discouragement, some days, was also redoubled. If she did not follow the rules, he would tell her, the exercise was a waste of time. Sometimes it took as long as half an hour for her to catch on (to the simplest point). Naturally it was all far too demanding, especially everything connected with the Urbanchich method, far beyond her strength, he would think, but nevertheless he went on repeating the exercises prescribed for each experiment without a pause until she actually collapsed. Most of the time she sat in her chair quite motionless, with her eyes shut more often than not. Still, in the many years in which he had subjected her to the Urbanchich method, she had gotten accustomed to his kind of experimentation. The sentence "In the Inn district etc." for instance, she had listened to for weeks on end, hundreds of times a day, every day, until he raised his hand to signal: exercise completed. The sentence, "In the Inn district etc." was after all a basic sentence in his experiment, says Fro. He would say it and she would instantly comment on it. He recited it faster and faster, she commented on it faster and faster, Konrad is supposed to have told Fro. After hearing her complain a thousand times that he took too long with his experiments, he finally turned a deaf ear to it, until in time he got into the habit of turning a deaf ear to her. There was no way to avoid using the Urbanchich method on her, for the sake of the book it simply had to be done. He claimed that he always finished by saying, now we can permit ourselves to stop working, and then followed it up immediately by asking: would you like me to play your record? then she would ask him to play her favorite recording, Mozart's *Haffner* symphony it was, it always relaxed her. Always the same record, the same record year after year, he thought, but as long as the *Haffner* is what she wants, she shall have it, he said to himself time and again. Most of the time, Konrad said to Fro, he was so exhausted by the time he played the *Haffner* for her that he nodded off to sleep while it was still on. Probably they both were aging more rapidly in the lime works. If only he could get his book written before he grew too old, absolutely too old and unfit to write it, he is supposed to have said to Fro and to Wieser. The minute he got to his room he went to bed. But the inner restlessness into which he was driven by the outward quiet would not let him sleep even when mortally exhausted, and so he wandered all over the lime works, several times all over the lime works, and spent the rest of the night lying on his bed quite unable to fall asleep. Once you have passed that boundary line between fatigue and exhaustion, it is absurd to believe that you can fall asleep, absurd to try to sleep, to force yourself to sleep; you weren't going to fall asleep. Instead, he got the opposite of the hoped-for relaxation, the serenity he meant when he dreamed of finding a quiet place to work; instead of being able to relax, he only grew increasingly restless, so restless that he inevitably broke his own rest by doing something or other that brought unrest into it. Here he was at last, actually at the lime works he had taken such infinite pains to get into because it was such a quiet place, the outward quiet which was of its essence and which he had always believed would give him the inward quiet he needed for his work, but he soon found out what a fundamental mistake that was! Though he realized his mistake soon enough, it was too late just the same. A terrible self-deception, a terrible disappointment. But he had worked out for himself a mechanism, he said to Fro, by means of which he could control the outward quiet, in fact the extreme outward quiet so characteristic of the lime works and its environs, gradually to gain control of it and ultimately to exploit it wholly for his own purposes, i.e., for his work. This mechanism enabled him at all times to induce inward quiet by means of the outward quiet, not by nature but by using his brain, using the mechanism itself without any special manipulation of the mechanism. To exploit and transform the outward quiet, even the extreme outward quiet, for the sake of and into inward quiet was a high art, beyond comparison with any other art not only of self-control, control of one's nerves, that is, he thought, and even though he had reached a high degree of mastery in it he did not claim to have mastered this art at all times. Instead of concentration (on his work), he is supposed to have said, nonconcentration (on his work) suddenly manifested itself. In a word: you had to be able to break away from your outward quiet at the moment when it had ceased to induce inward quiet; in the long run outward quiet never did induce inward quiet, it did so only briefly, much too briefly for intellectual purposes. The weather played a most important part in this, as in every other respect. For instance, when the foehn, that maddening mountain wind, suddenly started to blow: the longer he walked back and forth, this way and that, in the lime works, the greater grew his inward unrest, because he then had no control over the mechanism for inducing inner quiet. He then would try various expedients, substitutes for the mechanism which wouldn't function, such as reading his Kropotkin, or the Novalis, a book that was basically hers, but even the Novalis did not help him to calm himself, he would try sitting down, standing up, sitting down again, standing up again; alternate between opening the Kropotkin and the Novalis, pace the floor in his room, first in one direction then in another, try putting his papers in order, mix them up again, open the chest, close it again, pull out various drawers, always the same drawers, of the chest, pull out bills, notes, toss them all in a heap, pick up one or the other, read through them, drop them again, move the chair from the window to the door, the one near the door over to the window, turn out the light, turn on the light, follow a line, two lines, several lines, on a wall map. It did no good to go into the kitchen, to carry the logs from the kitchen into his own room, to get the ashes out of the fireplace, empty the pail, none of it was any use. To remind oneself of one thing or another was no use. It did not help him to speak aloud what he was thinking, or feeling, or to utter sentences, as he is supposed to have said to Fro, sentences he had just made up, totally meaningless sentences, or possibly sentences already used as material for the Urbanchich method. He would wander around, Konrad said to Fro, all over the lime works without getting anywhere near calming himself, everywhere, that is, except one place, his wife's room, because he did not want to aggravate his wife's depression by his own restlessness, considering that she was already in a state of deepest depression, constantly, in fact, he said to Fro; like him she would delude herself into thinking that times of unrest would alternate with times of inner peace, but in reality neither one of them ever came inwardly to rest, and so they both lived a permanent lie, not only did they lie to each other but each lied, side by side with the other, to him- and herself, while she lied to him and he to her and then simultaneously they lied to each other, in any case they lied that they were having a bearable life in the lime works, lied incessantly, although they were both trapped in an unbearable life, but if they did not simulate bearability, its unbearableness could simply not be borne, Konrad is supposed to have told

Fro, an unwavering simulation of leading a bearable life while actually and incessantly enduring the unendurable is simply the only way to get on with it, Konrad is supposed to have said to Fro, he also said something like it to Wieser, he even spoke to me about the bearability of the unbearable being made possible by the pretense of bearability, in the same words, with the same invisible gestures, as I recall, that time in the timber forest; but to get back to what he was saying to Fro, he said that he would wander all over the lime works which on days of that particular kind indeed seemed boundless to him, and try to come to the end of them, but could not get to the end of the lime works because one could walk and run and crawl through the lime works and never get to the end of them, he is supposed to have said, and finally, reaching a sort of climax in the utter shamefulness of his situation, he was often reduced to putting his hands on the walls, those ice-cold rough masonry walls, the ice-cold doorframes, the ice-cold trapdoors to the attic, the icy window glass, the ice-cold wood of the few remaining pieces of furniture, saying to himself, with his eyes shut, over and over, steady now, steady, steady, man. The lime works is not exactly an idyll, he is supposed to have said to Wieser, though it is all too easy to regard the lime works as an idyllic place because one happens to have gotten stuck in one's superficial prior judgment of the lime works; that the lime works is idyllic is only the judgment of people who judge the place on sadistic grounds, or on masochistic grounds, while in fact the lime works, as distinguished from its environs, is quite the opposite of an idyll. Visitors, for instance, tended to expect an idyll when coming to the lime works, even if they merely came to the vicinity, summer visitors as much as winter visitors, starting with their decision to visit the lime works, were expecting to enter an idyll, when in fact they had unknowingly decided to enter the very opposite of an idyll, had in effect quite unconsciously fallen victim to a total error at the very moment of their decision to go to the lime works. An idyll, they think, Konrad is supposed to have said to Wieser, as they step through the thicket, an idyll, as they brace themselves to knock on the front door. All the signs, before entering the thicket, when stepping out of the thicket, point to an idyll. But when they have actually stepped free of the thicket, they are horrified and turn back, if they set foot inside the lime works they are horrified and escape, some turn back as soon as they have stepped free of the thicket, and escape, the others turn and run as soon as they have set foot in the lime works, a minimal few get as far as entering the rooms inside and in no time at all they can't bear it. People don't instinctualize any longer, Konrad is supposed to have said to Wieser, mankind no longer instinctualizes. Aha, so that's the idyll the Konrad couple have moved into, they may think, Konrad is supposed to have said to Wieser, but in reality the Konrad couple, Konrad is supposed to have said to Wieser, moved into quite the opposite of an idyll when they moved into the lime works. The return to an idyll, they think. Compared with the lime works, everything else is idyllic, Konrad is supposed to have said to Fro, London is an idyll compared with the lime works, Wuppertal is an idyll; the ugliest, the loudest, the most malodorous place is an idyll in comparison. But even the surroundings of the lime works have been deliberately falsified into an idyll. An intelligent person arriving in the area, of course, will realize at once that the place is no idyll, but most human beings, Konrad said to Wieser, are not pos-

sessed of intelligence, you know, though they may look intelligent; people appear to know, appear to understand, when
in fact they know nothing and understand nothing. A dimwit
is likely to be unobservant and notice nothing even after he
has stepped forward out of the thicket. Konrad himself now
knew without a doubt that to have gone into the lime works
was to have gone into a trap. To Wieser: Last fall his wife had
still been able to dress, get herself ready, unaided, but when
winter came she could no longer do any of it without his help,
which meant that Konrad had not only to do his room,
making the fire and so on, but then had to make the fire in her
room, dress her, make the bed and so on, with the inevitable
catastrophic effect on his work; while for her, of course,
nothing could be more depressing than being suddenly unable
to dress herself any longer. How long would it be, Konrad
is supposed to have said to Wieser, before she could no longer
feed herself without help, not even the smallest bite? So far
she had managed to feed herself, if he cut up her meat for her,
broke her bread in pieces and so on, anything further she refused to let him do for her, but the time was coming when
she would no longer refuse to let him feed her, and then he
would have to stick the meat and the bread in her mouth bit
by bit, he would have to spoonfeed her the porridge, dribble
the milk behind her teeth spoonful by spoonful. Merely to
pull on her stockings had become an effort unutterably dreary
to make and to watch, he could see that she could no longer
bend over, nor could she any longer stretch out at full length.
When she stood up, she could not stand straight, when she
walked, she could not walk straight, and when she lay down,
she could not lie straight, her posture was about as crooked
as it could possibly get, her head hung down like an awkward

weight. Everything hurt her. Frequently she could no longer say where she was hurting the most, in the body or in the head, she didn't know whether to treat herself for bodily pains or for headache, head and body had for a long time now been one continuous pain, a pain that had become the best proof she had of her existence. All of her body and all of her head were now nothing other than one single pain, she is supposed to have said to Konrad four weeks before Christmas, that is, four weeks before her violent death. He simply couldn't stand this any longer, he is supposed to have said when he was arrested; apart from this he is supposed to have said nothing at all. But there is no telling what our courts will do, Wieser says, depending entirely on the way a court happens to be constituted, how the jury happens to be constituted, Konrad might get the minimum sentence, or the maximum, or else he could be declared insane. As daily experience teaches, it was all anybody's guess until the very last moment of every court trial, every time. In the last analysis there was nothing more spineless and more subject to whims and weather, sympathies and antipathies than the courts and especially juries, who could be swayed by the most unpredictable circumstances. Speaking to the public works inspector, too, the Konrad woman once said that her pains were by now all the proof she had that she was still here (alive). Konrad saw how she wanted to get over to the window and couldn't, wanted to stand up and couldn't, wanted to take a few steps and couldn't, that she was cold but couldn't pull up her blanket; and so he went and pulled up her blanket. She no longer noticed that he was wearing a dirty jacket, torn pants; that, after months of neglect, he had come to look like a derelict. The whole lime works is filthy from top to bottom, and she doesn't see

it, Konrad is supposed to have said to Wieser. That above all
the bed linen was filthy dirty because it hadn't been changed
in months was something she did not see, and he couldn't possibly clean the bed linen, he no longer had the strength to
do it, because he simply didn't have the time; as recently as
six months ago she had still taken care of such things as the
bed linen etc. from her invalid chair, she had swamped
Hoeller with orders to clean things, but she could do this no
longer, she had lost her grip on the situation, what with
having to concentrate on enduring her pains, Konrad is supposed to have told Wieser, and how he would see that she
wanted to get out of her room, but couldn't, that she wanted
to go to the woods and couldn't, to the village, and couldn't.
That she thought about traveling, but couldn't travel. That
she needed to see people, but couldn't see people, couldn't
have company, Konrad said. For years she had enjoyed no
kind of social contact with others, meaning social contact
with people congenial to both of them. However, there was
really no such thing as congenial company, because in the
whole world there was no person really congenial to another
—an observation typical of Konrad, Wieser said. Such people
as did come to see them, not recently but until about the end
of October, these so-called congenial people, had not been at
all congenial, they were all mere curiosity seekers, legacy
hunters, swindlers, Konrad is supposed to have said. Compared with them, the works inspector, the chimney sweep,
Hoeller, and he, Wieser, and Fro, were far more congenial
than those so-called congenial visitors, but seeing people socially was, as far as the Konrads were concerned, anachronistic
in principle. Nevertheless one could not live entirely without
seeing other people, Konrad is supposed to have said, adding

that it did not embarrass him to say over and over again what everybody tended to say over and over again, no matter how ridiculous, simplistic, trite it was, except that he said it in full awareness of what he was doing, unlike most people; that was the difference, as Wieser undoubtedly knew, since it did after all always make a difference who said what and how he said it, and a serious person, or, more precisely, a person who was to be taken seriously, could just go ahead and say whatever he pleased without needing to worry whether he was uttering something banal or trite, a so-called truism, because if the person who said something banal or trite or platitudinous was a serious person, a person to be taken seriously, what he said ceased to be any of these things. For the longest time they had not been seeing people at all, Konrad is supposed to have said to Wieser, because all of the people they had to see, such as the baker, Hoeller, Stoerschneider and the rest were people they had to see on business, not at all the same thing as people one saw socially. He could see that his wife was constantly thinking of people she was longing to see, friends, relatives, it was no use at all to try talking her out of wanting to see them, no use trying to explain to her that there was no such thing as friends, and that kinfolk were basically anything but kin, that kinship was a deception, a self-deception; a mistake, in fact. At the beginning all these kinfolk and friends had still come visiting to the lime works from the Tirol and Carinthia, from Switzerland, all the Zryds from the other side of the mountains and her other kin from the north, her East Friesian relations for instance, all of them people with a lifelong conspiratorial passion of curiosity, said Konrad to Wieser, but none of them came any longer, the lime works had gradually purged itself of this kinfolk garbage. We don't need any of these people, Konrad is supposed to have told his wife over and over again until they all finally stayed away and no longer even dared to write. He had begun, Konrad is supposed to have said to Wieser, by talking her out of being interested in seeing these people, and ended by showing her how impossible they were. That they would have to make do with just each other and no one else in the lime works is something he made clear to her soon enough after they moved in, but it took years for the resulting total lack of contact with her relatives to become final, not even to mention his own relatives whom he had dropped decades ago. She ultimately became resigned to this state of affairs. At first he had sacrificed himself to her, Konrad said to Fro at one time, for decades he had sacrificed himself to her and her crippled state, but now his work demanded that she sacrifice herself to him, body and soul; his conscience on this point was clear. After all, they, the Konrads, had been on the go, traveling incessantly for two decades, in every imaginable country, in every part of the globe, and always under the most tortuous circumstances; as anyone could imagine, after all, he is supposed to have told Fro, to take a totally crippled woman traveling all over the world for years is no picnic, think of what it means to drag a totally crippled woman from city to city, from one museum to another, one tourist attraction to another, one celebrity to another, what it means to put up with a minimum of existential elbowroom, freedom of action, to please a crippled woman who, like all cripples, had to indulge an insatiable craving for novelty all over the world, insatiable for everything conceivable and inconceivable, in addition to being at that time so demanding (!) in every respect that it actually overtaxed his strength to have to be with her at all times. Subsequently, of course, once he had begun the work on his book, she had to curtail her demands, gradually impose limitations on herself, subject herself to him and his conception of their life together, and this abrupt and unnerving reversal, namely that henceforth all the demands to be satisfied would be his and no longer hers, perturbed her at first, in fact he might say that she had lived for years in a state of self-destructive shock more beside him and under him than with him, until in the end she had resigned herself to living for his sake. From a person who had actually seen everything worth seeing and had met so many people worth meeting, and who owed all this to the sincere and supreme self-sacrifice of a man whose free surrender of his most productive years, indeed the most important two decades of his life, those between his thirtieth and fiftieth year, was certainly not to be expected, certainly not to be demanded as a right, such a person must naturally expect to make a commensurate sacrifice in return, without anyone's having to appeal to her gratitude or some gratitude-connected principle involving guilt feelings. Konrad would after all have gotten his book written long since if his wife had not forced him to take her traveling all over the world. The book would have been completely written ten years ago at the latest, in London, in Paris, in Aschaffenburg, at the very latest in Basel, he is supposed to have said to Wieser. To Fro: every day she would ask him whether he had a clean shirt on, and he would answer that he did have a clean shirt on, though in reality he had been wearing the same shirt for a week or even two weeks; she no longer noticed anything, no longer saw the dirt, etc., nothing at all. When she wanted him to read to her, she of course wanted him to read her favorite novel, the one about the medieval knight-troubadour, the Minnesinger Heinrich von Ofterdingen, by her favorite Romantic poet, Novalis. So of course he deliberately read to her from his favorite, whom she couldn't stand, the Russian anarchist Kropotkin, just to annoy her, to punish her for her inattentiveness, her inattention; there was simply no more effective way to punish her for insubordination; he always punished her by reading to her from the Kropotkin. But of course I do read her the Novalis, Konrad is supposed to have said to Fro, when she asks me for it. I can never refuse to read Novalis to her when she insists on it. Of course she hated everything in Kropotkin, and on the other hand, she loved her Novalis. The right thing to do was to read to her alternately from the Novalis and from the Kropotkin, not only the Novalis, he is supposed to have said to Fro. After reading her a passage from the Kropotkin he usually asked her to tell him what he had just read to her, and she would not know the answer, proving that she had not listened attentively when he had read the Kropotkin to her even though she was all attention when he read her the Novalis. What was that I just read to you, my dear? he would ask abruptly, and of course she hadn't listened to the Kropotkin and floundered pitifully in trying to make up a plausible answer. Toward the end she no longer dared to let her attention wander off when he was reading Kropotkin to her, she had learned to fear that he would make good his threats—as he did more and more often, in fact—threats to withhold food, to prolong the exercises, not to air her room. Or else he might suddenly, without warning, air the room by letting an ice-cold draft she had no way of escaping hit her directly from the window; suddenly, he read her twice as much from the Kropotkin as usual, etc. Not knowing, often, whether her failure to hear the Kropotkin was intentional or not, he often punished her unjustly, which he regretted, he said, so that to make up for it he read her the Novalis at greater length than usual, though it was exquisite self-torture for him to read the Novalis. Still, reading her the Kropotkin, he always suspected her of turning a deaf ear deliberately, because she was always able to recount flawlessly everything he read to her from Novalis, but if he asked her to repeat a Kropotkin passage she couldn't remember a thing. Konrad also complained that she always wanted a fresh clean dress, every day, and he told Fro that he refused to give in to this, a change of dress once a week seemed quite enough to him, especially as he had to help her put it on and take it off, after all a woman could certainly wear the same dress for a week, especially when it was so much trouble to get dressed, Konrad said. He would get a bit impatient when he had to dress her, there were times when he hurt her while changing her clothes, or so the baker says who is reputed to have been present often when Mrs. Konrad was changing. Nor did Konrad leave the choice of dress always to his wife; sometimes he insisted on a dress of his own choice, and sometimes they had unrepeatable arguments (works inspector) whether he would put on her the dress he preferred or the one she wanted, but nearly always his will prevailed; Konrad is reported to have taken advantage of his wife's extreme exhaustion to win the argument. On the one hand he would ask himself why she had to change her dress at all, after all he had long ago ceased to change his clothes, but on the other hand he would think that she couldn't really sit in that chair for years in the same dress, so he is supposed to have told Fro. And she did still have heaps of dresses, while he still had heaps of shoes, but for a long time now he had been putting on the same pair of shoes every day, so why couldn't she wear the same dress every day? he asked himself, he said. He was constantly kept busy airing out her room, she had to have fresh air, and there he was all day opening and closing her windows and fretting that he was not getting his writing done, feeling totally at his wife's mercy, with no will of his own, while she did with him as she pleased and had her revenge, as for instance when she insisted that he comb her hair, and so he combed her hair for hours with neither of them uttering a syllable the whole time (Fro). Actually there was often a terrible smell in her room when left unaired for longer than usual because he was irritated with her. But sometimes she said she wanted the room aired when he had just finished airing it, she would ask him to open the window when he had just shut it, as her special way of tormenting him. Several times a day, whenever he was most likely to feel irritated by it, she would announce that she felt a draft from the door; there's a draft, she would say, to let him know how angry she was, even though there was no discernible draft in the room, certainly not with all the doors and windows shut as they were, but she made a habit of resorting to this kind of thing as a weapon against him, until one day he told her that if she spoke to him of a draft just once more he would make a point of opening all the doors and windows, and go away, and stay away all night, and then he might come back next morning to see what had become of her. To this she is supposed to have retorted: Why don't

you, why don't you open all the doors and windows and
leave them open all night and give me a chance to freeze
to death! But she knew only too well he would never carry
out his ridiculous threat, she said. Still, he had to admit that
she did obey him sometimes, and then again he would obey
her, but she naturally ought to obey him more often than
he her, he is supposed to have said to Wieser; actually it was
incorrect to say that he obeyed her, he merely acceded to
her wishes. All day long I submit to her entirely, he said.
Then suddenly he would rebel and that would be the beginning of a new phase when she had to obey him implicitly,
and when no wish of hers was granted at all. His work required absolute obedience not only from him but from her
as well. Most of the time they were both concentrating intensely on the Urbanchich exercises, which meant weeks of
uninterrupted self-discipline, without a moment's unruliness
from her to be tolerated. But at times she could no longer
bear to go on sitting in that chair of hers, and she would
come close to losing her self-control. It happened every two
or three weeks, especially on weekends, he couldn't say why.
Suddenly she would fail to answer when he asked her a
question. He would ask it a second time, a third time, a
fourth time—no answer. To elicit an answer from her was
of the utmost importance for his book, yet she would not
give him an answer. He then walked over to the window
and let in some fresh air, as the air in the room actually did
turn foul after those hour-long sessions of Urbanchich exercises. But even the fresh air would bring no response from
her, not even when the room had become completely cooled
off. He would then close the window again and begin to
read the Kropotkin aloud to her, believing as he did so that

this was an infallible prod to make her talk, and while he was not surprised by resistance, protests, etc., on this occasion he would find that even a lengthy reading from Kropotkin got no reaction from her at all, except to deepen her silence, Konrad is supposed to have said. When that happens he shuts the book, stands up, walks back and forth in the room, says Wieser, faster and faster, more and more noisily, tries to say something but doesn't really know what to say, sits down, gets up again. He could of course read some Novalis to her, he thinks, but he doesn't read the Novalis; it would mean surrender, he is supposed to have said to Wieser. To Fro: But inasmuch as I simply had to go through the exercises on *i* with her that day, and so little was accomplished by that time, it was quite impossible for me to turn around and walk off to my own room. Suddenly he hit upon the idea of asking her whether he should bring her something to eat from the kitchen. But he got no response at all to this. Was she in pain? Even this question brought no response of any kind. If she was in pain, something had to be done about it, would she take a pill? he asked her; no answer. He had just decided to read some Novalis to her after all, but as he was about to start she finally signaled that she wanted to get up and walk a few steps, Konrad is supposed to have told Fro, and she actually let him help her up and walk her to the window and back, and again, and a third time, to the window and back to her chair, at which point she was so exhausted that he barely managed to get her back into the chair where she ended in total collapse. If only I had the patience, she is supposed to have said, if only I had the patience, but I have no patience, when he quoted her Konrad even tried to imitate her voice, according to Fro, who says that Konrad repeatedly said to him, to Fro, that is, if only I had patience, if only I had patience. But I have simply run out of all patience, she is supposed to have said. Afterward he read her a long passage of the Novalis, taking care to read in a level tone of voice, with an even distribution of emphasis, his style of delivery could certainly be described as monotonous, he is supposed to have said to Fro, an absolutely monotonous delivery was the most effective, he felt. One hour of reading aloud to her like this, and he was at last able to continue the Urbanchich exercises with her until far into the night. While reading the Novalis to her he held both her hands firmly, thus gradually calming her down. This situation recurred at intervals of a week or a week and a half, but it naturally had begun to recur at ever-decreasing intervals. As his experiments went on, she naturally did not hear him equally well at all times, as for instance if he pronounced the words *all the same, power,* or *powerlessness* loudly, she might not understand, no matter how clearly he said these words, she would fail to understand them, and yet he might pronounce the same words, *all the same, power,* or *powerlessness* in the merest whisper, and as indistinctly as possible, and she would nevertheless understand. It was a complete mystery to him how her hearing could be so absolutely unpredictable. He would say, for instance, *what an effort, to walk,* say it loudly and clearly, and she did not understand, whereupon he would whisper the same words almost inaudibly, *what an effort, to walk,* and she instantly understood him, etc. He realized, of course, that a mere change in the weather, a pain that resulted from such a change in the weather, was enough to make a different woman of her at times. But by and large he was continuing to achieve remarkable results with her using the Urbanchich method, which he was constantly expanding even as he applied it. For some time now he had been experimenting with consonants, until it became impossible to experiment further with consonants, whereupon he switched to vowels, then suddenly back to consonants, and so forth. If she suddenly showed signs of being unable to go on, a glance out of the window would invariably reveal the reason, he could see by the look of the air outside that the weather was changing, etc. From disconnected words, words that formed no sentences, he would shift to whole sentences and vice versa, from sentences to disconnected words. The ear, and her ear in particular, was so extremely sensitive to even the most inconspicuous changes in the weather, which go on incessantly, as you know, Konrad said to Wieser. There's a change in the weather every instant, another kind of weather every instant, he said. To me: even just looking at the trees, I can see a change in the weather, looking at a rock spur, at a body of water, at the walls, there it is, a change in the weather. Fro reports: Konrad had turned abruptly from using vowels to using whole sentences in the exercises, he would pronounce the following sentence: *Justice, when someone kills another,* and she would hear this sentence even though he had spoken it quite indistinctly, she indisputably heard it when he mumbled it into her left ear; her comment: the *i* in *kills* stayed in her ear for about eight seconds; naturally, he thought. There were times when, merely looking out of the window in the morning, he instantly knew that the exercises of that day should involve only vowels, or only consonants, or only sentences with *u*s or only sentences with *e*s, or only rather long sentences with *o*s, or only short sentences. Looking out the window, for instance, and taking a deep breath, he knew what today's experiment should be. Or else, standing by the window, he would decide momentarily: now, up to her room and say to her quickly: *swarms of birds, more and more swarms make the park swarthy,* and demand her instant comment on this. On Christmas Eve, exactly a year before her violent death, he had gone to her room at about five o'clock and repeated to her the sentence: *Mingling with men and women one only messes oneself up the more,* saying it alternately into her right and her left ear. He said that he murmured this sentence into her ears eighty or ninety times, and exacted a comment on it every time, until she collapsed in a coma, it never occurred to him until nearly eleven P.M. that it was, after all, Christmas Eve. She had forgotten all about it on account of being so intensely preoccupied with the Urbanchich exercises, and he had failed to remind her, and so they both went to bed that night at about one A.M. without his remembering to mention it to her, next day he is supposed to have said to her: Tonight is Christmas Eve, actually it was yesterday but for us it is Christmas Eve today, of course I knew it was Christmas Eve yesterday but I didn't draw it to your attention because we were in the midst of our experiments, so it will have to be Christmas Eve for us today, he is supposed to have said, and then she said: You terrible man! this "Terrible man!" Wieser says Konrad mimicked, using exactly her tone of voice. She often believed that there were times when he was not experimenting with her, Konrad, is supposed to have told Wieser, though in fact he was experimenting incessantly, even when he was merely saying Good Morning, or Good Night, when he asked her whether she wanted to change, or needed him to comb her hair, or was interested in eating something, he was always experimenting with her. He might ask her: Shall I read Novalis to you? but he was actually experimenting. Whether he was standing up or sitting down, pacing the floor, keeping silence, he was always consciously experimenting. His whole relationship with her was nothing else than one continuous experiment, Konrad is supposed to have said to Fro. To the works inspector: "Using the Urbanchich method, I am experimenting her (his wife) to death." Of course her earache grew worse, it went without saying that the pain in her ear would gradually spread to her whole head, since he was intensifying his experimentation, moving on to ever harder, ever more strenuous exercises, he is supposed to have told Fro. What worked the most in his favor was that all the people with whom he experimented, meaning everybody he had anything to do with, had no inkling of the fact that he was experimenting with them whenever he was with them, and not only then. For a whole year he studied only the effects on the hearing of scratching sounds, slaps, drilling, drops, sounds of a rushing, whirring, humming sort, he is supposed to have told Fro. Blowing sounds. He had tried out hundreds of thousands of scraping noises. Her receptivity for twelve-tone music, he is supposed to have told Fro, had played the most important part in his experiments, including the orchestral works of Webern, Schoenberg's *Moses and Aaron,* the string quartets of Béla Bartok, all kinds of music. But it was all done with a view to the book as a whole; how easy it would be for a dilettante to fritter himself away, lose himself in a sea of details, Konrad is supposed to have said. To keep everything relating to the sense of hearing under surveillance simultaneously required a nearly superhuman effort. Why, his researches into the auditory sense of various kinds of animals alone had taken him not less than two years, supposedly. Konrad might often let a whole hour go by without letting his wife know that he was experimenting, only to say suddenly: Hearing Experiment I, get ready to go, and then the words *lust, lost, least,* followed by a so-called auditory sound-color control quiz: Is the *u* a somber sound? Is the *o* somber? Is the *e* somber? He often followed this up with the word *streamlet,* the purest word of all. He had experimented with the word *streamlet* for ten years, he is supposed to have told Wieser. Fro: the following procedure was repeated every day: Konrad went into his wife's room and said something, on which she had to comment. He would accept no so-called excuses. Sometimes she dared to ask him a question, such as: Is this an experiment or not? and he would answer *Yes,* or *No,* because she believed that there were times when he was not experimenting, not knowing that he was experimenting incessantly, that to him *everything* was an experiment. Even though he had the whole book quite finished in his head, as he believed, he never ceased experimenting, so as to complete his work even further, to perfect it, even though it was quite complete in his head already, and although he might at any moment sit down and write it all up without fear that he did not have it fully worked out in his head, if the possibility of suddenly writing it all down should arise. He was simply filling up the time with experiments until the moment arrived, as he confidently and unwaveringly believed it would, when he would finally write it down. Once such a piece of work had been embarked upon, it was possible to do all that could be done with the Urbanchich method, he is supposed to have told Fro. His kind of experimentation, pursued for such a long time, could not suddenly be dropped without ruining everything. Without his wife, who had sacrificed herself to him entirely, he would never have the entire book worked out in his head as firmly as he did. Every day, every moment, it was she alone who made it all possible. Demonstrations of fact, again and yet again, were what made the book possible. The experimenter, he felt, had to go on experimenting, that was his job, until he ceased asking himself why he was experimenting, a question it was not his province to ask himself, he was supposed to experiment himself to death if necessary. It was simpler to experiment with short sentences, he is supposed to have said, even simpler than that to use single words, simplest of all to use vowels only. It was more complicated, more strenuous, especially, of course, for his wife, to work with long composite sentences, the longest, most intricately complex sentences, the kind it admittedly gave him the greatest pleasure to experiment with, or such sentences as this, for example: *The connections which, as you know, are quite independent of the interconnection of the whole, but are nevertheless connected, in the most delicate ways, with the connections of the connection which is independent of the interconnection,* and so forth. You could say, of course, that the whole thing was crazy, but then you would have to say that everything was crazy, which is the simple truth, that everything is in fact crazy, still, nobody would dare say such a thing because, if he did, everyone would say *he* was crazy, which could only lead to everything coming to an end, everything gradually coming to a stop of its own accord, Konrad is supposed to have said. Human beings (all mankind) owed their very existence, after all, to inconsistency (the utmost).

As for himself, Konrad, there was nothing left that meant anything to him except experimental sentences, he is supposed to have said, experimentation was all there was, all he cared about, the whole world was an experiment, everything was; and then he is supposed to have said: It's not so much the length of the sentences that matters, nor the brevity of sentences (or words) that is decisive, not just, for instance, the *a* and *o* and *i* and *u* sounds, but all of it together, always. Suddenly, he once told Fro, he was standing at the window, he could not see a thing, he could hear but he could not see, not a thing. His eyes must be failing him, he thought; they had been getting worse all the time. At such times he would have to stand at the window with his eyes shut for a long time before he could open his eyes and see again. He is also reported to have complained about the problems he had heating the place in winter; he could not let Hoeller do it because Hoeller made so much noise and such a mess doing it, so that if Hoeller does it (gets the furnace going) I lose two or three valuable hours of experimental time. But if Konrad undertook to do it himself, it cost him an enormous effort just to overcome his inner resistance to doing it. Our chimneys don't draw, and so our stoves don't draw, he is supposed to have said. He had to go around endlessly checking up on the stoves and stoking them. It was a good thing that the lime works stoves could be stoked from the hallways. It had taken him years to learn how to stoke the stoves in the lime works. Every single stove had to be tended differently from every other, it was a regular science! he is supposed to have said, actually a science! The temporary failure of his eyesight lasted a little longer each time, he should have seen a doctor about it long since, but he wouldn't see a doctor.

Only a year ago his eyes failed him only every three to four weeks, but by now he was stricken every day, Konrad is supposed to have told Wieser. Of course it was connected with his work. Anyone who used his eyes as intensively as he did was bound to damage his eyesight, it was to be expected. His wife did not have this kind of eye trouble, although she had always suffered from poor vision, but her poor vision had not deteriorated any further in the course of time. But Konrad himself had been naturally endowed with the keenest eyesight, which he had, however, been subjecting to the severest strain, he is supposed to have told Wieser. He also had an extraordinarily good ear. His kind of eye trouble not infrequently led to total blindness, Konrad is supposed to have said; he happened to know that a close relative of his had suffered the same kind of eye trouble and then suddenly went completely blind; Konrad was afraid of this happening to him, too. One tended to think that this eye trouble would clear up, but it didn't clear up, and one found oneself suddenly blind, from one minute to the next, no matter what one did to prevent it, nothing was any use. To Fro, Konrad is supposed to have said two days before the murder: When we moved in, we put in mostly new flooring, I think, and here I sit in a chair opposite my wife's chair, looking to her as though I were reading my Kropotkin, but in fact I am not reading Kropotkin at all, I can't seem to concentrate on it, and even though I have the Kropotkin open and though I am reading in it line by line and word for word, my mind is on something entirely different, what I am thinking is that when we moved in we put in new floors, larch wood floors; larch wood darkens with time, I ordered the widest planks obtainable, irregular planks but laid by one of the best flooring men anywhere, a man who had moved from Toblach, my wife's home town, to Sicking. Plank by plank, tongue in groove, groove to tongue, I keep thinking, and in the second story, I am thinking, I had all the window sills redone, on the third floor it was the window jambs, all the door frames on the first floor, the ground floor. On the first floor it was also necessary to install a new ceiling, I am thinking, sitting opposite my wife and pretending to be reading my Kropotkin, I turn the pages in the Kropotkin as if I had just finished reading a page. At first I did not intend to do any repairs or restorations in the lime works, but I ended by doing so much. This area is famous for its good but unreliable craftsmen, I keep thinking, but all the work I had done here in the lime works was beautifully finished, in the shortest possible time. If it's to be done at all, I thought, then I might as well let them restore all the stucco work on the ceiling of the ground floor reception hall, and no sooner had I thought this than I ordered it all done. But no one looking at it must suspect, I said to the plasterer, Konrad is supposed to have said to Fro, that any of this stucco work has been restored, and the plasterer understood perfectly, in fact there is not the slightest suggestion anywhere that a restoration of the stucco work on the ground floor reception hall ceiling has been effected. An excellent man, it seems to me, Konrad is supposed to have said to Fro, I was thinking while pretending to read Kropotkin, the kind of work he did on that ceiling had to be totally inobtrusive, and he did in fact patch up and restore the stucco ornamentations on the ceilings in the most inobtrusive fashion. Wherever you look these days you can see stucco ornamentation ruined by amateurish restorations and patching, Konrad is supposed to have told Fro. And we put new stoves in almost every room, in all the places that were never heated before we came, he said. He had gone into the lime works and exclaimed: Why, everything is in wrack and ruin here, the place has been totally neglected, it's hopelessly run down! and he thought of how shocked he had been by all that neglect and deterioration, while his wife believed he was reading his Kropotkin, he is supposed to have said to Fro. Still, it turned out that the neglect had done only superficial damage, the dilapidation was only superficial, he is supposed to have told Fro. Basically the lime works were an incredibly solid piece of construction work! The lime works, in fact, represented an excellent historical record of the past four or five centuries, architecturally, Konrad is supposed to have told Fro, anyone who had the time and felt like it could find here a record of every historical detail of all those centuries. Finally the senselessness of pretending to read Kropotkin all along while thinking about something quite different, in fact the opposite of Kropotkin, made me shut the book. All that continuous reading, said my wife just as I was shutting the book, weakens your eyes, Konrad is supposed to have said to Fro, it's because you are incessantly reading your Kropotkin that you have all that eye trouble more and more often. Note that she doesn't say it is my reading that does it, but that it is my reading of Kropotkin that aggravates my eye trouble. He then gets up, he says, and goes to look out the window, where he sees Hoeller passing by down there, Hoeller always passes by at this time, Konrad thinks, wearing his blue coat and swinging his ax; funny how talking with Hoeller always is so relaxing. Whenever he starts talking with Hoeller, about hunting and the weather, right away he feels more relaxed. Konrad felt he had an intimate understanding of Hoeller's ways, and there could be nothing mysterious to Hoeller, either, about Konrad and about the way Konrad and his crippled wife had been living in the lime works for several years now, Konrad thought, as he said to Fro. The first time Konrad and I met (in the timber forest) Konrad said that although he ought to be expressing himself, if at all, with the greatest circumspection, because of his eleven or twelve previous convictions for so-called libel in this country, he nevertheless did express himself, or, as you might say, he daily committed the error of expressing himself, of expressing opinions, of telling facts that always fitted the definition of a so-called libel of somebody; no matter what he said, he always turned out to have said something libelous, but strictly speaking, you might say that everything he could say about this weird country, with its extremes of inhumanity and irresponsibility all on the increase as they were, could be considered a so-called libel, entailing the highest probability of his being hailed, in consequence, before an invariably prejudiced, biased court; such a possibility faced him at all times, especially considering his many previous convictions for libel and simple or aggravated assault, he was in perpetual danger of being denounced, slandered, charged, and convicted, no matter what he might say, or come out with, in the ears of the people around here it always registered as a so-called libelous statement, and it was only by chance that charges were not preferred against him every day of his life, because he did go out every day and saw people and inevitably expressed the opinions he held to them, because he knew the truth and so he expressed the truth, and although the opinions and truths he expressed were decidedly worth expressing and hearing, still, those involved, part and parcel as they were of this degenerate country, full of mistrustfulness as it was, his facts and opinions were invariably legally actionable and punishable. Life was not easy for a man of character, his kind of character, to endure life the way he was made, to get through it somehow, demanded the most strenuous intellectual and physical self-discipline, the utmost spiritual and physical tension, all of which indescribable inner pressures forced out and conditioned, as it were, all the things he had to say, so that he had to be resigned to being a man expressly made, designed, and bound to give offense, always, a problem he intended to solve but which he apparently did not succeed in solving. A world, he said, in which one could be hailed before a court for defamation of character, so called, and which maintained that it had such a thing as character, when obviously character was precisely what had disappeared from this world, if character had ever existed in it; not only was it a terrible, a horrifying world, but it was also a ridiculous world, but unfortunately each one of us had to resign himself to existing in a world that was not only terrible and horrifying but also ridiculous, each and every one of us had to come to terms with this fact; how many hundreds of thousands, how many millions of people had already come to terms with it, even in his own unquestionably terrible, horrifying, and ridiculous country, our own country, the most ridiculous and most terrible of them all. Speaking of his country, his own homeland, a man could not exist in it, get along in it for a single day, except by never once telling the truth, to anyone, about anything, because the lie alone kept things moving in this country, the lie with its seven veils and embroideries and masquerades and intimidations. In this coun-

try the lie is valued above all, the truth only gets one prose-
cuted, condemned, and ridiculed. Which is why Konrad did
not conceal the fact that his entire nation had taken refuge
in the lie. To tell the truth was to make yourself culpable and
ridiculous, the mob or the courts decided whether a man had
made himself culpable or ridiculous or culpable *and* ridiculous, if the truth-teller could not be made to appear culpable
he was ridiculed, if he could not be ridiculed he was penalized,
a man who told the truth in this country was either ridiculous
or a criminal. But inasmuch as hardly anyone wanted to make
himself ridiculous or legally punishable, people were terrified
of being penalized, to pay high fines or go to jail or prison
simply did not come naturally to people, so they all lied or
kept silent. Unfortunately there were characters like himself
who could not keep silent, who had in the course of time
come to their senses and gotten to the bottom of the truth
and therefore could not keep silent, who had to express themselves, so that they exposed themselves to criminal prosecution and ridicule over and over again, then became more and
more exposed to criminal prosecution under the ruling
criminal code, more and more exposed to ridicule under the
ruling social code. He would have to change his character
from the ground up, but no one could change his character,
one's character could not be changed. So he had locked himself in, here at the lime works, to avoid yet another sum-
mons; for twenty-two days now he was completely locked
up inside the lime works and had let no one enter the lime
works, either. This was the first time in twenty-two days that
he had set foot outside the lime works, for a walk in the
timber forest, because he was in fact a restless man who needed
to see people. For all those twenty-two days he had desperately

needed to get out of the lime works, but he had not set foot outside the lime works, not even as far as the tavern, not even to the sawmill. He kept reassuring himself that Hoeller would certainly never inform on him, but he did not go even to the annex. People did of course continue to come to the lime works, but I never let them in, Konrad said, if I open the door, the law will get me. But then all of a sudden the works inspector arrives, and the mayor arrives, and I have to open the door, they are town officials after all, I have to open the door to the municipal council, to the district superintendent, to the section chief of the flood control unit. They all come here on official business, or else they pretend to come on official business, and if I don't let them in they resort to official authority, forcing me to let them in, and I am terrified of getting into trouble with the law as it is, because of the things I say. However, with these so-called officials he naturally had only practical necessities to talk about, so there was no danger of getting into legal trouble on account of the things he said. And so, while he no longer set foot outside the lime works in order to avoid being charged and convicted and locked up—now that he had a criminal record, even a conviction for libel would mean imprisonment—he did speak to the so-called officials, including of course the forestry commissioner and the works inspector, but only with the greatest circumspection. To Fro, two years ago: at breakfast he would be silent while she did the talking. He was silent because he had made a habit of being silent, she talked because she had made a habit of talking (at the breakfast table). She talked incessantly at the breakfast table because she had no other opportunity to talk incessantly. He would wake up thinking about his work, but soon dropped the idea of writing and decided to start right after breakfast on the hearing exercises. Standing in the east corner of her room, he would plan to call out to her words with the *u* sound: *Urals, uremia, Uranus, usual, union, Uruguay, usury, Utopia,* etc. etc. This would be followed by words with *o*: *Oklahoma, odious, ore, oil, open,* etc. Then words with *k*: *Caste, card, Khartoum, carefree, catastrophe, catafalque, Cabbala, Kabul, catharsis, cataracts,* etc. Then words with *es*: *Esther, Estragon, escudos, España, Eskimo,* etc. Then words with *al*: *Albania, Alba Alarcon, Alhambra, algebra, alkaloid, Almira, alms,* etc. Then words with *is*: *Istria, Ismail, Istanbul, Islam,* etc. Getting out of bed he would be thinking that he could start the exercises during breakfast, so as to include the conversation (or the silence) at breakfast in the exercises. He would talk about the difference between listening and hearing, starting with an explanation of listening, then of hearing, giving ear, hearkening, pricking up one's ears, auscultation, overhearing, jointly hearing, etc. Listening in, mishearing, lending an ear. Then suddenly he would say to her: Trying not to hear. Listening hard, he would say. He had prepared their breakfast the previous evening, so that he merely needed to carry their tray into her room in the morning, they had always breakfasted together in this way since the first day they were living together. While carrying the tray up to her room he usually had the most brilliant ideas for his book, on the use of the Urbanchich method. Holding the tray in his hands he slowly felt his way up the stairs in the dark of the vestibule, to the first floor, then the second floor, then to her room which he said he entered without knocking. Set the tray on the table, he thought, so he put the tray on the table, thinking that she was watching him doing it. At the same time he thought of her bungled efforts to dress herself, wash herself, comb herself, to stretch out, all of which, all the misery of it, he could see clearly in her face. He then tried to wash her, dress her, comb her hair, help her to stretch out. Her hair certainly needed a washing, he thought while washing her; an impression that naturally grew stronger as he combed her hair. But he had not washed his own hair for weeks, he thought, while combing her hair. The dishes must be moved from the tray to the table, he would be thinking as he speeded up the combing of her hair. First he put the water on to boil, then he hastily buttered the bread—actually, he was using margarine instead, these days. She would ask him: Did you sleep well? and he asked her: Did you sleep well? and then they answered each other; she would say: Of course not, and he: Of course not. Then he saw that the water had come to a boil and he poured the boiling water into the teapot, saying, as he told Fro: Two minutes more, and then they would ask each other, wordlessly, whether they should begin at once with the exercises. He might, for instance, decide about beginning the exercises (expanded Urbanchich method) while he was pouring the tea. Words with diphthongs, he said to himself, and it seemed to him that she realized he had begun the exercises already, at breakfast, because she was not oblivious to the expectancy with which he watched her reactions, controlled her reactions to everything he said or didn't say (to her), how impatiently he awaited her reaction to the least trifle, or controlled her ability to react. Yesterday we indulged ourselves, he would say to her, in the most flagrantly undisciplined conduct, when we broke off our exercises two hours short of what our schedule calls for, so we cannot indulge ourselves in slacking off today, not to mention the fact that we were continually interrupting the exercises, even though we have no right to permit such interruptions. She listens to me, says nothing, eats with much appetite, Konrad said to Fro. Shortly after starting breakfast I tell her enough time has now been spent on having breakfast; I prefer short breakfasts, while she prefers to stretch breakfast time as long as possible. So he drained his cup, saying one cup is enough, and cleared away first his and then her breakfast dishes. Dawdling over breakfast is bad for creativity, he is supposed to have said, the cups go on the shelf, the bread into the breadbag, the first exercise on diphthongs begins. He would then experiment on her till eleven or half past, by which time she had been for hours impatiently awaiting lunch, to be brought either by Hoeller from the tavern or by Konrad from the kitchen; her constant waiting for him to feed her irritated him, it distracted him to the point of making him lose his temper with her, he ordered her to concentrate, why don't you concentrate, he is supposed to have said to her time and again, hundreds of thousands of times, here I am concentrating to the very limits of my capacity while you are not concentrating at all, all you ever think about is food, or about Hoeller's being supposed to bring the food, about meat and cauliflower and pastries, and meanwhile my mind is totally intent on applying the Urbanchich method, one would think it was only fair to expect her to concentrate one hundred percent on the Urbanchich method too, but she was so quickly exhausted, her responses lagged behind, her alertness visibly diminished from sentence to sentence, word by word, sometimes she heard nothing at all, then again not enough, whether he screamed into her left ear, her right ear, she heard nothing.

The exercise ended miserably, like most of them in the last six months, a wretched performance, absolutely wretched, disgusting, he said; he would get up, pace the floor, until he suddenly caught himself listening intently for Hoeller's step, bringing the food. But lunch never came until half past one, no telling why, unless it was a wedding breakfast at the tavern that was holding things up, he said to Fro, in which case they'd forget all about Mrs. Konrad, because the innkeeper and his staff could think of nothing but their wedding party. The moment he heard Hoeller knocking downstairs Konrad instantly left his wife's room, says Fro, and as he was descending to the vestibule he planned to call Hoeller to account for bringing the food so late, but then he thought, better not call him to account, just ask him, but I will call him to account, and so on, but by the time Konrad opened the door he had forgotten his intention to call Hoeller to account. When he hears the knock on the front door, Konrad says to his wife, lunch is here, that's Hoeller downstairs, and suddenly she looks completely relaxed, he instantly sees what a great relief it is to her, and goes down. Going down the stairs to the vestibule he is thinking that the food will be cold because Hoeller has been loitering too long on his way through the icy cold of the woods or along the water's edge, but as he opens the door he sees the steaming food hamper, it seems that the food is actually still hot, so we're getting a hot lunch today, I won't have to heat any of it in the kitchen, I can take it right upstairs to my wife, it won't take more than a minute to set the table and serve it, she's always amazed at how fast I serve a meal, this time they're both amazed when they discover that the food hamper contains baked liver, with a fresh lettuce salad, and last but not least, a semolina soufflé, their favorite dish. Right after lunch, he thought, we will go on with the exercises, all the more energetically for having just had our favorite dish. At first she refused to go back to the exercises right after lunch, Konrad is supposed to have told Fro, you think that just because we've had our favorite dish you are entitled to go back instantly to the exercises, she is supposed to have said, as Konrad told Fro, but he did start the exercises at once and she gave in, he stood at the corner near the window and called out the word *labyrinth* to her, quickly at first, ten times in succession (forcing instant comments from her) and then at longer intervals again and again the word *labyrinth* (without comments from her). At not quite half past four in the afternoon he decided to go to his own room, saying to her, you take a rest now, I have an idea for my book. But as he enters his room his idea for the book is suddenly gone, he cannot recapture it, pace the floor as he will, it's gone forever. To calm himself he sits down at his desk, however, and—starts to read his Kropotkin. I've got to read my Kropotkin now, because this evening I shall have to read Novalis to her, he says to himself, I promised to read Novalis to her tonight, so he reads all he can of the Kropotkin now. Just as he has started to read "A Change for the Better" he hears a knock at the front door. My method is always the same, he is supposed to have said to Fro, when I hear someone knocking at the front door, I decide not to go down, then whoever it is will stop knocking. But the knocking doesn't stop, and I finally go down. It's the works inspector at the door, saying he must have left his measuring tape behind last time he was here. I haven't seen it, I tell him, Konrad said to Fro, your tape must be somewhere in the vestibule, meanwhile I am thinking if only

I had waited a little longer before answering his knock, he might have left, but as it is the inspector is already inside the vestibule and both of us are searching for the missing tape. But we can't find it. It simply has to be here, the inspector is supposed to have said, but where can it be? says Konrad, so the inspector bends over, Konrad bends over, both of them searching the floor inch by inch for the tape measure, without success. Could the tape measure be up on the first floor? the inspector asks Konrad, and Konrad replies at once, but you weren't even up there! then the inspector: You're right, of course, I never did go up to the first floor, so it can't be up there, and they continue their search, primarily in the so-called wood-paneled room on the ground floor, and Konrad asks if the inspector might not have lost the tape measure at the tavern; or the sawmill, where he had surely been too? says Fro, but the inspector insists that he is certain he lost his tape measure at the lime works, but then he wavers and says, is it possible, after all, that I didn't lose it at the lime works? could I have lost it in the village? left it somewhere in my office? but no, I remember clearly that I still had it when I came to the lime works, I put it down somewhere here in the lime works, somewhere on the ground floor, could someone have removed it from here? the works inspector asked Konrad, who said: I am all alone here at the lime works, my wife, who never gets out of her invalid chair, doesn't count after all, she can't get up out of her chair, and I, Konrad is supposed to have said firmly to the works inspector, do not remember the tape measure at all; Konrad did not even know what the inspector's tape measure looked like, it was a brand new tape measure, the inspector told him, but Konrad did not remember even seeing the new tape measure, the old tape measure was kept inside a green case, a green leather case, Konrad is supposed to have said to the inspector, I can visualize your old tape measure in its green case, but I cannot recall the new tape measure at all, and they both allegedly spent over an hour searching for the tape measure without finding it, in the darkness of the vestibule it was impossible to find anything anyway, the inspector is supposed to have said to Konrad. They both ended up totally exhausted, lying on the floor of the ground floor vestibule, when suddenly the inspector cried out, here it is, my tape measure! and sure enough the inspector had found the tape measure, it was right inside his big outer coat's breast pocket; he had completely forgotten that he had slipped the tape measure into his big breast pocket. Here we are hunting for that tape measure all over the place for over an hour, and all the time it's inside my breast pocket! the inspector is supposed to have exclaimed, adding: What's more, I probably interrupted you (Konrad) at work on your book, I am so sorry about that, whereupon Konrad said that the inspector had not disturbed him in the least, that he, Konrad, had done no writing at all all day long. I'll never make it, Konrad said, even if all the conditions are favorable, all the human conditions, Konrad reiterated, according to Fro, but I cannot seem to make any headway on writing my book; you have not disturbed me, though of course when I am trying to work everything constitutes a disturbance, but when I am not working, you (the works inspector) cannot have disturbed anything, and so forth. While saying all this to the inspector, Konrad, according to Fro, was thinking: I am lying, everything I say is a lie. And he cursed the works inspector inwardly. This time he did not invite the works inspector to a glass of brandy as usual, not even in the wood-paneled room, in fact he did not invite the man in at all, not even into the coldest room there was, in short, absolutely not at all, and the inspector suddenly found himself outside the building again. Konrad was eavesdropping inside the front door, listening to the inspector walking away in the snow, the inspector always walks ten times more laboriously than usual in snow, Konrad is supposed to have told Fro, claiming that he, Konrad, had seen the works inspector furiously throwing the tape measure, which he had just recovered with so much trouble, into the snow-covered road, gesturing violently, before he picked it up, dusted it off, and rolled it up again, the inspector was enraged at having made such a fool of himself in Konrad's eyes, after all he was the first to start creeping around on the floor on hands and knees searching for a lost tape measure which he actually had in his breast pocket the whole time. The works inspector is a mess of neurotic complexes, Konrad is supposed to have thought as he watched the man stomping off through the snow, in that uncomfortable posture (for Konrad) one has to hold when looking through a keyhole, which I have gotten accustomed to in the course of time, Konrad is supposed to have said to Fro. The moment the inspector had vanished into the thicket Konrad went back to his room and back to reading his Kropotkin, but he had barely read two pages, basically not more than a quick review of what he had already read of "A Change for the Better," when he heard a bell ring, this time upstairs, his wife demanding attention. He instantly went upstairs to her. Think of it, my dear Fro, everything I am telling you, describing to you, intimating to you, Konrad is supposed to have told Fro, basically goes on here every day, over and over again! everything that goes on here goes on day after day after day, it's the height of absurdity, and by dint of being the height of absurdity it is the height of terribleness, day after day after day. It's true, Fro's testimony agrees in every respect with Wieser's testimony, the works inspector confirms everything Fro and Wieser have said, and conversely, both Wieser and Fro confirm what the works inspector says, basically one confirms the other, they all confirm each other's testimony. What is it? Konrad is supposed to have said to his wife when he got to her room; he had been reading his Kropotkin, he had gotten no work at all done on his book that day, he had been interrupted by the inspector, then, finally, he had at least managed to get back to his Kropotkin when she rang and there was no way he could avoid going up to see what she wanted, he intended no reproach to her, he had reached the point where he never reproached her with anything in any way, but as soon as he entered her room, he said, she said at once: Read to me, meaning that he had to start reading Novalis to her. To Wieser: For many days now Konrad had noticed that his wife's eyelids were inflamed, not that he ever mentioned it to her because he assumed she knew her eyelids were red with inflammation, after all she looked into her mirror often enough and intently enough, there were many times she would sit for an hour staring at herself in the mirror, so she was bound to know that she had inflamed eyelids, Konrad said to Wieser. Causes: dry air, solitude, age. He did not mention his observation to her, because he had given up wasting another word on any of her ailments; for him to draw her attention to some new infirmity was out. For instance, only six months ago she had still been able to sit up so straight that you could not see a certain miniature painting

representing her paternal grandmother, which hung behind
the invalid chair in which she sat. Now, only six months
later, her posture was so slumped, Konrad is supposed to have
told Wieser, that not only could you see the miniature in its
entirety, almost, but she was bent over almost three or four
inches below it. Week by week, sitting opposite his wife,
Konrad claimed to have seen more and more of this miniature
portrait behind her, though for weeks he had refused to believe it, but in the end he had to admit it: his wife was
gradually slumping lower, the miniature rising behind her,
so to speak, until Konrad felt able to calculate precisely the
moment when he would see the portrait in its entirety, not
that he actually worked it out, he just knew he could if he
wanted to calculate the precise moment of full visibility. He
thought about this, and about the fact that nowadays his
wife, when he helped her up and walked with her a bit,
took steps just half the length of those she could take only
six months ago, Konrad is supposed to have told Fro, soon
she would not be able to walk all the way to the window,
not even to the center of the room; soon she would not be
able to get out of her chair, in fact; suppose that moment has
suddenly arrived, he would think; he realizes that she can
no longer stand up—and a new phase of their life together
has begun. Nowadays when he reads Novalis to her she sometimes fails to understand whole passages, he is supposed to
have told Fro, he asks her if she has been listening and she
says yes, she has been listening attentively, but she hasn't
understood everything she heard; in this connection, it is
necessary to explain that the Novalis, though she loves it, unlike him who can't stand the Novalis, is nevertheless a difficult
book, as commonly understood; this has nothing to do with

the fact that when he reads her his beloved Kropotkin, to punish her for something, she deliberately pretends not to understand more than half of what he is reading. When she fails to understand her beloved Novalis though she listens with might and main, there's no pretense about that. Now at the Laska, where I sold another of our new policies today, they say that there's a cripple living in the lime works, the Konrad woman, that's whom they mean in the hostelries hereabouts when they refer, as usual, to "the woman," and this cripple, they say, is cared for, according to some, or shamefully used, according to others, by her husband, the owner of the lime works, and a mad despot to his wife. According to the gossip he is terrible, devoted, sadistic, attentive, all at the same time. They praise him for fetching her meals from the tavern, but say he is destroying his wife by using her ruthlessly as a guinea pig for his scientific experiments, his so-called Urbanchich method, of which they have no conception except what they get from Hoeller's weird descriptions after years of watching Konrad's practices with his wife. They say that Konrad torments his wife by saying, shouting, whispering, either very quickly or with excruciating slowness, all sorts of incomprehensible things into her agonizingly inflamed ears and then forcing her to comment on each and every one of his utterances until she comes close to fainting. Even after Mrs. Konrad has reached a point of exhaustion when she can't react at all any more, her husband will keep at her for hours after she has collapsed into total apathy, they say at Laska's, sometimes until four in the morning, etc. He started out being fabulously rich, they say, but it's all gone because he's an idiot with money, and anyway his obsession with his so-called scientific work, something to do with the sense of hearing, has left them in straits, not that you could consider him actually impoverished, but there were rumors about an impending forced auction sale of the lime works. Nevertheless, they seem to think of him as a rich man still, but you have to remember that to a common working man, anyone who has one good suit and doesn't have to go to work in overalls at six o'clock in the morning like himself is a rich man. Konrad himself, says Wieser, would probably never have called himself a rich man, though he might reluctantly have admitted to being well-to-do, back in Zurich or even as late as his Mannheim period, even though at that time he could still be considered a rich man by even the most exacting standards, yet Konrad himself said to Fro about two years ago: I am actually poorer than any of the people who call me a rich man, but how am I to make people understand that I am telling the truth? Talking with the woodcutters and other workmen who hang around the various taverns far into the night, toward the end of winter, was Konrad's favorite recreation, he enjoyed their conversation more than anyone's, he is supposed to have told Wieser. But he had not gone to any of the taverns for months now, what with the way things were getting worse for them at the lime works, he even missed his tavern-going habits less as time went on. For months on end he had not talked with the workmen, woodcutters, gamekeepers, etc., nor gone even once to the woods, he had not seen the village for six months, in fact, though he did go there, but only to the bank where he would cash a check and go straight back to the lime works, having drawn out a negligible amount of money, not enough to keep one alive, but too much to let a man croak. He had not even spoken to Hoeller for weeks, unless you counted telling Hoeller to chop some wood, or not to chop wood, or taking the food hamper he brought from the tavern and handing back the empty hamper. This year Hoeller had become a changed man, Konrad did not know why he seemed to have lost the confidence of this man of extraordinary integrity, he could only guess that it might be for the same reason he had lost confidence in himself to a degree. A simple question had in the past always elicited a simple answer from Hoeller, Konrad is supposed to have said to Wieser, but nowadays all he ever got were ambiguous answers to the same simple questions. These days there was only mistrust between them, which made them uncertain with each other, full of unspoken reservations that entailed a daily circling around and around the unacknowledged source of their trouble. It was Hoeller's cousin, the one with the seven or eight convictions for sexual offenses, who had taken to living with Hoeller in the annex, secretly, behind Konrad's back, without his or Hoeller's asking Konrad's permission; ever since the cousin's arrival Hoeller had ceased to come near Konrad except when he brought the food hamper or asked if he should chop some fire wood. According to Wieser, this means that Konrad has had to do without his conversations with Hoeller, an important source for his book; in fact, Konrad has also been deprived of the talk he valued so much with all the simple men of the region around the lime works. The Konrads preferred to spend their mornings mulling over what they would have to eat, Konrad is supposed to have told Fro, instead of Konrad simply going down to the kitchen to fix something, anything, when Hoeller was not going to the tavern for their lunch, whether because he was sick or had to chop wood or the like, so that Konrad was prevented from working on his book, what the Konrads would do was to sit and talk for hours, endlessly, about sauerkraut, cauliflower, meat, egg dishes, soups and sauces, salads and cooked fruit, unable to decide in favor of any specific kind of meal. To waste the entire morning like this on planning what to eat, thinking about what to eat, was absolutely disgusting. Encounter III: at about two A.M. Konrad said, he had heard a shot nearby, it had to have been fired quite close to the lime works, he thought, but he could see nothing, even after opening the window and looking outside, nothing. But somebody had just fired a shot, he said to himself, and there's a second shot, and a third, after the third it was quiet again . . . before the Konrads moved into the lime works the annex had been a meeting place for the hunting men of the area; Konrad despised hunters as much as he did the hunt, all of his ancestors had been hunters, woodsmen, all their lives their heads were full of hunting to the exclusion of everything else, a hunter was invariably a stupid man, a hunter was always and every time a congenital dimwit, a hunting moron. Konrad had never been interested in hunting. The moment he moved into the lime works he abolished all the hunting privileges associated with the lime works; no more hunting meets in the annex, he declared, and ever since then the hunters naturally hated him and he was always terrified when he walked through the woods, even just setting foot outside the lime works, afraid of being shot at or shot down by a hunter, a hunter could always feel free to gun down any man he hated, Konrad said, though he would be brought to court, but the courts would let a hunter go scot-free, or else, if a hunter was convicted of murder, they would sentence him to a ridiculous suspended sentence, hunters could kill people to their hearts' content in this country and go scot-free. Konrad hated hunters, he said, but he loved guns, especially hunting rifles, it was a paradox but he could explain it. Then: he greased his boots with concentrated beef fat, using the ball of his thumb. Greasing his boots was already beginning to cost him a tremendous effort, it had to be done with the ball of the thumb, as he learned before he was four years old from his father, he could still remember his father teaching him how to grease his boots with the ball of his thumb, never with a rag, only the ball of the thumb, no brushes; rags were a poor substitute for the ball of the thumb, which left the leather beautifully supple, if you worked it always from the inside out and with growing intensity; Konrad always liked the smell of boot grease, Polish or Slovakian, he loved the smell of his room after greasing his boots there in the wintertime, the only time he greased his boots in his room, the rest of the year he did it out in front of the house, but he particularly remembered the wintertime greasing of his boots indoors as a pleasant chore associated with a pleasant smell. But in recent years he found himself totally exhausted after greasing his boots, on such a day he could hardly do the Urbanchich exercises, not even to mention the writing, merely to think of the book on such a day was an effort to be shunned, even if an idea for his book should occur to him after greasing his boots, it could only be an insignificant idea. After such a chore as greasing his boots or any such physical effort, these days, Konrad said, he would have to lie down on his bed, made up for the day as it was, in an indescribable state of collapse, and take several deep breaths, with his eyes on the ceiling which seemed to be in constant motion up there, he said, trying to clarify his conception of the book, divided as it was into nine parts, but in his weakened state after greasing his boots or some such effort as that, he found it impossible to think, all he could muster was a hazy outline of the book which had nothing in common with the real book except for his fear of the hard work involved, which drove him in desperation to try to think of other things, anything else rather than the book, but when he succeeded in driving the book from his mind it made him even more desperate, because to find himself thinking of anything else than the book naturally drove him to despair at once. Relax and breathe deeply, he would say to himself then, inhale, exhale, calmly now, he would say, in constant anxiety that he would be torn away from this by the sudden ringing of his wife's bell, her so-called signal that she needed help, afraid of having to go up to her room and witness one of her bouts of helplessness, always some new form of helplessness, infirmity, incapacity. Sometimes a good idea for his book would come to him precisely during such a state of weakness in consequence of having greased his boots, etc., on occasion some of his best ideas would occur to him then, ideas of a kind that never came in the beginning, twenty years ago, because they happened to be typical of old age, the very best ideas in fact, but they usually deserted him as quickly as they had come, which reduced their value for him to nil, and viewed from this perspective they were of course the most worthless, actually the most terribly worthless ideas one could have or imagine, ideas of a worthlessness a young man could not even conceive of, because a young man could not have such ideas, could not remotely understand such ideas. All that was left was the recollection of having had a good idea, a recurrent experience of having had a good, an excellent, a most important idea, a truly fundamental idea, but one never remembered the idea itself from one moment to the next, memory was something you simply couldn't depend on, a man's memory set him traps he'd walk into and find himself hopelessly lost in, Konrad said, a man's memory lured him into a trap and then deserted him, it happened over and over again that a man's memory lured him into a trap, or several traps, thousands of traps, and then deserted him, left him all alone, alone in limitless despair because he felt drained of all thought; Konrad had come to observe this geriatric phenomenon and had begun to be more and more terrified of it, he was in fact prepared to state that a man's youthful memory was capable of turning into an old man's memory from one moment to the next, with no warning whatsoever, suddenly you found yourself with an old man's memory, unprepared by such warning signals as a failure, from time to time, in trifling matters, brief lapses or omissions, the way a mental footbridge or gangplank might give a bit as one passed over it; no, old age set in from one moment to the next, many a man made this abrupt passage from youth to age quite early in life, a sudden shift from being the youngest to the oldest of men, a characteristic of so-called brain workers who tended, basically, not to have a so-called extended youth, no gradual transitions from youth to age, with them the change occurred momentarily, without warning, suddenly, mortally, you found yourself in old age. A thinking man with an old man's memory instantly lost all his ideas, the most important, the best, unless he noted them down at once, so the thinking aged man had to carry paper and pencil with him at all

times, without paper and pencil he was totally lost, while a
thinking young man needed no paper and pencil, he remembered everything that occurred to him, he could do
anything he wanted with his brain and with his memory,
effortlessly store whatever occurred to him in his brain
and therefore in his memory, hold on to the most extraordinary ideas as long as he needed to and almost without effort
until, suddenly, from one moment to the next, he was old.
An old man needs a crutch, he needs crutches, every old man
carries invisible crutches, Konrad said, all those millions and
billions of old people on crutches, millions, billions, trillions
of invisible crutches, my friend, no one else may see them
but I see them, I am one of those who cannot help seeing
these invisible billions, trillions of crutches, there's not a
moment, Konrad said, in which I do not see those billions,
those trillions of crutches. Those millions of ideas, he said,
that I had and lost, that I forgot from one moment to the
next. Why I could populate a vast metropolis of thought with
all those lost ideas of mine, I could keep it afloat, a whole
world, a whole history of mankind could have lived on all the
ideas that I lost. How untrustworthy my memory has become!
he said; I get up and note down an idea I have just had (in
bed), my best ideas all come to me in bed, and as I start to
note it down, shivering with cold at my desk because I
couldn't take the time to wrap myself in a blanket, the idea
is dissipated, it's gone, no use asking myself what became of
it, it's irrecoverable, gone, I know I had an idea, a good idea, a
prime, extraordinary idea, but it's lost now. It happened to
him over and over again: he would have an idea, unquestionably a good idea, perhaps not an epoch-making idea, but those
are best discarded at once, because in fact there is no such

thing, those so-called epoch-making ideas are all phony, he
said, what he had was a useful idea, but in the very act of
noting down this useful, practical idea, it gets lost. You could
call this whole thing a farce, of course; everything is farcical,
if you like, to call it a farce is a way of keeping oneself on the
move, getting on with this whole evolutionary farce and one's
role in it, why not, but it did of course keep getting harder to
do, after one's sixtieth year it required an enormous effort to
catapult oneself through this farce day by day, moment by
moment, the effort became a torment, because it was the most
insincere, most unnatural effort-against-the-grain, he said:
While losing the idea in the midst of noting it down, I say to
myself, I'll just throw this bescribbled slip of paper away, into
the waste basket with it. At his age he had begun to regret all
those feeble ideas, he did not scruple to call them feeble-
minded ideas he had lost in the act of trying to note them
down, and that had vanished in their thousands as so-called
incipient but lost ideas in his waste basket. *What an idea!* he
had thought, and *What a miserable blank* was what he noted
down. Words ruin one's thoughts, paper makes them ridiculous, and even while one is still glad to get something ruined
and something ridiculous down on paper, one's memory
manages to lose hold of even this ruined and ridiculous something. Paper can turn an enormity into a triviality, an absurdity. If you look at it this way, then whatever appears in
the world, by way of the spiritual world so to speak, is always
a ruined thing, a ridiculous thing, which means that everything in this world is ridiculous and ruined. Words were made
to demean thought, he would even go so far as to state that
words exist in order to abolish thought, and one day they will
succeed one hundred percent in so doing. In any case, words

were bringing everything down, Konrad said. Depression derives from words, nothing else. To Fro, three years ago: I looked up at the ceiling, and lo and behold, the quiet that suddenly filled the whole lime works had momentarily ceased to be the sinister quiet I had become accustomed to through the years; suddenly it was a comforting quiet: not a person, not a sound, how blissful! instead of: not a person, not a sound, how terrible! It was comforting, one of those rare times when one feels that suddenly everything is possible again, Konrad is supposed to have said to Fro. Suddenly everything was evolving out of me, and I was evolving everything, I was the possessor of possibility, capacity. Of course I did my best to hang on to this state of mind for as long as possible, but it didn't last, the unquestioning assurance of earlier times; just now recaptured, was gone as suddenly as it came, the ideal constellation, ideal construction of the mechanism of revulsion had turned into its opposite. How easy it was once for my brain to enter into a thought, my brain was fearless then, while nowadays my brain is afraid of every thought, it enters a thought only when relentlessly bullied into it, whereupon it instantly conks out, in self-defense. First: a natural marshaling of all one's forces, possible in youth, Konrad is supposed to have said, then, in old age, which is suddenly all there is, the unnatural marshaling of all impossible forces. While I was not defenseless when entering into my thoughts, in earlier times, nowadays I enter into my thoughts defenselessly, unprotected though heavily armed, whereas in earlier times I entered into my thoughts totally unarmed and yet not defenseless. These days his brain and his head were preoccupied and timid compared with former times when they were neither preoccupied nor at all timid, now they were timid in every respect, every possible or impossible manifestation, and so timid a brain must unquestionably withdraw from so timid a head as his, so timid a brain and so timid a head had to withdraw from the world, and yet it was a fact that head and brain, or rather brain and head could withdraw from the world only into the world, and so forth. You could, in fact, withdraw everything from everything and again into everything, meaning that you could not withdraw at all, and so forth. This resulted in a constant state of moral despair. You could try to circumvent nature by every conceivable means, every trick you could think of, only to find yourself in the end face to face with nature. There was no escape, but on the other hand, there was no real mystery in this, either, because the head, meaning the brain inside the head, no matter how high it holds itself, is only the height of incompetence, inseparable from the piece of nature it heads up, so to speak, which it cannot really control, and so forth. Some people whom the world dares to call philosophers—a classification that constitutes a public menace —even try bribery, Konrad said to Fro, who bought the new life policy from me yesterday. Nothing is ever mastered, everything is misused. And so: this quiet that suddenly reigned again in the lime works, Konrad is supposed to have said to Fro at one time, this quiet, a false quiet as I explained to you before, because it cannot be real, so that there can be no real quiet in the lime works, and therefore no real quiet in him, Konrad; in any case, this false quiet, for which he had no actual explanation, did make it possible for him even in his old age to approach ideas, from time to time, ideas no longer rightfully his, because they were the ideas of youth, so that in his case they could not be real ideas, as he allegedly expressed it. At such times he would be lying on his bed, listening, but hearing not a person, not a sound, nothing. At such moments he would believe that it was now possible for him to sit down at his desk and begin to write his book, and so he would sit down at his desk, but even while he felt he could now begin, he could not begin. It set him back whole decades, because what he experienced was a total setback in every respect in one single moment. This book of his would not be a long one, he is supposed to have said to Fro, not at all, it might even be the shortest book ever written, but it was the hardest of all to write. It might be only a question of the beginning, what words to begin with, and so forth. Perhaps it was a question of the right moment when to begin, as everything is a question of the right moment. He had been waiting for the right moment for months, for years, for decades, in fact; but because he was waiting for it, watching for it, the moment would not come. Although he understood this quite clearly, he nevertheless kept waiting for his moment, because even when I am not waiting for this moment, Konrad is supposed to have said to Fro, I nevertheless am waiting for this moment, still waiting for it, even now, regardless of whether I am waiting for it or not, I keep wearing myself out waiting, which is probably my real trouble. While waiting, he kept refining his points, he said, incessantly altering details, and by his endless alterations, refinements, unyielding preoccupation, unyielding experiments in preparation for writing, he made the writing impossible. A book one had completely in one's head was probably the kind one couldn't write down, he is supposed to have said to Fro, just as one cannot write down a symphony one has entirely in one's head, and he did have his book entirely in his head. But he was not going to give up, he said, the book probably has to fall apart in my head before I can suddenly write it all down, he is supposed to have said to Fro, it has to be all gone, so that it can suddenly be back in its entirety, from one moment to the next. Encounter IV: With regard to his stay in Brussels of about twenty-two years ago, at which time he had briefly placed his wife in a clinic in Leeuwen, Konrad said the following, not quite but almost word for word: When I can no longer stand it in my room, because I can neither think nor write nor read nor sleep and because I can no longer do anything, not even pace the floor in my room, I mean that I am afraid that if I suddenly resume pacing the floor in my room, after having already paced the floor in my room for such a long time, even this resumption of pacing the floor will be made impossible for me because someone will knock, and because of this fear, it actually does become impossible for me to pace the floor. They knock because I am disturbing them, because my pacing the floor is disturbing someone, they knock or they shout, which I find unbearable because I am afraid that they will soon knock again or shout again or knock and shout together . . . then I leave my room, because I can't stand it there any longer, and go down to the third floor and knock at the professor's door . . . I knock and wait for the professor to answer the door, I stand there and wait for the professor to invite me in . . . and as I stand there waiting I think how cold it is, I am freezing, I don't know whether it is eleven or twelve or one o'clock in the morning . . . my incessant pacing of the floor in my room has left me in a state of near unconsciousness, I keep waiting, thinking all this, every time I am standing at the professorial door, waiting to hear the professor say "Come in!" or: "The door isn't locked!" and then I open the door and go in, I see the professor sitting at his desk . . . and so I wait, but I hear nothing. Nothing. I knock again. Nothing. I go on waiting and knocking until at last I decide that I ought to turn around and go back to my room, because the professor will not open his door, not today . . . he opened it yesterday, and the day before yesterday, and the day before that, too, he opened his door to me every day last week, every time I knocked he opened the door . . . but today, I start to worry, the professor won't open up . . . I knock, and knock again, and listen, and hear nothing. Is the professor out? Or is he in, but out of earshot, perhaps? Could he have gone to the country again? How often the professor takes a ride out into the country, I say to myself, off he goes, unexpectedly, to the country. To all those hundreds of relatives, I guess. Suppose I were to knock a little louder? I think. Louder still? But I've already knocked twice or three times as loudly as before . . . Knock again! I say to myself. Knock again! By this time I am knocking as loudly as possible, everyone in the house must have been able to hear me, because I keep knocking more loudly than ever, and still more loudly! Someone must have heard me by now . . . these people all have sensitive ears, the most sensitive hearing of all . . . but I knock just once more, the loudest ever, and I listen, and I hear the professor, he is walking toward the door and opening it, though he opens it only half way, and I say: I hope I'm not disturbing you, though I know it's late, but I do hope I am not disturbing you . . . I see now that the professor has been immersed in his work . . . My morphology! he says, according to Konrad, My morphology! and I say to him, Konrad says, if I am disturbing you I shall go back to my room immediately. But! I say, and the professor says: My morphology! and meanwhile I am wondering, says Konrad, why the professor has opened the door only halfway? only wide enough, in fact, so that he can stick his head out to talk to me, but not to let me inside . . . But listen to me, I said to him, says Konrad, if I am disturbing you I shall go back to my room at once. If I am disturbing you . . . at this point I see, says Konrad, that the professor is already undressed, quite naked, in fact, under his dressing gown, I can see it, and I say: You're already undressed for the night, I see! then I must be disturbing you, and if so I shall instantly go back to my room! you need only say the word, that you do not wish to be disturbed this late . . . but if you wouldn't mind, if I may just once more, I would like to come in to see you for just a few moments, I say to him, I shall leave right away, I don't even have any idea what time it is, I tell him, I've been pacing the floor in my room all this time, with this problem of mine, I'm afraid I'm going crazy . . . as you know, my dear professor, I haven't been working for days now, I can't write at all, not a line, not an idea, nothing . . . again and again it seems to me, stop, here's an idea, but no, in reality there's nothing, I tell him . . . and so I go about all day long, obsessed with the thought that I can't think, as I walk back and forth in my room, actually thinking the whole time that I haven't an idea, not one single idea . . . because in fact I haven't had an idea for the longest time, I say . . . and I wait, and pace the floor, but what I am waiting for is only you, all day long I wait for you to come home . . . Today you came home two hours later than usual, I tell him, yesterday it was one and a half hours later than usual, actually it was two and a half hours later than usual today . . . I hear you because my hearing gets keener from one day to the next, I can hear you when you are still out on the street, when you turn the key in the lock of the front door, and when you lock the door on the inside, then I hear you entering the vestibule, all day long I wait for you to enter the vestibule ... Today you must have done your shopping, your errands, you probably paid your bills, went to the post office ... once you are inside the vestibule, I anticipate your unlocking the door to your apartment, and when you have unlocked your door, I imagine you entering your room, taking off your coat, your shoes, then you sit down at your desk, perhaps ... then you take a bite to eat, begin to write a letter perhaps, a letter to your daughter who lives in France, to your son who lives in Rattenberg ... or a business letter ... or else you are working on your morphology, perhaps ... I seem to hear with increasing keenness how you turn the key in the lock—lately you have been unlocking the door much faster than formerly, in the beginning—then you walk quickly into your room, you pull off your coat ... then I imagine you considering whether to lie down on the bed or not, whether to lie down in your clothes or not, lie on the bed without taking off your shoes, perhaps, or else not to lie down on your bed before you go back to your work on your morphology, to lie down ... then, when you lie down on your bed, when you have lain down on your bed, you realize the senselessness of your work and the senselessness of your existence ... I imagine that this realization of the senselessness of everything must come to you ... that you have to earn your living so miserably, to continue your research so miserably, that everyone must earn his living so miserably, must continue his research so miserably ... in such growing misery, you are thinking ... and that you have no one in the world, after all, Konrad is supposed to have said to the professor ... that, whether you sit down at your desk or not, lie down on the bed or not, you are bound to realize the whole extent of your misfortune in life, a misfortune that seems greater every time you think about it . . . At this point the professor admits Konrad into the room . . . and, says Konrad, I go straight to his bed and I say to him, I see that your bed is already made, you have made your bed already, you evidently intended to go to bed already, or perhaps you have already been to bed? and I say to him, please don't let me get in the way, do lie down if you feel like it, all I want is to pace the floor a bit in your room; as you know, I can no longer do it in my own room . . . when I pace the floor in my room, I tell him, it seems to me that everyone in the house can hear me doing it, just as you know, I am sure, when I am reading in my room, that I am reading in my room, and when I am thinking in my room, you know that I am thinking in my room, you know that I am writing when I am writing in my room, you know that I am in bed when I am in bed . . . I believe that all the people in the house know what I am doing . . . because, you know, these people know it when I am thinking, when I am thinking about my book in my room . . . which makes it impossible for me to do any thinking in my room, impossible to think about my book in my room, which is why I have been such a mental blank for such a long time now . . . and if it is impossible for me to think in my room, imagine how terrible it is for me to have to formulate a letter in my room . . . as a result of all this I have been unable to read for the longest time now, unable to think at all . . . but in your room, I said, I can still pace the floor . . . I can walk back and forth in your room, and relax . . . little by little, and after a while I can relax more deeply, I tell him, and then I can go back to my room . . . you see, I tell him, I am relaxing already, my whole body is relaxed now, and this relaxation slowly goes to my brain as well; when I relax in your room it is a simultaneous relaxation of body and brain . . . actually, I tell him, I need merely enter your room and I feel relaxed already . . . Isn't it strange? considering that it has become quite impossible for me to look up anybody, ever . . . but I set foot in your room, and instantly I feel relaxed . . . Today, I tell him, you came home so late, those silly errands of yours . . . all those silly letters you get day after day and have to answer day after day, all your silly people . . . I get no letters and I answer no letters . . . and those repulsive colleagues of ours that you have to put up with at your university, that you have had to put up with all these years . . . all the annoyances that prevent you from coming home earlier . . . then, as you are turning the key in the lock, I tell him, each time you do it I feel you are saving me from this frightful situation, I tell him, because you know, I always feel as if I were going to suffocate, I tell him . . . as if I am bound to end my life by suffocating, to suffocate in the end, how grotesque to have to end in suffocation . . . simply because you had a few extra errands this day, and came home too late . . . and by the time you got to your room, I would have long since suffocated, Konrad said to the professor, actually I expect every day at the same time that I will suffocate, here I am, suffocating, I tell myself, choking on an absurdity, because you are out, as it might be, as it certainly could turn out, on one of your errands, perhaps taking the long way home, or paying an unusually extended visit to your aunt or something . . . but then I hear your step outside, I hear you turning the key in the lock . . . and I say to myself, now I can relax; you can see for yourself how much more relaxed I am since you let me into your room, I tell him, but I do hope I am not disturbing you, I think I have disturbed you often enough already, Konrad said to the professor, but if I have to be alone one more moment, he said, I always feel ready to suffocate . . . and then I hear you . . . What a lovely miniature you have here, on your wall, I tell him, I've never noticed these lovely miniatures before . . . and then I hear you unlocking your apartment door, and locking it again, and I hear you lying down on your bed and sitting down at your desk and getting up again from your desk . . . and then I pace the floor in my room a hundred times, back and forth, again and again, and I say to myself: now you can go down to the professor's, at last, and then: no, not yet, not yet! no, not yet! then again, go ahead now, go down, quickly now, this minute . . . the indecision drives me nearly crazy, this incessant do-I-go-or-don't-I, might I, but perhaps not . . . then I think: now! now I can! and in this way an hour has gone by, and I say to myself, but what if the professor is busy with his morphology . . . you were, in fact, busy with your morphology just now, I tell him, says Konrad, but you were too tired to work, too . . . you are too tired, I say to him . . . yet how busy! I say, and I walk over to his desk and I see that the professor has been busy working on his morphology . . . while I spent an hour wondering whether or not to go down to see him . . . Well, if I am disturbing you . . . do tell me if I am disturbing you . . . you must say that I am disturbing you, if I am disturbing you . . . that of course I am disturbing you, that I have been disturbing you for some time; I tell him, Konrad says: All these years I have been disturbing you . . . all these years I have been living in the same house with you . . . of course I am a harassment to you! . . . but you see, I tell him, says Konrad, I have been waiting for two hours, four hours, six hours, eight hours . . . and still I don't go down to see you . . . here you are, I say to myself, waiting all this time, and still not going down to see him! . . . and then of course I do go down and knock on your door, I go on interminably knocking on your door until you open it and let me in . . . and let me pace the floor in your room, so that I can gradually begin to relax . . . and I do relax, and I say: Possibly tonight I shall finally make a bit of headway with my book, even if it's only the least bit . . . possibly, I say, but I do say this to myself day after day, every day, I say to myself that today, when the professor gets home, you will go down to him and pace the floor in his room and then you will go back to your own room and get going on writing your book . . . it is exactly what I still say to myself, as you know, Fro, to this day, that now, I always say to myself, now, this time, I shall begin at last to write my book down . . . and to the professor I say, Konrad reported, if only I'm not disturbing you . . . if only I didn't know how easily people are disturbed, a man who needs his peace, a man like yourself, professor, a man like myself, professor, . . . whom people disturb when he is longing only to be left alone . . . but unlike myself, who can no longer stand being alone, I say to the professor, you do want to be alone, and what's so strange about this is that you have become so old being the way you are, but you do want to be alone, because of course you have to be alone . . . and you always do tell me when I come in to see you that you want to be alone, I say to him, says Konrad, you tell me that you must be alone, and even when you do not say it, even when it is not you who says it, even when you say nothing at all, I can hear it, I hear you saying that you want to be alone . . . my dear professor, I tell him, I shall leave you now, I am quite relaxed, it is altogether thanks to you that I have been able to calm myself like this . . . though probably even you will soon be unable to help me relax, just as my wife can no longer help me to relax, nobody, nothing can help me, I tell him . . . thank you, thank you, I say, walking to the door, the professor opens it for me, and I tell him that I did not intend, certainly did not mean to disturb you and I turn around and I hear the professor going back inside his room . . . how quickly I got back to my own room, I think, it's astonishing, and I sit down at my desk and get ready to write, but I can't begin to write . . . I must be able to write, I think, but I can't write . . . and I get up and pace the floor in my room, on and on, just as I do here at the lime works . . . an unfortunate natural predisposition is what makes me pace the floor in my room all night long, all night and in the morning, when the professor has long since left the house, I keep on pacing back and forth, and I feel afraid of this pacing back and forth, as I still feel afraid of it today, just as I felt afraid of it all that time ago in Brussels, I still fear this pacing back and forth today in the lime works and I pace back and forth and I walk and wait and think, I wait and walk and walk and walk . . . and walk . . . To Fro: Konrad said that he and his wife preferred to spend the entire morning, in that unsurpassable, deadly togetherness of theirs, deadly from the moment it began, in mulling over the menu, viz., what Hoeller should bring them to eat from the tavern, Konrad being either too busy with his stepped-up experimental work to go, or too exhausted physically by his work: should they have a meat course or a pasta; or perhaps neither meat nor pasta but fish, instead? and what about soup and a salad as well, both of them prized a salad beyond anything, and he would rather, said Konrad to Fro, do without meat or fish and even without soup, in fact, but, if at all possible, he did not wish to do without a salad, so they went on for hours mulling over such questions as whether Hoeller would be taking twenty or thirty or even forty minutes to bring the food from the tavern to the lime works, and it was heartbreaking (Fro) how much time and energy they would give to guessing at the possibility that Hoeller might be unusually late, impermissibly late, that is, as a result of running into someone on the way and dawdling over a conversation, instead of Konrad concentrating, as he should, all his available forces upon getting his book written; he would welcome any distraction at all, nothing was too absurd or too trivial or too insignificant to serve as a distraction from his work, his writing, even though he would awaken in the mornings smothered in a horrible miasma of conscience trouble that positively tasted like brain rot and pressed painfully against the back of his head, at the mere thought of writing his book, in fact, he no longer thought of his writing, he is supposed to have told Fro, because as time went on this thought had become the most excruciating torture to him, though he was nevertheless in any case confronted with the problem of how to go about writing his book, regardless of what he was thinking or doing or considering, anything whatever was inescapably connected with his book, with getting it written, darkening his defenseless head with shame (he never explained to Fro in what way shame entered into it). Shall we have sauerkraut or potatoes, or will they have meringues today or even those fluffy beef roulades they both loved so much, and what about apple crumb cake or apple strudel or possibly pot strudel? or bacon-dumplings or pickled meat or spleen soup if not baked-noodle soup, or boiled beef with horseradish,

perhaps? on the other hand, there might be a well-aged veni-
son with cranberry sauce; they wondered at length whether
Hoeller might bring them news, political or farming or
social news from the tavern, news of a death or a wedding, a
baptism, a crime, and how, where, and when something might
have happened that even two well-traveled people like themselves might regard as sensational, something that had been
kept secret for a long time but could no longer be kept secret,
and to what extent the work on the roads had progressed, as
well as the so-called shore improvements and the damming
of the mountain streams, how cold the lake was, how dark the
woods, how dangerous the precipice, whether people were
talking about Mrs. Konrad and what they were saying, at the
tavern, at the sawmill, in the village, whether the rumors
about themselves were still making the rounds (works inspector), just how much people really knew about the
Konrads' affairs, or really did not know, how they felt about
Konrad's not having set foot in the village in such a long time,
about his not being seen in the woods for such a long time,
or in the sawmill, the tavern, at the bank; whether the market
had drawn a good crowd last market-day or not, what people
were saying about the new church bells, whether the cost of
funerals had gone up, whether the new members of the gov-
ernment had taken hold, whether the deer and the chamois
were fewer this year, whether things represented as true were
indeed true, whether things that had seemed to be true for
years had turned out to be untrue, whether things that had
seemed to be in doubt had cleared up, all this and more they
wondered about, says Fro, and they kept thinking up more
questions, more things worth looking into, for hours on end,
distracting themselves with all this nonsense (Fro) so that he

could forget about his book, and she about her disease, her crippled condition. It is alleged that they put it to a vote as to which of their favorite two books he should be reading to her as a reward for subjecting herself to his experimentation with the Urbanchich method, for decades now they had always filled the breaks between exercises by his reading aloud to her, either the Kropotkin memoirs, that is, his book, as in recent weeks, or the Novalis novel, her book; of course he read to her from her book if she wished it, incidentally the book that had been her declared favorite all her life, and he did read it to her for weeks on end, again and again, but he also read her his admired Kropotkin, against her will and despite her resistance, she had at first refused to listen when he read the Kropotkin aloud, but he paid no attention to her obstructionist tactics vis-a-vis Kropotkin, and by ruthlessly persisting in reading the Kropotkin to her in a loud voice week after week and then day after day he had prevailed against her, although she insisted to the very end on her instinctive dislike for this Russian book, not that she still hated it as in the beginning but she never ceased to feel mistrustful toward it. Actually Konrad believed that despite her constant grumbling he had converted her to the Kropotkin long ago, by persuasion so artfully and tirelessly applied that she hardly noticed it. They spent whole days bargaining, Wieser says, trading an hour of Kropotkin for an hour of Novalis, two hours of Kropotkin for one and a half of Novalis, or no Novalis for no Kropotkin, or a chapter of Kropotkin for one or two chapters of Novalis, etc., in which bargaining process Mrs. Konrad was naturally always at a disadvantage, according to Wieser. Basically it was always Konrad who decided what was to be read aloud. Every reading ended with a discussion of the text he had just read, conducted of course by Konrad, says Wieser, never by his wife. Now and then they would, for instance, try to relate Kropotkin to Novalis, on the basis of the passage just read, in a purely scholarly way, nothing bellettristic, an analysis that would lead them to touch on all sorts of related matters, as Konrad is supposed to have expressed it to Wieser. The most interesting kind of reading to him was the kind that opened out in every direction, he did not say in every direction of the compass, exactly, but his special preference had always been for scientific books, thoughtful twentieth century nonfiction, or books like his Kropotkin, future-oriented books, in short, while her preference was always for the humane letters of the second half of the nineteenth century, naturally, said Wieser. He, Konrad, had always despised a reading not followed by discussion or debate, at least an effort to analyze the subject, or some such immediate commentary. Of course it had taken years of the most strenuous effort on his part to make his wife at least passably familiar with this attitude of his. But if a man had the necessary patience, Konrad is supposed to have told Wieser, he could in the end win over the most refractory opponent to the most refractory cause, by the sheer forcefulness of his honest, fanatically precise logic; ultimately even a person like his wife could be won over by this means. A man possesses from birth what a woman has to be taught, Konrad maintained, often by the most grueling, even desperate pedagogical methods, by the use of reason as a surgical instrument to save an otherwise helplessly dissolving, hopelessly crumbling corpus of history and nature. It was decidedly possible to take a hollow head, Konrad is supposed to have told Wieser, or a head crammed with intellectual garbage, and transform it into a thinking or at least a rational head, if one had the courage to try. There would be no dolts in the world if intelligent people refused to tolerate doltishness. On the other hand, Konrad is supposed to have said immediately afterwards, in the end it was really quite senseless and useless to try, though one might think of something, still it would be useless, one might do something, but it would be done in vain, whether it was done or left undone, it was no use, whatever one thought or did was no use, so a rational man tended to leave things alone to develop however they would. The intelligence itself, the man himself, was oppositional by nature, Konrad said. One came to be a man by consciously taking the opposition, by daring to act in conscious opposition. A woman did not follow suit, because this was not her way, she tended to confront the man's, or more precisely, her husband's solitariness without comprehension or respect, mostly, even though to have respect required no special knowledge or cultivation of the mind, bogged down as she was in her stultified world of a vulgar subculture. Konrad's wife, as he himself said to Wieser, at least deeply respected him, though with certain reservations, in every phase of their shared life, despite the inborn resistance she shared with all others of her sex against the so-called masculine element, i.e., specifically against her own husband. Wieser and Fro both describe the last afternoon they saw Konrad, each in his own way, their statements confirming each other, though from time to time Wieser will be contradicting Fro, Fro contradicting Wieser, yet they nevertheless end by confirming one another. Fro claims to have been with Konrad, about a week and a half before the sad end of Mrs. Konrad, in the so-called wood-paneled room, oddly enough there was a fire laid on in the so-called wood-paneled room that afternoon, Konrad was expecting a visit from the so-called forestry commissioner, for a consultation about the damming of the mountain streams behind the rock spur, the forestry commissioner was due at eleven A.M., but had not yet put in an appearance at the lime works at twelve nor even at one P.M., until finally a woodcutter from the sawmill had shown up with a message that the commissioner was unable to make it, and proposed another appointment for next week, to which Konrad agreed. He poured the woodcutter out a glass of brandy and sent him back with regards to the forestry commissioner. It was shortly after this that Fro arrived at the lime works where Konrad led him straight into the wood-paneled room which was warm because he had been heating it for two days straight in anticipation of the forestry commissioner's visit. But now the forestry commissioner is not coming, but you are here, what a rare opportunity for a chat, Konrad is supposed to have said to Fro, when this room is heated one notices for the first time what a good room it is for conversation, even though it is furnished with nothing better than these dreadful, tasteless few pieces, though they are comfortable, you will have to admit; Konrad and Fro then sat down together, Fro said, in the wood-paneled room, Konrad saying that for two days now he had made no effort to think about his book, which he had not yet begun to write, because of his expectation that the forestry commissioner would be arriving to talk about damming up the mountain streams behind the rock spur, so I was concentrating on that, Konrad said, I was concentrated on that one hundred percent and totally neglected my book, he said, knowing that he simply could not afford to neglect his book at all, but it was unavoidable, the forestry commissioner had insisted on seeing him, to refuse was impossible, a man like the forestry commissioner was after all a state official with so-called high authority and could simply enforce his will, he could command admission to the lime works, demand a consultation, etc. When their expectation of the forestry commissioner had been at its height, Konrad's wife had also been wholly concentrated on the impending visit and had instructed Konrad on the reception to be accorded the forestry commissioner, viz., to have ready sliced ham, brandy, cider, etc., and she had put on a new dress, had gotten Konrad to comb her hair quite early in the day instead of as usual starting the day with their experiments using the Urbanchich method, she asked for a manicure, ordered a new tablecloth; in short, everything on them and in them had been intent upon the promised visit, but at the height of their expectation a woodcutter had arrived, bringing the forestry commissioner's regrets, Konrad told Fro. Now that Fro was here, sitting in the wood-paneled room, the heating of the room and the other preparations of the forestry commissioner's visit had not been wholly in vain, since Fro could now profit by the forestry commissioner's failure to show up, and enjoy these excellent slices of ham and the rowanberry wine which Konrad kept in reserve for only special guests such as the forestry commissioner or the district supervisor or the chief of police, and, most of all, enjoy his visit with Konrad who, in expectation of his distinguished visitor, had banished all thought of his pressing work from his mind, and even Mrs. Konrad was in an unusually sociable frame of mind, almost cheerful, Fro says, because the forestry commissioner's cancellation had apparently taken the two of them so much by surprise that there simply was no time for their disappointment to surface, indeed it had seemed to Fro that their inability to shift quickly enough from expectancy to disappointment had caused them simply to transfer their attentions to Fro, who had as unexpectedly appeared at the right moment, so that they simply received and treated Fro as though he were the forestry commissioner, as it were, Fro said, it was the first time in all these years that I was ever received by them so graciously, their cordiality untroubled by any shadow, in fact I was received and treated as the forestry commissioner was always received and treated in the Konrads' home, said Fro. For years Fro was accustomed to being regarded as a so-called familiar visitor to the lime works, everything pointed to this being the case, and everyone knows how so-called familiar visitors are treated everywhere, but on that day, the last day he visited the lime works, the Konrads outdid themselves in graciousness, cordiality, even noblesse, as compared with previous visits. Fro recalled that Konrad had offered him the more comfortable of the two chairs in the wood-paneled room and not, as usual, the less comfortable one, that Konrad slipped the deerskin rug under his guest's feet, a courtesy that quite stunned Fro, and that a glass of rowanberry brandy was offered him the moment he had set foot in the room, but before the two of them sat down in the wood-paneled room together, Konrad most politely escorted Fro upstairs to visit Mrs. Konrad on the second floor, making polite conversation all the way up the stairs, such as: My dear Fro, what a long time since you've been here, and how are your children? My dear Fro, have you rented your fishpond yet, and you know, my dear Fro, I don't even know whether your daughter is married or not? and: My dear Fro, your visits to us here at the lime works are growing so rare, and: My dear Fro, if ever you should want to borrow a book from my library, consider it at your disposal, I do have an excellent library as you know, it contains the most beautiful editions of the best, the most famous, and most important books, first editions only, of course, and: My dear Fro, my wife is looking forward most particularly to seeing you, I can't tell you how glad I am that you have come to see us, my wife still remembers with such gratitude your excellent advice regarding the bushes we imported from Switzerland, my wife's home country, as you know, my dear fellow. Exactly as if I were the forestry commissioner, Fro reminisces, that's how Mrs. Konrad received me, in a new dress and really putting herself out to be charming. She chatted with him for half an hour about Novalis and questioned him about Kropotkin, she actually wanted him to express adverse criticisms on Kropotkin, but Fro doesn't know Kropotkin at all, though he was careful not to admit it to Mrs. Konrad, so he wisely confined himself to responding only with *certainly, oh yes,* or: *no, oh no no,* in reply to every remark of hers on the subject of Kropotkin's memoirs, in unwavering agreement with whatever she was saying, Fro feels that the presence of Mrs. Konrad during his visits to the lime works always activated, made operational, the good manners he had been taught, his proper upbringing which meant knowing always when to insert a *yes, indeed* or a *oh no, certainly not* in all the right places, a knack that would see anyone through hours of polite conversation. The Konrad woman had seemed remarkably relaxed that afternoon, when she somehow kept in check the chronic restlessness of every part of her body, so apparent at all other times, concealing it on this occasion by an unparalleled mental and emotional effort (Fro, verbatim). She ended by saying, Do come again, my dear Fro, we are always so glad to see you, after which Fro went back to the wood-paneled room on the ground floor with Konrad. Going down the stairs, Konrad continued pouring out civilities in the style originally meant for the forestry commissioner. My dear Fro, Konrad is supposed to have said on the stairs from the second to the first floor, to see a man like yourself at the lime works is always a pleasure, and, he added, on the way from the first to the ground floor, when a man like you arrives, somehow it clarifies things, all the pieces fall into place. Once seated inside the wood-paneled room they chatted about everything, on and on for three hours, sipping schnapps, nibbling ham. You see, Konrad said (as reported by Fro), her family blames me for our gradual deterioration, as they have the insolence to put it, and as they have the unquestionable right to put it, too, they say that my wife's life and mine together are turning into a catastrophe. On the other hand, my family, excepting myself that is, Konrad said to Fro, all the other members of my family, which has sunk from the heights of a so-called classic traditional family of means to the level of a negligible family, a family of no significance, they all blame her. My side blames everything on her sickness, on her being a cripple, while her side blames me for it all, they blame it on the way my head works, on my book. In the end both sides may come to agree, Konrad said to Fro, that all of our misery can be laid to the book, so that ultimately it's the sense of hearing that bears the whole responsibility. People are always looking for a simple basic cause behind a lot of chaotic circumstances, or strange circumstances, or in any case extraordinary circumstances, it's natural to look for a basic cause, and it's equally natural to grasp at the most obvious, the most superficial factor involved, the one that is easily recognizable as the most superficial factor even to an inferior intelligence, and so in our case, my dear Fro, they have seized on my book as the basic cause of what everybody agrees to consider the catastrophe leading to the inevitable complete disintegration of my wife. One's fellow men, including of course one's neighbors, one's nearest and dearest, etc., tend to overestimate precisely that which is least estimable, or deserves to be regarded with the most disdain such as, for instance, the members of one's own family, etc., even those held in the lowest esteem are still rated too highly, one tends to overestimate persons to whom one has happened to give authority over oneself, though in fact one is most likely to have delivered oneself into the hands of the lowest human element there is. In fact, every time you take your fate into your own hands you have handed yourself over to the lowest kind of human being, but this is a kind of truth no one can face up to day after day, as he should, because if he did, he would simply have to give up, give in, fall into total despair, shamefully fall to pieces, dissolve into nothing. There are plenty of people who think they can save themselves by filling up their heads with fantasies, Konrad said to Fro, but no one can be saved, which means that no head can be saved, because where there is a head, it is already irredeemably lost, there are in fact none but lost heads on none but lost bodies populating none but lost continents, Konrad is supposed to have told Fro. But to tell this kind of truth to my wife is exactly like talking to a rock that has taken millions of years to go deaf. I grant you that to be unable to put your finger on the real cause of all our troubles is a torment even to a man with a complete idiot of a wife around his neck, a lifelong torment if you like, but the real cause can never be found, whatever cause you think you can spot will turn out to be a fake, all of our contemporary so-called scientific research into what causes what, all of it misapplied because it is misunderstood, inevitably comes up with nothing but fake causes, because it is in fact possible to understand the whole world, or what we believe to be the whole world, or what we think we recognize as the world on a day-to-day basis, as the result of nothing but fake causes arrived at by fake research. You could waste decades of your life trying to get the better of this self-perpetuating duplicity, but all you would get out of that was to grow old, that was all, to go under, that was all. Suppose you make a statement, Konrad is supposed to have said to Fro, only one sentence, say, no matter what it is, and suppose this sentence is a quotation from one of our major writers, or even one of our greatest writers, all you would succeed in doing is to besmirch, to pollute that sentence, simply by failing to exercise the self-control it would take not to pronounce that sentence at all, to say nothing at all, you would be polluting it, and once you start polluting things, the chances are you will see everywhere you look, everywhere you go, nothing but other polluters, a whole world of polluters going into the millions, or, more precisely, into the billions, is at work everywhere, it is enough to shock a man out of his mind, if he will let himself be shocked, but people no longer let themselves be shocked, this is in fact precisely what characterizes the man of today, that he refuses to be shocked by anything at all. Distress has become transformed into hypocrisy, distress is hypocrisy, the great movers and shakers of mankind, for instance, were merely even greater hypocrites than most people. Since we have nothing but polluters in the world, the world is polluted through and through. The vulgar will always remain the vulgar, and so forth. Konrad went on to say that people no longer took risks, they were cowards, every one of them, and so forth. Facing consequences was a thing of the past, nobody and nothing was consistent any more, which made everyone extremely vulnerable, and so forth. An animal was mistrustful in advance, which is how you distinguished an animal from a man, and so forth. Konrad himself, he said to Fro, had with his wife withdrawn altogether from society, which had become long since only a so-called society, one fine day they had simply withdrawn themselves from society by an act of philosophical-metaphysical violence, and so forth. A constant lack of human company, however, was as deadening as a constant immersion in company, and so forth. But what if you sat down to dinner, suddenly, with the family of a bricklayer, for instance, as if it were the most natural thing in the world, like me sitting down to dinner with Hoeller, say, Konrad is supposed to have said, forcing him (and myself) to think, merely to think, that it was natural, that it was where I belonged; and what if I perpetrated this swindle in full awareness of what I was doing, and so forth? His wife was, in fact, still keeping in touch, decades after her sickness had forced her to withdraw from society, with that same society, despite the fact that she has been parted from society for decades by the lime works, by Konrad himself, by his concentration on his book, and on her own part by her crippled condition, her invalid chair, all because the doctors are incompetent, she nevertheless keeps in touch with people, most devotedly and intimately in touch, to a degree that more than approaches perversity but actually uses perversity as a ruthless means to the end of keeping in touch, of clinging to society body and soul, Konrad said to Fro, at the same time that I keep telling myself, in every way I can, that society is nothing, that my work is everything, my wife insists that my work is nothing and society is every-

thing. While he based his very existence on the fact that society was nothing, while his work was everything, she quite
instinctively drew her being from the fact that his work was
nothing, society was everything, and so forth. Given his being
of sound mind and in possession of the necessary means,
Konrad is supposed to have told Fro, he would first of all and
instantly open all the prison gates and so forth. Furthermore:
religion was a clumsy attempt to subject humanity, a mass of
pure chaos, to one's will, and: when the Church spoke, it
spoke as a salesman; listening to a cardinal we seem to be
listening to a traveling salesman's pitch, and so forth. On the
other hand we all had a tendency to think we had already
heard everything, seen everything, done everything already,
come to terms with everything already, but in fact it was a
process that repeated itself on and on into the future, which
future was a lie, and so forth. The greatest crime of all was
to invent something, Konrad is supposed to have said to Fro.
To resume: the future belonged to no one and to nothing.
People kept coming around to weep on your shoulder, about
their children, about their scruples, about this that and the
other thing they were suffering though they had done nothing
to deserve it and so forth. Maybe so, but the trouble was that
for having children, for having scruples, for suffering, they
expected to be compensated, and so forth. Society might pay
compensation, but nature did not pay compensation. Society
was setting itself up as a sort of surrogate nature, and so forth.
Then: he read in the paper that Hager, the butcher, had died.
Only a week ago Hager had personally brought the Konrads
fresh sausages all the way to the lime works, in an old carry-
all of a kind it was a pity they were no longer making; it was
so immensely practical. When Konrad finished reading the

item about the butcher's death he went up to his wife's room, knocked on her door, waited for her *Yes?* then he walked in and told her: Hager, the butcher, is dead. Then she said: Well, so Hager, the butcher, died after all! a statement on her part that Konrad is supposed to have told Fro was deeper than met the eye, it was well worth a scientific study in depth. Two days later Konrad went up again to tell her that he had just read in the paper about the tobacconist, who had doused himself in gasoline, struck a match, and so incinerated himself, whereupon Mrs. Konrad is supposed to have said: Aha, so the tobacconist doused himself in gasoline, did he? and again Konrad felt that her comment was highly interesting, it was not the death of the tobacconist that was of scientific interest but Mrs. Konrad's statement in response to the information that the tobacconist had doused himself in gasoline, struck a match, and so incinerated himself. Prior to doing it he had willed everything he owned, cash, merchandise, including not only the tobacconist's specialties but stationery, piles of pencil boxes, carnival masks, etc., to his, the tobacconist's, wife. Mrs. Konrad commented that naturally the tobacconist willed everything to his wife; again, material for investigation, you see, Konrad said to Fro in the wood-paneled room, Fro says. It took the fire brigade an hour to put out the fire, Konrad is supposed to have said to his wife, by which time there was nothing left of the tobacconist but ashes, and those firemen really made a shambles of the whole shop, whereupon Mrs. Konrad is supposed to have said: Those firemen make a shambles of the tobacco shop and ruin more than they save. About this remark of his wife's Konrad said he would like to write a book. Don't you see, Fro, he said, women are always saying this kind of thing, and if I were not so concentrated on my study of the auditory sense, I would not scruple to write a book about "Noteworthy Statements By My Wife In Response To Domestic Trivia Of Conversation." The Konrads had loved the good-natured butcher and they had hated the malicious tobacconist, as Konrad allegedly reminded his wife, whereupon Mrs. Konrad said: *Nihilist!* and Konrad instantly realized that the word *Nihilist!* could have been aimed only at the tobacconist. The tobacconist had done his wife in by slowly strangling her, until he finally strangled her to death, Konrad is supposed to have told his wife, who said: Mutual dependence drives people apart, one way or the other. For the longest time Konrad and his wife had exchanged only the most laconic remarks, Fro says, they barely spoke except to say the absolutely necessary, in the fewest possible words, as Konrad is supposed to have told Fro once, for ages there had been no so-called exchange of ideas between them at all, only words, and now, after all that has happened, Fro says, the chances are that in communicating only by way of the limited range of daily commonplaces and formulas of daily necessity they were communicating nothing except their mutual hatred. Fro says that certainly in the final weeks, but possibly in the final months of their life together, verbal exchanges between Konrad and his wife had dwindled down to an absurd minimum; for instance, according to Konrad, his wife had for a long time spoken to him about a pair of mittens she was making for Konrad, she had been working on this one pair of mittens for six months, because she unraveled each mitten just before she had finished knitting it, or she might finish it completely and then suddenly insist that it was the wrong color, that she must have wool of another color for his mittens, and when she had gotten him to agree would unravel

the finished mitten and start knitting a brand new one, in a
new color or shade and so forth, every few days or weeks, depending upon how much of her time or his time or the time
of both was taken up with the Urbanchich exercises, there
she'd be, knitting a new mitten in a new color, each choice of
color in worse taste than the preceding choice, her preference
running to every possible shade of ugly green, until Konrad
came to loathe those mittens, in fact he came to loathe her
knitting as such, her constant preoccupation with her knitting,
but he never let on how much he hated it, according to Fro:
hypocrite that I had to become because of her endless knitting
and her incessant preoccupation with her knitting, he is supposed to have told Fro, I pretended that I was pleased with
her knitting and that I was pleased with the mittens, consequently, no matter what color the wool was, I like these
mittens, Konrad is supposed to have said over and over to his
wife, nevertheless his wife would suddenly say, every time
she had finished one of those mittens, she would declare suddenly that she must unravel it, it was the wrong color, she
must have new wool in the right shade, after all she had the
time, and while she was saying all this she had already begun
to unravel the finished mitten, the mere thought of her these
days brought on a vision of her unraveling a mitten, Konrad
is supposed to have told Fro, that unpleasant smell of unraveled wool was permanently in his nose by now, even in his
sleep, Konrad told Fro, in the kind of nervous waking-sleep
characteristic of his last weeks in the lime works, he would
hallucinate his wife unraveling mittens, imagine what it's
like, he said to Fro, considering that there is nothing in the
world I hate more than I hate mittens. All his life long he had
hated mittens, beginning with his earliest childhood when they

had hung his mittens on a yard-long cord around his neck,
oh how he hated them, it's always mittens mittens mittens
with her, Konrad is supposed to have said to Fro, no matter
that I am concentrating on the Urbanchich method, concentrating on my book, on making a little headway with the
method and the writing, she has nothing in her head but
mittens, mittens she is knitting for me, even though I loathe
mittens, imagine, my dear Fro, Konrad said, except for my
earliest childhood I have never worn mittens in my life, I have
tried telling her, I often said, but I never wear mittens, why
do you have this mania about knitting mittens for me, I shall
never wear them and yet here you are knitting away at them,
he is supposed to have told her, just as she had formerly spent
decades sewing nightgowns for the poor and for orphans,
Konrad is supposed to have said to Fro, these last few years
she had taken to knitting mittens, not, that is, hundreds of pairs
of mittens but only the one pair of mittens, always the same pair,
for her own husband, she knits them and unravels them and re-
knits them and unravels them, she knits dark green mittens and
bright green mittens, a pair of white mittens, a pair of black mittens, knits them and then unravels them again, Konrad said
to Fro. She made him try on the same mitten hundreds of
times, that terrible business of having to slip into the mitten,
every time, he is supposed to have said, with her knitting
needles dangling from her half-finished mitten, as he tried
it on. This was not the only tic she had, Konrad is supposed
to have told Fro, there were also the Toblach sugar tongs
she always kept asking for, an heirloom she had from her
maternal grandmother, not a minute would go by but she
would ask for them, give me the Toblach sugar tongs, she
would say, without any visible reason, Konrad always got

the tongs for her out of the table drawer, she asked for them several times a day but not, as one might suppose, only at such times when it seemed reasonable to ask for them, as for breakfast, perhaps, or when needed during meals, but at any time, suddenly when he was reading to her, for instance, especially when he was reading a favorite passage of Kropotkin to her, Konrad told Fro, that was the kind of time she chose to ask for the Toblach sugar tongs, when he handed them to her she placed them in front of her on the table, then after a while, when she hadn't even touched her so-called Toblach sugar tongs, she is supposed to have told Konrad that he could put them back in the drawer. Konrad could have recounted a whole series of such peculiarities, he said, but he didn't care to, such a recapitulation of his wife's most extraordinary peculiarities would in all probability, and quite superfluously, he felt, lead to the most terrible misunderstandings; apart from which, Konrad is supposed to have said to Fro, he, Konrad, was himself afflicted with such peculiarities, little oddities of his own, I am quite conscious of these peculiarities of mine, Konrad is supposed to have said, I can assure you of that, my dear Fro, I might even say that I am *hyperconscious,* Konrad is supposed to have said. But after all, even you (Fro that is), Konrad is supposed to have said, freshening Fro's schnapps, are not free of such peculiarities, oddities, even absurdities, we observe such things in every person we have anything at all to do with, in fact, but they trouble us only when the person involved is one with whom we live in close intimacy, so that we are forced to notice their tics repeatedly, so that these peculiarities become most unpleasant, terrible, nerve-wracking, even though the same peculiarity we find so unpleasant, so terrible, so cata-

strophically nerve-wracking and nerve-destroying in a person
we live with we might find quite attractive, not at all terrible, not in the least irritating and so forth, in another person,
someone outside our lives, a person we encounter not constantly but rarely. Actually, Konrad is supposed to have said
to Fro, if it isn't the mittens or the Toblach sugar tongs,
then it is her pronunciation of the word *unbridled* or *comical,* a whole series of words my wife enunciates in the oddest
way, she exploits the words as a way of exploiting the people
around her. As for myself, Konrad is supposed to have said,
I may feel suddenly compelled to walk over to the so-called
chest we picked up in Southern India, open it, take out the
Gorosabel rifle, slip off its safety catch and aim through the
window at the extreme outcroppings of the rock spur; after
holding my aim for two or three seconds I stop, put the rifle
back into the chest we picked up in the South of India (a
place near Moon Lake!) and lock up the chest, then I take
a deep breath and my wife says behind my back: Did you
take aim again at the extreme outcroppings of the rock spur?
and I tell her, yes, I did take aim at the outermost point of
the rock spur. Come, she says, sit down here with me, I think
I have earned a chapter of my Novalis, and I actually do
sit down and read her a chapter of her Novalis. When that
is done, I say: and now, of course, a chapter of the Kropotkin. Right, she says. This has been our routine for years
now, and not a movement, not a word more, not a movement, not a word less, Konrad is supposed to have told Fro.
One could say, of course, that this sort of thing puts us right
next door to madness. His wife, too, was always reaching for
her gun, the Mannlicher carbine fastened to the back of her
chair, she had done it a hundred thousand times, Konrad

told Fro, for no reason at all, pure habit, absolutely unneces-
sary, not even a safety exercise, or automatic reflex of any
kind, that made her reach for her Mannlicher carbine, a
weapon, incidentally, designed to be effective at short range
only, at no more than fifteen or twenty yards, Konrad told
Fro, as Fro remembered instantly when the so-called bloody
deed became public knowledge. Mrs. Konrad is also alleged
to have nagged her husband incessantly about his criminal
record, while he countered with criticisms of her family, her family history being singularly rich, as Konrad told
Fro, in every kind of morbidity and rottenness. Konrad's
previous convictions, says Fro, are so overshadowed by the
enormities of his latest crime, unless you'd call it his unquestionably monstrous act of madness, that they no longer count.
Basically, Mrs. Konrad is supposed to have said repeatedly
to her husband, she was married not so much to a madman
as to a criminal, Konrad told Fro in the wood-paneled room.
Later Konrad is supposed to have said: My wife and I both
know that we are done for, but we keep pretending, day
after day, that we are not done for yet. They had in fact
come to take a certain satisfaction in feeling that they were
done for, there being nothing else left to take satisfaction in.
We tell each other from time to time that we have reached
the end, Konrad is supposed to have told Fro, actually we
do so several times a day, but even more often during our
increasingly, even totally sleepless nights, relaxed in the knowledge that we say what we think, regardless of concern for
a future we simply no longer have, we have at last stopped
pretending, we can relax now, knowing the worst as we do,
horrible as it unquestionably has been, my dear Fro, though
others might see it differently, therefore act differently, there-

fore be treated differently, because they have always been
treated differently, dear Fro, but for us the horror it has been
will soon have ended, and we find it relaxing, to think that
we shall soon have put it all behind us. Their coexistence
(to Wieser: life together) had been all wrong from the beginning and yet, speaking man to man, which couple's life
is not all wrong, which marriage is not totally perverse, is
not revealed, once it has come into being, as insincere and
hateful, when even friendship is always based on a fallacy;
where will you find two people living together who can
honestly consider themselves happy or even intact? No, my
dear Fro, the so-called shared life, regardless of who is involved, regardless of the persons, of their social position, ori-
gins, profession, turn and twist it as you like, remains as
long as it lasts a forcible imposition, always painful by nature and yet, as we know, the most understandable, the most
gruesome test-case of nature's ways. But even the worst of
torments can become a habit, Konrad said, and so those who
live together, vegetate together, gradually become accustomed
to living together, vegetating together, to their shared torment which they have brought upon themselves as nature's
way of subjecting her creatures to nature's torments, and in
the end they become accustomed to being accustomed to it.
The so-called ideal life together is a lie, because there is no
such thing, nor does anyone have a right to any such thing,
whether one enters upon a marriage or upon a friendship,
one is simply taking upon oneself, quite consciously, a condition of double despair, double exile, it is to move from the
purgatory of loneliness into the hell of togetherness. Not
even to mention their particular kind of togetherness. Because the double despair and double exile of two intelligent

persons, two people capable of reasoning their way to a clear awareness of everything involved, is, if not always, at least temporarily, from time to time, a redoubled double despair and a redoubled double exile. She could not rise from her chair, so he had to help her up, she could not walk by herself, so he had to help her to walk, she could not do her own reading so he had to read to her, she could not relieve herself unaided, so he had to assist her with that, he had to help her to eat, and so forth. But if he, for his part, tried to tell her how overwhelmingly great the Kropotkin was, for instance, she did not understand, or how much his own book meant to him, she did not understand, or what he was thinking about, she did not understand. When he said: natural science is all there is, nothing else matters, she did not understand. When he said: politics is what counts, politics is the thing, she did not understand. If he said Pascal or Montaigne or Descartes or Dostoyevsky or Gregor Mendel or Wittgenstein or Francis Bacon, no matter who, she did not understand. When he spoke of his scientific research she would say, with her usual abruptness: You could certainly have become a distinguished scientist; or, when he talked about politics, she would say, you could certainly have become a leading political figure; when he tried to explain the importance of Francis Bacon, she would say: You could certainly have become a great artist. What she did not say, though he could read it in her face, was that he had become, instead of all that, nothing at all, a mere madman. But then, what is a madman? She simply did not believe what he tried to prove to her day after day, though he knew it could not be proved, namely, that he had perfected in his head a scientific work of fundamental importance. Of late he had become so desperate about this deadlock that he boldly called it an absolutely epoch-making scientific work. But she only laughed and said: Whatever it is that you have in your head, I'd rather not see it; if your head could be tipped over to empty out its contents, what is likely to fall out is some ghastly mess or other, some indefinable, horrifying, utterly worthless kind of dung or rot. Your so-called book—this is how the Konrad woman dared to refer to her husband's work-in-progress toward the end, knowing how weak he had grown—is really nothing more than a delusion. He had come to fear the very word *delusion* as a weapon she brandished several times a day, Konrad told Fro; she has the effrontery to say it right out, always waiting for the right moment to throw the word *delusion* at my head, the deadly moment whenever she thinks I have reached the point of utter defenselessness. To think that for twenty years I have believed in that delusion of yours! she is supposed to have said more than once on the very eve of the bloody deed, as they refer to it at Laska's. It could have been the word *delusion* alone, Fro thinks, that brought Konrad to the point of pulling that trigger. But at Lanner's there are some who maintain, quite to the contrary, that on the eve of the murder Konrad treated his wife more tenderly than he had in ages. At The Inglenook they say that Konrad had been planning the murder for a long time, while at the Stiegler they call it a sudden, unpremeditated, so-called impulse killing, but what if it is a case of common, premeditated murder, an opinion also represented at the Lanner, or, as they say at The Inglenook, the act of a madman, while at Laska's there's some speculation that Konrad had no intention at all of shooting his wife, that he had merely tried to clean the gun, which had not been cleaned for a long time, nor had it been fired for a long time, most probably, after months of disuse a gun is likely to get dusty, especially when kept in the open in a dusty room where all the wood is infested with hundreds of deathwatch beetles, and the carbine went off while he was cleaning the barrel; still, the fact that the bullet happened to enter the back of her head, or the nape of the neck, whichever, had to be more than a coincidence, they say at Laska's, especially since at least two, maybe more, shots had been fired from the Mannlicher carbine, which was something to think about. At Lanner's they even talk of five shots, while at the Stiegler they talk about four shots in all, two in the back of the head and two into the temples; Konrad himself has not uttered a word about it to this day to shed any further light on it, the word is that he is squatting in his cell at the Wels district jail, a completely broken man, and answers none of the hundreds of thousands of questions being put to him. Fro says that he ordered some shoes to be sent to Konrad in prison, at the same time that he actually wrote Konrad a letter expressing his hope that Konrad would let Fro have Konrad's notes for the book, he offered to put back in order the stacks of notes that had been left scattered all over Konrad's room after the police had searched the scene of the murder for days on end, leaving the place a shambles. Fro explained in his letter that he was the best man for the job of putting the notes in order because he was the only man—apart from Wieser, who was too over-burdened with his work at the Trattner estate to concern himself with Konrad's notes—the only man Konrad had taken into his confidence respecting the notes, more so than he had Wieser, toward whom Konrad felt a certain reserve,

while Fro and Konrad had always been on the closest of
terms (Fro!) and so Fro explained that he was sending shoes
to Konrad with this request to authorize Fro to pick up
Konrad's notes for his book in the lime works, since the
authorities had permitted access to Konrad's room as long as
eight days ago, even though the room of the murdered
woman was still officially sealed, along with the whole second floor, unlike the first floor where Konrad's room was
situated, of course, and where Konrad's notes for his book
should be. Fro said that he believed these note slips, crazy or
not, were of great interest, if not for the science of otology,
as Fro puts it, then certainly they were of interest from a
psychiatric point of view, says Fro (who speaks only of his
own interest in the book itself when writing to Konrad in
prison, emphasizing his respect for Konrad's scientific work
which he pretends to take very seriously indeed; but whenever he talks to me about it he always calls it the so-called
book, a way of stabbing Konrad in the back, it seems to
me), and this batch of notes for the so-called book, says Fro,
is of the greatest interest to a lot of people, not for what it
purports to be, but in another way, says Fro, and eventually
they could turn out to be of quite serious consequence and
of the greatest significance, depending entirely on which
heads, which people, when and where. As soon as he could
get his hands on these note slips he would put them in order
and then pass them on to a psychologist friend of his in
Gugging (Fro, verbatim), a native of Linz, though he, Fro,
would keep it a secret from Konrad, of course, he knew he
could trust me not to say anything about it to anyone; if the
psychiatrist who was a friend of Fro's found Konrad's notes
to be of genuine interest, then Fro could have them photo-

copied and put the originals back in Konrad's room. For the moment he was still waiting, Fro said, for Konrad's answer, he was prepared to wait because to get a letter from the district prison would certainly take at least ten times as long as from anywhere else, Fro says. Fro claims he is confident that Konrad will agree to allow him to pick up the notes for Konrad's so-called book, because Konrad believes that Fro takes him quite seriously and is bound to feel that his notes could not be in better hands than Fro's, and so forth. Incidentally Fro, to whom I explained his new life policy today in the last detail, though I do not have the impression that he will close the deal, he is much too cautious a man—Fro incidentally confirms Wieser's story that Konrad dreamed about the murder a long time before he actually did it, it was about a year ago that Konrad told the following dream: Konrad dreamed that he had gotten up in the middle of the night, because of an idea that came to him for his book, and that he sat down at his desk and actually began to write it down, and by the time he had written about half of the book down he felt that he would succeed in getting down all of it, this time, that he would get it all down on paper in one sitting, so he kept at it and wrote on and on until it actually was all down on paper, all complete, finished; instantly his head dropped down on his desk in total exhaustion, as if he had fainted, but as his head lay there in near-coma on his completed manuscript on the desk, he was nevertheless observing himself in his unconscious state and observing everything else in the room, to sum up the situation: Konrad has actually been able to get his work down on paper, as he had so often imagined it, for decades on end, he had written it all in one sitting, suddenly, from one moment to the next,

as he had always dreamed he would, but now that he has
set down the final word on paper he has fainted dead away,
fallen where he is, but observing himself in this unconscious
state from every angle of his work room; it is the ideal
moment, the ideal situation of his life, as for hours on end
Konrad sees himself lying there unconscious in the full possession of his completed manuscript, having just finished the
complete text and ended by writing on the title page, in his
old-fashioned large calligraphic hand, *The Sense of Hearing,*
his last act before his head dropped like a stone onto the
title page he had just written, afterward seeing himself in
this state from every possible angle, seeing the whole scene
which he later described as the happiest of his life, though
in fact it is unquestionably the unhappiest, basically, of his
life, and then suddenly, abruptly, Konrad is supposed to have
told Fro, the door opened and Konrad's wife walked in, this
crippled woman chained to her invalid chair all those decades
and who in reality could not have managed to take one single
step unaided, in fact she could not even have pulled herself
upright in her chair unaided, suddenly is standing there in
Konrad's room and comes over to the unconscious Konrad,
her husband, who is watching closely the whole time, and
bangs her fist down on the manuscript under his head, and says:
So, behind my back you have written down your book, have
you, behind my back, a fine thing, she says over and over
again, behind my back, she says, while Konrad watches and
hears everything all the time he is lying there in his coma
with his head on the completed manuscript, even the shock
of his wife's fist banging down on the manuscript right next
to his ear hasn't torn him out of his coma, and here comes
her fist banging down on the manuscript a second time, can

you imagine, a woman whose energy has been totally drained away long since, after decades of huddling as a paralyzed cripple in her invalid chair, brutally bangs her fist on his manuscript, saying: That's what you think, that you can sit down here in secret, you sneak, and get your book down on paper, just like that, all in one sitting, think again! and with that she grabs up the whole pack of manuscript and flings it in one powerful motion into the flaming stove. Konrad wants to leap to his feet and stop her, but he can't budge, he can't. So, she says, the Konrad woman says, now your book is up the chimney, your whole work gone up in flames, and: now you can start all over, wracking your brains about getting it written, for the next twenty or thirty years, it's all gone, your book is gone, every scrap of it! At which point he suddenly wakes up, finds he can move, and realizes: a dream. I was incapable of leaving my room, Konrad is supposed to have told Fro, beginning with feeling incapable of getting out of bed, incapable of doing anything at all. For two days after that dream I did not leave my room at all, of course my wife rang for me, she rang incessantly, because of course she needed my help as always, but I could not and did not give her a sign, for two whole days I stayed in my room. I went on brooding about this dream for months afterward, as you can imagine, but I never told my wife about it, I never even hinted at it, though there were times when I came close to telling her what I had dreamt, but again and again I refrained from doing so, you mustn't tell her this dream, I kept saying to myself, every time I was tempted as I often was to tell it to her, in fact, tempted to tell it to her in all its utter ghastliness, as I often planned to do. I still see it all, vividly, how my wife enters the room and bangs her fist down on my manuscript, the first time and then again, a second time, bang, on the manuscript, and I unable to move a finger, unable to prevent her from tossing it into the fire, flinging the whole, complete finished manuscript into the fire! Even in my dream I felt it was spooky, Konrad is supposed to have said to Fro, what with me lying there in a dead faint, her sudden outburst of monstrous energies while I lay paralyzed, her lightning-like movements while I was totally motionless, powerless, my absolute physical passivity, though I noticed everything with surrealistic keenness as against her decisiveness in action, her horrible decisiveness, if you can imagine it, Fro, her utter ruthlessness in action! There are times when I am sorely tempted to tell her my dream, Konrad said to Fro, the whole dream, every last particle of it, and without sparing her my comments on every detail, either, but of course I don't do it, I'm too sure it would kill her. To tell a person who figured like this in such a nightmare, to tell her in every remorseless detail, is to destroy that person, Fro, Konrad said. Wieser's account of this dream is in complete accord with Fro's account of it, but while Fro tells it in a highly dramatic, emotional way, as befits his own character and the degree to which he is influenced by Konrad and by Konrad's narrative style, Wieser's manner in retelling the dream is perfectly cool. Consequently, Wieser's version is incomparably more effective than Fro's rendition of the same story. Fro adds: for the first time in three or even four decades, Konrad saw his wife in that dream as she once really was, tall, stately, beautiful, even though she behaved abominably. She was always sending Konrad to the cellar to bring her up some cider, Konrad is supposed to have told Fro, Fetch me some cider! she is supposed to have said practically every five minutes,

Go on, get the cider! and he went down every time she asked
for fresh cider, all the way down to the cellar. A jugful?
Konrad is supposed to have asked her again and again, so
that he would not have to go down cellar so often, but: No,
a glassful will do, she is supposed to have answered every
time, be sure to fetch only a glassful, I want fresh cider every
time, and so he would get her a glassful at a time, never a
jugful of cider, although he always offered to bring a jugful,
but she refused every time, and so he had to go down cellar
several times a day to fetch her a glassful of cider, Konrad
told Fro, although it obviously would have made sense to
bring up a large jugful of cider from the cellar so that she
could drink her fresh cider all day long without his having to
make his way to the cellar and up again every single time,
because if you kept your large jug of cider in the cold lime
works kitchen and kept it covered with a wooden board, you
could freshen your glass of cider all day long just as much as
if you had to go down specially for every mouthful of cider,
Konrad explained, she drove him nearly crazy all day long
with her orders to go down to the cellar and come up from the
cellar, he wouldn't be surprised if she took a special, malicious
pleasure in watching me every time going down to the cellar
or climbing up from the cellar, or even merely knowing that
now he is going down to the cellar, now he is climbing up
the cellar stairs, it takes a more grueling effort every time, you
know, my dear Fro, Konrad is supposed to have told Fro (he
said the same thing to Wieser, too) verbatim. That last time
they talked, in the wood-paneled room, Konrad drew Fro
into a lengthy and detailed consideration of the cider-pressing
and cider-storing processes: how the casks had to be cleaned beforehand, was one of the things Konrad explained to Fro,

scraped and cleaned and aired and stored while airing, which kind of pears made the right mix for a strong cider and which combination of fruit-varieties would make for a sweet cider, and that all-in-all it did not depend so much on the combinations of the varieties of pears, nor even on the method of pressing them and preparing the cider in general, what it really depended on was the kind of cellar, Konrad is supposed to have told Fro; the lime works boasted the best cellar in the country, which is why in fact they did have the best cider anywhere at the lime works. Ask whomever and wherever you would, the lime works cider was the best there was. His cousin Hoerhager, Konrad is supposed to have said, had still taken a hand personally in pressing the cider along with Hoeller and the other lime works men under Hoeller, but Konrad left the work to Hoeller and two or three of the sawmill workers recruited by him, the cider press had always been Hoeller's affair, Konrad is supposed to have said to Fro. Four barrels for the Konrads (which in fact they are supposed to have polished off together in the course of each year), two barrels for Hoeller, who had always managed to drink up his two barrels in a single year, visitors at the annex, including Hoeller's cousin who was known to be a hard drinker, didn't count one way or the other, considering that a barrel held over two hundred liters. But Konrad had brought up his story about the cider—which incidentally was losing ground in this country, known to be the foremost pear cider country in Europe, because the people nowadays preferred drinking inferior beer to the best cider, Konrad is supposed to have told Fro, it wasn't for nothing that the natives were called ciderheads—but the reason Konrad had brought it up was only to give Fro some idea of his wife's sadistic attitude toward

Konrad, her husband, whom she certainly did not keep sending down cellar because she could not live without drinking cider, and certainly not because she had to have fresh cider every five minutes, but simply because she meant to humiliate him, Konrad, as constantly as possible; as for the cider she made him bring up, most of it she never drank at all but poured it away, into the pail, out the window, Konrad told Fro, but she kept making him go down cellar for her cider every five minutes just the same, especially at such times when he had started to read aloud to her from his Kropotkin, or to talk about the book, or when he began to talk about Francis Bacon or Wittgenstein, whom he loved to cite, his quoting from Wittgenstein's *Traktatus* had in fact become a habit of his that was guaranteed to drive a woman up the wall, his wife had hated it from the first, so inevitably when he started on Wittgenstein she would send him down cellar for a glassful of cider; and Fro is supposed to have said to Konrad that this slavish obedience of his, Konrad's, to his wife's commands, an obedience Fro was forced to describe as doglike, nevertheless did not really exclude its opposite, as reflected in Konrad's general conduct, his character, the fact that he always prevailed in any difference he had with his wife, to which Konrad is supposed to have replied that of course he knew quite well why he permitted himself to be sent to the cellar every five minutes to fetch cider, etc., why he let himself be made a fool of by his wife, from time to time, Konrad said to Fro, because there is nothing more ridiculous than a man being sent again and again to the cellar for some cider and who actually goes, submissively, cider jug in hand, a man who would have to feel his way down the dark cellar stairs with an empty cider jug in one hand, then again, in the pitchdark of the lime works cellar, the brimful cider jug in his hands, blindly feeling his way up those stairs again and again, making a grotesque appearance besides, because in order to avoid catching cold in those icy cellars he was wrapped in a stinking old horse blanket or the like; all his wife was aiming at was to make him ridiculous, it was the one idea left in her head, to make a fool of him, to cut him down to size because he still considered himself a man of science, and in fact he did, he saw himself, to be quite candid, Konrad is supposed to have told Fro, as a scientific philosopher. Basically, Konrad is supposed to have said to Fro, my wife has been able to make a fool of me, make me her house buffoon, as it were, but only because for a long time now I have let her do it, without letting her realize the part I actually play; by deliberately making her think that I am a fool and that she prevails against me, I keep the upper hand, he said. A quite transparent strategy if you saw it, too intricate to be fully explainable if not. He knew exactly why he let his wife get away with sending him on those fool's errands to the cellar every minute, with letting him make himself ridiculous by throwing on whatever wrap was handy (horse blankets, etc.), letting her victimize him with her practical joke of nonchalantly knitting the same mitten for him year after year, and why he submitted without a murmur to trying on incessantly if not the identical mitten, then nevertheless the same mitten, again and again. Despite all that, he said to Fro, regardless of all of her sadistic tricks on him, all her endless nonsense, women were so inventive in resorting to ridiculous nonsense, absurdities, etc., he was all right, he was making headway with the Urbanchich method, the book was firmly established in his head, etc., and even though he had not been able to write any of it down to this day, it was far from a hopeless case, because, as he suddenly said to Fro, the actual writing down of an important intellectual undertaking can hardly ever be postponed too long! and, he quickly added: Admittedly, a postponement can also be ruinous to such an undertaking as this book of mine, yet in almost every case this kind of intellectual task stands to gain by a so-called conscious or unconscious postponement. Suddenly she would say: How much cider do we actually have in the cellar? and send him down to test the casks for their exact content by rapping his knuckles on them, or else she would ask: Do we have any garlic in the house? or: What time is it on your bedroom clock? so that he had to get up and go downstairs to his room to look at his wall clock there and then climb back upstairs to tell her the time on his wall clock, she could never trust either of their clocks, hers or his, only both of them together, Konrad is supposed to have told Fro, but, he added, there is no depending on both of those clocks either, ultimately (according to Mrs. Konrad). Is it dark outside? she would ask over and over, or: Is it snowing outside? always just when he had begun to read her the Kropotkin. Not that he always took orders with such alacrity, Konrad said to Fro, that would be unwise, so he very often pretended not to hear what she was asking. When she said: Is it snowing outside? meaning of course: get up immediately and look out the window and tell me whether it is snowing or not, he would start reading the Kropotkin with the utmost coolness as though he had heard nothing. She might often ask six or seven times whether it is snowing outside, Konrad said to Fro, but I react not at all, I merely read and go on reading until she gives up and stops asking. Most of the time he obeyed her so-called orders only when there might be an advantage in it for him, or when he really had nothing better to do, because actually an order from her when he was, for instance, reading Kropotkin to her or reporting on his progress with the book or the like, did not necessarily annoy him every time, unfortunately his own concentration on the Kropotkin or the book or some other intellectual concern was not always wholehearted, quite the contrary, occasionally it was a relief to be sent down cellar for cider, to go to the kitchen, to go to his room, whatever. Even during his morning or evening piano playing, literally *playing* because he was not, of course, performing seriously on the piano (Konrad said so himself), she is alleged to have taken the liberty of ringing for him, no sooner had he sat down at the piano when she rang, whereupon he got up, put down the cover over the keyboard, waited, then sat down again to play, at which point she rang again, they often went on like that by the hour. But it was some time now since he had ceased to play the piano at all, suddenly playing the piano no longer relaxed him, somehow, Fro reports Konrad saying pathetically: it no longer worked for him! In the early years at the lime works he had played the piano day after day, starting at four A.M. usually, improving amateurishly on the piano, Wieser calls it, and specifically trying his hand at the various classical piano pieces, strangely enough, though on the other hand it was not so strange, it was quite characteristic of a dilettante like him to insist on tackling the most difficult pieces again and again and so, as I was saying, he strangely enough tackled the most complicated sonatas and concertos, etc., but had hardly touched the piano at all in the last two years, as he is supposed to have said to Fro, the cover stays on the keyboard, at first I needed the piano to relax my nerves, but nowadays I need and have something far more effective to do the job (to Wieser) and his wife too, who had for decades loved her record player, one that Konrad had given her for Christmas long ago, an HMV from London, but for years she had not asked him to play anything for her on the record player, it too had outlived its usefulness for her, Konrad is supposed to have told Fro, the piano doesn't work for me any longer just as the record player doesn't work for her any longer, music has simply ceased to be effective for us. He used, for instance, to have to play her the *Haffner* symphony, conducted by Fritz Busch, for months on end, Konrad said to Fro, an excellent recording, but playing it day after day for so long he came to hate it more than any other, these days he could not even pronounce the word *Haffner* in his wife's presence, merely thinking of the *Haffner* symphony turned his stomach, they had even thrown out all the recordings that listed Fritz Busch as conductor, they had become altogether unable to listen to Fritz Busch, one of the most outstanding conductors, orchestra leaders, as Konrad is supposed to have put it. Music had gradually become totally played out at the lime works, Konrad told Fro, to think of the trouble I took to move the piano into the lime works, and now the piano just stands there, I never play on it. However, he had not sold the piano, either, understandably, since after all he might one day begin to play the piano again, etc. Still, I do not believe that I shall ever have to depend on the piano again, Konrad said, I hope my wife will not revert to wanting a record played for her every minute. Of course I could sell the piano, actually convert the piano to cash, I hadn't thought of that! but: No, it won't come to that, I shall never sell the piano, I shall never sell the Francis Bacon, the Francis Bacon and the piano will

not be sold. No, no more music at the lime works, Konrad is
supposed to have told Fro. To Fro: after breakfast, he had
stayed in his wife's room in order to proceed with the Urbanchich exercises right after breakfast. He planned to practice
words with *st* and *ts*. However, his wife had first made him
try on the mitten, then she needed help with combing her
hair, quickly combing through her hair, he noticed it was
dirty, but washing her hair was the ghastliest chore of all so
he did not tell her that her hair needed washing, instead he
answered her question: Is my hair dirty? with a simple *No*
and then she asked for a new dress and he did, in fact, put
another dress on her, not a new one, just another one. The
dress was one he had ordered made for her by a tailor once in
Mannheim, it had a stiff silk stand-up collar and was made
of light gray satin that reached down to her ankles; it had
long ceased to be fashionable, Konrad said to Fro. Finally he
was beginning to get impatient to cut all that short and get
on with the Urbanchich exercises, saying: Now then, let's get
started, but she only laughed and said he could do as he
pleased, she for her part had no intention of doing a thing
today, no Urbanchich exercises or anything, today she was
going to make a holiday of it, she suddenly felt like making a
holiday of it, which is after all why she had decided to put
on a new dress, have her hair well combed, let him cut her
nails, etc. Every two weeks or so, Konrad said to Fro, his wife
would suddenly, on an ordinary weekday, announce that she
felt like making a holiday of it, and refused to work, saying
to Konrad: I will not work today on the Urbanchich method,
not even for half an hour, though he would have settled for a
half-hour's work that day, using words with *st* and *ts*. When,
out of the blue, she proclaimed a holiday, she would subject

Konrad to what he described to Fro as exquisite torture by making him put on the table one or several cartons filled with ancient snapshots, which she proceeded to pile on the table and look over, hundreds of thousands of faded snapshots, one after the other, commenting on each one, her comments were always the same, Konrad said, look at that one, look at that one, she would say, picking up one snapshot at a time from the heaps on the table, staring at it, and saying, look at that one, now look at this one, after which she dropped the snapshot on another heap which thus became the one on the increase, dragging out this game which Konrad thought gave her the greatest pleasure, possibly the only pleasure she had left, for hours on end until the whole day had become a total loss as far as doing anything else was concerned. When she had finished with her heaps of snapshots and her incessant: Look at this one, look at that one, she forced Konrad to haul in several cartons full of old letters, all addressed to her five or six, but mostly ten or twenty or thirty years ago, and forcing him to read them to her aloud, incessantly breaking in, with her: Listen to that, listen to that, as her habit was, a habit that drove him up the wall though it did not drive him so far as to make him throw the whole heap of old letters at her head, although, as he said to Fro, he could barely restrain himself from doing just that. On one of these so-called holidays of hers he always knew right away that the day would end as a total loss to him, all its momentum lost to his experimental work; these so-called holidays made him feel disgusted with his wife, disgusted with himself as well, all in all a deep disgust for the revolting condition they both were in. Then there was a knock at the front door; Hoeller had brought their dinner. She is having one of her holidays, Konrad is supposed to have

said on this occasion at the front door downstairs as he took
the food hamper containing the dinner from Hoeller's hand,
and Hoeller instantly knew what Konrad meant, the food
was still warm, so it seemed on that particular day Hoeller had
not fallen in with anyone to gossip with on the way over
from the tavern to the lime works, the chances were that he
had not run into anyone at all, Konrad is supposed to have
said to Fro, small wonder, what with that snowstorm we
were having, and I immediately went back to my wife's
room, after all no stopover in the kitchen to warm the food
was necessary. When Mrs. Konrad saw what was in the
hamper she said: Isn't it just as if the tavern people knew we
were having a holiday? she was referring to the generous
pieces of well-done baked liver, the beef soup with ribbon
noodles, lots of so-called bird salad, and a pastry that turned
out to be, after Konrad had lifted it out of the hamper and set
it on a large platter, a pot cheese strudel. That kind of a day,
of course, Konrad said to Fro, with a snowstorm outside,
possibly can't be spent in a better way than in eating well,
drinking well, all that kind of nonsense. Anyway he couldn't
care less, nor could they both care less, he is supposed to have
said to Fro, what, basically, Hoeller might bring them to eat
from the tavern, they were both totally indifferent to what
there was to eat, though there was a time when they had set
a high value on good eating, but that was a long time ago,
Konrad said, twenty years or so. These remarks about eating
reminded him of the dead sawmill owner, he is supposed to
have said to Fro, three weeks ago, just as I was trying to slice
some boiled salt pork into very fine (they had just slaughtered
a pig at the tavern not too long ago), extra thin slices, that's
how my wife likes it, but I like it that way too, trying to cut

those slices finer every time, there was a knock at the front
door downstairs. At first I thought, suppose I ignore that
knocking? nevertheless I did go down at once and there was
Hoeller at the door, surprisingly, because I thought Hoeller
would be in town that day, but there he stood, suddenly, and I
asked him what he was doing here. What's up? I asked him,
I was just slicing the pork, we're having lunch, I said, and
Hoeller says, the sawmill owner is dead, this is the way it
happened, says Hoeller, at five o'clock this morning the sawmill owner climbed on his tractor just after calling out to his
wife to get the chains out of the barn, he needed the chains for
lashing on the load of tree trunks he was picking up in the
wood, his wife ran to the barn for the chains, it didn't take
her more than two or three minutes to get back with the
chains from the barn, Konrad is supposed to have said to Fro,
but there was her husband hanging dead from the tractor
seat, head first, he had plummeted from the driver's seat but
was still hanging from it by the seat of his pants, it was
lucky the motor was turned off; his wife had thought at first
he was alive, just trying to lean down from the driver's seat
to the hub of the wheel to repair something there, but as she
came up to him she realized that her husband was dead already, she immediately thought that he must have had a
stroke, and in fact the doctor she called diagnosed a heart
attack, nothing unusual, the doctor is supposed to have said,
heart attacks are a common cause of death for men between
forty and fifty, the sawmill owner had just passed forty-two,
they eat and drink and then they climb on their tractors, full
of cholesterol, and fat from lack of exercise, riding their
tractors incessantly as they do, their bodies almost motionless
on and around their everlasting machines, so that the men who

work the land nowadays are the most in danger of heart
attacks. The sawmill owner's wife had dragged her man off
the tractor all by herself, he had fallen on the grass, imagine,
Konrad said to Fro, the sawmill owner's heavy body on the
grass, a fine fellow though, the wife did not have the strength
to carry her man into the house, she called in a few woodcutters and day laborers from the dam project, so with four or
five others the heavy body was soon lifted up off the grass and
carried into the house; once inside the house, the sawmill
owner's wife started to wonder where she could lay out her
husband's corpse, and decided that the former pigpen, which
at the moment contained only a huge cider press and nothing
else, would be the most suitable place for laying out her husband, she had decided on this even before she called in the
doctor, and had the laborers help her wash the body, because
her sisters happened to be in town that morning; the dead
sawmill owner had been quickly undressed, washed, and
combed, Konrad said to Fro, no sooner had the doctor left
than they all went to work carpentering a temporary bier in
the former pigpen, by which time the children had come
home from school, and the sawmill owner's wife's sisters were
back from town, and they all did what they could to lay out
the sawmill owner on his bier in state as quickly as possible,
Konrad told Fro, Hoeller described it all carefully in the
smallest, seemingly insignificant detail, Konrad said. The
dead man's children had been remarkably quiet, considering
that they had come home from school to find their father had
suddenly fallen off his tractor and was dead, and the sawmill
owner's wife's sisters, who had always lived at the sawmill, as
Konrad is supposed to have said to Fro, did their best to collect
flowers for the dead man's lying-in-state, they had wrapped

him in a linen shroud which the sawmill owner's wife had
kept along with her own in one of her bedroom clothes chests,
so in no time at all the sawmill had that atmosphere characteristic of a wake, Konrad said, that very definite odor of
flowers and fresh linen and lifeless body and fresh wood and
holy water; the news of the sawmill owner's death had gotten
around the entire region with incredible speed, Hoeller himself had heard of it within half an hour after the death from
one of the wife's sisters who had come round to the annex to
tell Hoeller and ask him to come to the sawmill and help
them put the bier together and of course Hoeller who had
been busy chopping wood immediately dropped what he was
doing and went to the sawmill with the sawmill owner's wife's
sister, but by the time they got there his help was no longer
needed because they had already put up a provisional bier
on two trestles and even laid out the corpse on it; Hoeller
arriving just three-quarters of an hour after the sawmill owner's death found the corpse already lying in state surrounded
by flowers and candles though, oddly enough, Hoeller is
supposed to have told Konrad, Fro says, there was blood
trickling from the left corner of the dead man's mouth, his
widow kept trying to wipe the blood away with a bit of linen
rag, but she did not succeed in preventing the dead man's fresh
linen shroud from showing some rather large blood stains.
The children knelt, as the children of dead people always
kneel, Hoeller told Konrad, as he said to Fro, beside the
corpse, and little by little the room where the bier stood, which
happened in the case of the dead sawmill owner to be the
former pigpen with the big cider press inside, was filling up,
as always in the case of a death, with condolers. Hoeller is
supposed to have given Konrad an exact description of the

first several hours after the death of the sawmill owner at the
sawmill, finding some characteristic little thing to tell about
every single one of those present at the house of mourning, for
instance how the sawmill owner's widow had said to Hoeller,
while he was standing in the entry to the sawmill planning
the text of the death notice, to be ordered from the Sicking
printer's, with the widow's older sister, the widow said to
Hoeller that her husband's death had not taken her completely
by surprise, in fact the two of them, she and her husband, had
talked about the possibility of his having a stroke just two
days previously, though of course they had ended up laughing
together, which now seemed strange, yes indeed, the sawmill
owner's widow is supposed to have said to Hoeller in the
entry to the sawmill, as Konrad reported it to Fro, who knows,
she said to Hoeller, what will happen now, and what kind of
man will be coming into the house, meaning, as Hoeller
thought, that the sawmill owner's widow was alluding to the
likely successor to the sawmill owner, after all she could not
live there alone with all those children, still so little, she is
supposed to have said to Hoeller not two hours after the death
of the sawmill owner, and: the children were no help, but
what with the sawmill being after all a property worth
millions, she would unquestionably find a man before not
too long, you must remember, Konrad said to Fro, that the
sawmill owner married into the sawmill, originally, as the
sawmill was part of the widow's original property. Getting
back to his own wife, Konrad said that if there was a man in
the world who could put up with her, then he was that man,
and she alone in the world was the woman who could endure
him, Konrad said to Fro. Today I asked her to let me read
her the Kropotkin for two hours, Konrad said to Fro, but

she refused, but in the end we agreed to the following: she
would put up with listening to two hours of Kropotkin if he,
her husband, would help her put on the black, gold-embroidered dress, as she described her wedding dress; good,
Konrad said to his wife, first you put on the dress, then you
listen to me reading Kropotkin for two hours. But she had no
sooner put on the black, gold-embroidered dress, meaning,
naturally, that he had put it on her, than she said she wanted
to take it off again, now that she had it on she could see quite
clearly in the mirror that the black, gold-embroidered dress no
longer suited her, I mean, she said, of course it suits me, but
only in a frightening sort of way. So I took off her black, gold-
embroidered dress again, Konrad is supposed to have said. No
sooner was it off than she asked me to put on her gray dress
with the white velvet collar, so Konrad hung the black, gold-
embroidered dress back inside the wardrobe, took out the gray
dress with the white velvet collar, feeling all the time that his
wife was watching him closely, You are watching me, aren't
you? he is supposed to have said, waiting a bit before he
turned around to hear her answer, but she kept silent, Konrad
said to Fro. He had hardly put the gray dress with the white
velvet collar on her when she straightened up as best she could
to see herself in the mirror and then said: No, this dress won't
do either. I'd rather get back into my old dress, the one I'm
always wearing, and Konrad patiently took off her gray
dress with the white velvet collar again, and helped her into
what she is always supposed to have called her terrible everyday dress. This is the smell that suits me, my everyday smell,
she is supposed to have said, as soon as she had on her so-called
terrible everyday dress once more. Now where did I have this
terrible thing on for the first time, she asked, and he an-

swered: In Deggendorf, don't you remember, in Deggendorf, it was made for you by your niece's seamstress in Deggendorf. Right, by my niece's seamstress in Deggendorf, Mrs. Konrad is supposed to have answered. I wore it to the ball in Landshut, too. Yes, she repeated, says Fro, the ball in Landshut. Then Konrad read to her, as agreed, Kropotkin, for two hours straight. To Wieser: Hoerhager, Konrad's cousin, would undoubtedly have let the lime works fall into disrepair. When the Konrad's announced that they would move into the lime works, people laughed at them. You would have to be crazy to move into the lime works, the Sickingers are supposed to have said, Konrad said to Wieser, and: those people, my dear Wieser, were right. Only two years ago I was still of the opinion that the lime works would be good for my work, but now I no longer think so, now I can see that the lime works robbed me of my last chance to get my book actually written. I mean that sometimes I think, he is supposed to have told Wieser, that the lime works is precisely why I can't write it all down, and then at other times I think that I still have a chance to get my book written down precisely because I am living at the lime works. The two ideas keep alternating in my head, namely that the lime works will enable me to write my book, and that I shall never be able to write my book, because I am here at the lime works. Not so long ago I was of the opinion that the lime works was my only salvation, which meant that it was also hers, (his wife's) and yet today I am surprised that I could have had such an opinion at all. Though I must admit that the moment I have said the lime works will never let me write my book, hope springs up again that the lime works will be favorable to my writing it. But if you can't get your book written here, his wife is supposed to have

said again and again, why did we move to the lime works?
If you can't get it written here, why are we making the sacrifice of living here at the lime works when we could be living
so much more pleasantly anywhere else, surely there can be
no doubt, Wieser reports Mrs. Konrad saying to her husband,
that living at the lime works means being committed to extreme self-sacrifice, let's not fool ourselves, to immure ourselves in the lime works is madness, unless there is a so-called
higher aim to justify it. Though it was true that they had by
now gotten accustomed to their existence at the lime works,
the question remained in any case: what was it all for, if it
was not for the sake of the book, for the sake of *The Sense of
Hearing?* Or as she once phrased it, was it possible that this
greatest of all possible sacrifices had been made in vain? While
she did not really believe in the value of his book, Mrs. Konrad had once said to the works inspector, she could not really say
that the book upon which her husband had expanded the major
part of his intellectual life was worthless and so forth; the
value of his book, Mrs. Konrad once said to the works inspector,
might actually lie in quite another direction; possibly its value
would be quite the opposite of what her husband believed it
to be, Mrs. Konrad said to the inspector, but in any case the
work had to be written, if only because it was necessary to
scotch any notion that her husband, Konrad, was no better
than a madman, one of the many fools who ran around everywhere claiming that they had something, no matter what, even
if it was some kind of ominous scientific work, in their heads,
none of which anyone ever got to see, and if only to save herself, primarily, from unbearable disgrace, she was always
pleading with him to get the book out of his head and down
on paper, and so forth. To be quite frank about it she had no

way of knowing whether her husband was just another fool,
but on the other hand it was possible that he was both a fool
and a genius, who could tell? she is supposed to have said
to the inspector, because she believed her husband showed all
the characteristics of genius as well as all the characteristics
of a fool; Wieser surmises that she may possibly have said this
kind of thing on the very day when Konrad shot her dead
with one or several blasts from her Mannlicher carbine, that
she might have happened to call her husband a fool on that
catastrophic day, the day of the murder (Fro), all of a sudden,
as she had done so often before, but this time he had lost
control and killed her, because she had too often irritated him
beyond endurance by calling him a fool, a madman, and even
a one hundred percent highly intelligent mental case, and on
such occasions, says Wieser, and this is not merely rumor but
fact, on those occasions Konrad had threatened to kill her. It
is my theory, not merely my suspicion but my theory, which
quite possibly may turn out to be fact soon enough at the trial
in Wels, Wieser said, that Konrad probably killed his wife
because she had just once too often called him a fool or a madman or, her favorite expression on the subject, when she was
speaking to Wieser, he said, a highly intelligent mental case.
In the room where the murder took place there was no clue,
of course, that such a quarrel had come about, or that she had
said anything of the kind, Wieser said. But all the indications
are that Konrad killed his wife because of what Konrad repeatedly referred to as her ruthless critical comments. What
could be more natural than that he should suddenly shoot her
down, after all, says Wieser, when he had gotten his fill of
her accusations and carpings that were increasingly violent of
late besides, Wieser said, of course it was the act of a madman,

but as such it was quite understandable and reasonable. Konrad was feeling close to reaching the goal of a lifetime, seeing it within reach, as Wieser says, at which moment of high tension he saw his wife as getting deliberately in his way, debarring him from his life-long goal, the writing of his book. He had to kill her, in the end he simply had to kill her, says Wieser. That to kill his wife was simultaneously to kill his book, Wieser said, was another matter entirely. A woman ceaselessly nagging at her man, Wieser says, is likely to cross the line until suddenly a point has been reached at which murder becomes inevitable. Such a murder tended to make an end of everything, it destroyed everything at one blow, exactly as in the case of the Konrad woman, when in one split second the intellectual life work of an extraordinary man was annihilated as two people were killed, because there could be no question about it that Konrad himself was a dead man, even though he might continue to exist for years, whether in prison or in a mental home, whichever the court would decide, but in any case, and no matter how long he continued to live on, the fact remained that he would have been already dead for a long time, for that length of time, when he was finally buried. It shocked Wieser every time he thought of it that a human being could, by a mere careless slip, a sudden relaxation of his mind's rational function, transform himself from an extraordinary being into the most miserable of creatures, and not himself alone but the person closest to him as well. How frequently the foremost runner in a race could be seen coming to a sudden stop. Basically, says Wieser, in killing his wife, Konrad had not killed primarily his wife but had, as it were in a sudden fit of abstraction, killed himself. For both the Konrads everything was destroyed in one moment. The

man who at this moment was restlessly pacing the floor of his
prison cell in Wels, or else lying stock-still on his prison cot,
probably knew this clearly. Whether or not Konrad had been
crazy all along, it was only a question of time when he would
be crazy for good. It isn't as if we had been compelled to move
into the lime works, Konrad is supposed to have said to
Wieser, we could have gone to a number of other places like
the Tirol, for instance, or Styria, as everyone knows there is
no dearth of so-called scenic spots in our country, but a scenic
spot was precisely what I sought to avoid, Austria is of course
full of nothing but these so-called scenic spots, Konrad is
supposed to have said to Wieser, there isn't another country in
the world where so many hundreds of thousands of so-called
scenic spots are crowded together in so relatively small an
area, but that's just it, that kind of beauty spot is the worst
place in the world for starting or even proceeding with an
intellectual undertaking well on its way, Konrad said, according to Wieser, why, if he was sure of anything he was sure of
this, that a so-called scenic area, a beautiful city, would never
fail to destroy the best, the most solidly planned intellectual
work, destroy it root and branch, a beautiful landscape could
only act as an irritant on the brain, a so-called wonder of
nature invariably undermined the mind. Which was why it
was harder in Austria than anywhere else, Wieser claims that
Konrad said to him, to get on with an intellectual task or complete it, there was no other country where you could point to
so many hundreds of thousands of neglected or abandoned
ideas, jettisoned plans, unrealized original projects, genuinely
immense undertakings in the sciences or the so-called fine arts
and where you could point, simultaneously, to so many scenic
spots; here in Austria, Konrad told Wieser in so many words,

every genius has frittered himself away, everything extraordinary has ended in self-destruction, the so-called creative element has let itself be killed by the beauty of nature. A graveyard of ideas, a wasteland of perversely aborted high flights of the mind, that's what the country was, its beauty made it our homeland, but it was the scene of incessant founderings, humiliations, suppressions of greatness. He once opened one of those huge trunks they kept in the attic at the lime works, one of those dirty, dusty trunks we all take on sea voyages, Konrad said to Wieser, as I have often told you, my wife and I traveled a great deal, during the early decades of our life together we were almost uninterruptedly on the move, partly because we feared that an abrupt change for the worse in my wife's various kinds of ill health might nail us down altogether, would prevent even the shortest of trips from one day to the next, so that we made the longest possible journeys, Konrad said to Wieser, sea voyages for the most part, though as late as '38, just before the outbreak of the Second World War, we took the Transsiberian railway as far as Vladivostok, then we went to China, to Japan, to the Philippines, nowadays this doesn't mean much but in those days such travels were still monstrous undertakings, and for both my wife and myself they were of course an extraordinary physical strain, though the strain, or rather the resulting exhaustion, never hit us with its full force until after we had completed the trip, when we would be overcome with the awareness of it, and so, you see, Konrad said to Wieser, we would keep going on ever more extensive trips on the assumption that each would be our last, for reasons of health, or else it would be our last trip because I might suddenly have to settle down on account of being fully preoccupied with my task, my book on *The Sense of*

Hearing, Konrad is supposed to have said to Wieser. When
I opened that heavy sea chest, out came a whole flood of
travel brochures, steamer tickets, railway tickets, the trunk
had been locked up for decades and my suddenly opening it
made its contents burst out in a sudden spate—hundreds of
thousands of brochures and ticket stubs from and to every conceivable place in the world came pouring out. To think that all
those travels of ours have ended by leading us here into the
lime works, Konrad is supposed to have said to Wieser. In
Paris, for instance, they had lived in an apartment on the
Boulevard Haussmann, and yet they had finally moved to the
lime works, Konrad had thought and had persuaded his wife
that no other place offered better conditions for getting his
work done, though he had not really convinced her of it, not
to this very day, and she was probably right, Konrad said the
last time he saw Wieser, I should probably have listened to
her and taken her to Toblach instead, that lovely little spot in
the mountains would surely have brought us peace, and if not
peace, exactly, at least my wife would have been happy there
for the rest of her days, it would have suited her, my dear
Wieser, because in Toblach she would have found what she
always sought at my side, a certain contentment among her
sisters and other relatives, a certain inner security and outward
shelter, but because I had to make my will prevail, as I begin
to see at last, or as I think I must admit to myself, by forcing
my poor wife to move with me into the lime works for the
sake of an altogether hopeless cause, I have destroyed her life,
annihilated myself as a person. At the time of the decision to
move to the lime works, back in Mannheim, Konrad was reduced to choosing between giving in to his wife and giving
himself up, sacrifice himself completely, by going to Toblach,

or else move to the lime works, with its harsh climate, compared with Toblach, and Sicking was a most unfriendly town, it meant the end of hope for Mrs. Konrad; to move to Sicking was to destroy her life. Though of course we could also have gone to live in the Wilhering Cloister, Konrad said, which is surrounded by an orchard in bloom, those Cistercians would undoubtedly have taken good care of us, or else we could have gone to Lambach, or to Aschach, or Lauffen, there was even nothing to prevent us from deciding to go back to London or to Manchester, all that stood in the way was my obsession about moving to the lime works, Konrad said to Wieser, and what drove me to surrender myself irrevocably to that obsession was my cousin Hoerhager's dragging his feet in consenting to the sale, had Hoerhager simply refused to accept Konrad's proposals to buy the lime works at any price, there is no doubt at all that the question of whether or not to move to the lime works would have resolved itself in the most painless way. But as it was, Hoerhager's teasing evasiveness had inflamed Konrad's mania that he must have the lime works at any cost, even though the idea that he must become the owner of the lime works, move in and live there and nowhere else, Konrad told Wieser, ultimately depended on nothing more than two or three visits Konrad had paid there as a child, at the age of four or five, and later when he was about eight or nine, for a few days in winter and a few days in summer chosen haphazardly by his parents, unsure of themselves as they were every time they had to choose a place to send him on his vacations from school, a place to send him on a brief holiday, and that was all he knew of the lime works and Sicking, and it was solely upon this experience all those decades ago, that his life-long wish to own the lime works was

based. Later in life he had taken his young wife there once, as
he remembered it, one October evening, rather wintry for the
date, on a visit to his uncle, Hoerhager's father, on which occasion he had found the lime works cold and unfriendly, and
yet even more fascinating than on the earlier occasions, he
told Wieser, and his wife had described the place as sinister
afterward, it was past midnight and they were on their way
to Scharnstein, as Konrad remembered, when she called the
lime works a sinister place in an equally sinister landscape.
She had found it oppressive, and inside the lime works she
felt scared; when Konrad asked her what she was scared of,
she is supposed to have said: *Suddenly, of everything.* To
force her to move into the lime works for good and all was
monstrous, Mrs. Konrad said to her husband, but then in her
eyes, Fro says, Konrad had always been a monster, and Wieser
says that Konrad, considering everything Wieser knew about
the couple, could never have seemed other than a monster to
his wife, as it was practically second nature for Konrad to
represent himself as a monster all his life long, not only to his
wife, until he had finally quite lost himself in the role of a
monster, universally so regarded but especially so by his wife,
treated as a monster by everyone around him all his life, so
that is what he ultimately became, and you could therefore say
that it was the people around him, especially his wife, who
had made a monster out of him, says Wieser, or rather a so-
called monster, it was not Konrad himself who should be
blamed for this, even though the people who had driven him
to the point at which it was possible for them to label him a
monster, or a so-called monster, would then not scruple to
blame it all on him, to blame him for being a monster.
Though on the one hand it was distracting to live in the

cities, life in the country, on the other hand, was distracting also, basically both cities and country places, the country as such, tended to distract one's mind from one's task in much the same way, from progressing in one's intellectual work, Konrad is supposed to have told Wieser, ultimately everything was nothing but distraction, because city and country, city ideas and country ideas, or conceptions of the city and of the country had in recent decades begun to overlap and become completely fused and confused with one another, it had begun to be basically absurd to try to distinguish between the city and the country, they had become so completely homogenized, Konrad is supposed to have expressed it like that to Wieser. The problem of the monotonousness of the prevailing current architecture played only a subordinate part in all this, even though the vista offering itself to the observer, of a scene, an atmosphere, was equally saturated with progress-and-machine-madness, regardless of where he found himself, country or city, the same assumptions prevailed everywhere. We were, all of us, undergoing, in every respect, what he called a process of social interfusion at the end of which the so-called processed man would emerge as a monster, that is, as a machine. Konrad had naturally expected that at the lime works he would suffer a minimum of distraction, if any; Sicking had no distractions at all, by comparison the rest of the world was nothing but distractions (from his work on the book). But whatever he may have thought about the lime works and about the book it had all been a mistake, every bit of it, Konrad is supposed to have said to Wieser. In the last analysis a man tended to yield instinctively to a form of indirect blackmail exerted on him by his own personality. Though of course he had carefully gone over every pro and contra having to do with their moving into the lime works, as had his wife whom, however, he did not really consult as a person who would have a deciding vote in the matter; he merely took her into consideration. What was so fascinating about their move was that it was an abandoned lime works they were going into. Besides, after decades of extensive but ultimately aimless traveling, the Konrads had finally had enough of traveling. At least as far as he was concerned. Traveling ultimately wore you out, the new experiences came to lose their newness all too soon, the great varieties of people came to look all alike, the circumstances and connections in which they turned up came to have a sameness, as did the looks of the landscapes, always the same as one moved toward them and away from them, the conditions, climatic, social, hostile, political, natural, medical, etc. etc. had a sameness that tired one out. In time the world tended to use itself up simply, and what was most depressing of all in traveling around, Konrad is supposed to have told Wieser, you kept being increasingly confronted with the world's increasingly evident shabbiness, until this was what you were facing incessantly and on to the end, so to speak. To try to escape from all this by moving oneself into some remote shelter was also an error, of course, as he fully realized by now, but so would any other solution they might have hit upon have been an error. The lime works had offered itself as a turning point, though not as a radical about-face, there was no such thing, but at least as a quarter-turn in every degree, as Konrad is supposed to have expressed himself to Wieser, and Konrad had assumed that it would be possible for him to make one more such turn later, even if by no more than a few degrees. They could foresee that they would soon be suffocating in their Paris apartment, Konrad said to Wieser, and they had to face it, to suffocate in the thick of a human mass, for instance on the Boulevard Haussmann, Konrad said, was unquestionably the most terrible way to go. But, don't you see, Konrad is supposed to have exclaimed, to Wieser, there are so many ways to be ruined, to founder! in which connection several books, by a writer whose name he had forgotten, came to mind, an Austrian writer, and anyway the name didn't matter, the person didn't matter, no writer's person or biography ever mattered, his work was everything, the writer himself was nothing, despite the despicable vulgarity of all those who insisted upon confusing the writer's person with his work, the general public had been corrupted by certain historical and literary processes of the first half of the nineteenth century into daring, with the shameless impertinence characteristic of them, to confuse the written work with the writer's personal concerns, using the writer's person to effect a vicious crippling of the writer's work, always shuttling back and forth between the writer's private person and his product, and so forth, more and more confusing the producer and the product, all of which led to a monstrous distortion of the entire culture, bringing into being a culture which was a monstrosity, and so forth, but to get back to the man's writings, reading him was like reading a madman, a writing madman, but he was in fact quite the opposite of a madman, and Konrad recommended to Wieser some titles, fragments in which certain goings-on were described that were highly relevant to what was going on in his life, although the proceedings in the books were metaphysical in nature, while his own original undertaking was anything but metaphysical, in fact Konrad did not hesitate to describe his entire development as organic from first to last, and though it had a decidedly speculative bond with the metaphysical it did not in any sense derive its being from metaphysics, Wieser says. Basically Konrad's own development could not in any respect be regarded as a so-called thing of the imagination, absolutely not, it was strictly a physical process, Konrad is supposed to have said to Wieser, at bottom it was nothing more than an infinitely sad story of a marriage, astounding, shocking if you chose, and yet it could just as well be regarded as almost laughably commonplace, even though it might seem strange, extraordinary, crazy, to the superficial observer. But there was no use talking about it. The mitten: while watching her knit his mitten he asks himself: Why is she knitting that mitten, always the same one? but he also asks himself why, instead of continually working on that mitten, doesn't she take time out to mend his socks, patch his shirts, his torn vest, all my clothes have big holes in them, everywhere, he said to himself, but she sits here knitting that mitten. Her own cap needs mending, so does her blouse, too, but no, she keeps working away at that mitten. The lime works have been the finish of her, he thought, watching her at work on that mitten. A person like his wife could hardly be considered a living human being any longer, even if you made every conceivable kind of allowance, emotional, rational, anything you pleased, not in the condition she was in after nearly five years at the lime works, he would think as he looked on while she kept at her knitting. There had been nothing between them for a long time now, nothing more than what he could only call mutual ignoration. But on the other hand, whatever had been between them previously, all their traveling together and so forth, had ultimately predestined them for this very life of theirs at the lime works. The lime works were our destination, our destination was to be done to death by the lime works. Before we moved into the lime works, Konrad said to Wieser, we were constantly and to the greatest extent in the company of other people, but after we moved into the lime works we were totally deprived of human companionship, totally out of human society, which was bound to lead, first, to despair, then to spiritual and emotional desolation, then to sickness and death. Absolutely nothing at all happens here! Konrad exclaimed, according to Wieser. But even to consider the kind of senselessness it was to move into the lime works as a form of heroism was suicidal. Although even his wife had persuaded herself, during their first two years at the lime works, that their complete withdrawal from the world into the lime works would be his salvation, Konrad himself, though he had at first naturally regarded the move as his (my) salvation, Konrad said to Wieser, after only six months he said to himself that this would possibly be his (my) salvation, then, after a year or so, he thought this would probably be his (my) salvation, but after two years he said to himself that of course this cannot be his (my) salvation, and after three years at the lime works she, Mrs. Konrad, faced up to the fact that, to the contrary, the lime works meant Konrad's total destruction, although he himself was not yet aware of it, still kept suppressing his awareness of it while clinging to the hope that it might still be possible for him to get his book written here. In the end the two of them had taken to assuring each other that, as Wieser says, at least it cost next to nothing to live at the lime works. This was true enough, as everyone knows you could live at an absurdly low cost, by comparison with costs elsewhere, especially the big cities, in such remote country places as the Sicking area, but to let this fact come up as a reason for moving to the lime works, even if it came up only inside their own heads, had seemed to them extraordinarily humiliating. But at times they would actually settle for this as an acceptable reason, i.e., the thought that the lime works could actually be credited with having cut down on their living expenses necessarily seemed to be a saving thought for a few hours or days, as Konrad explained to Wieser. Considering, after all, that they had hardly any money left, Konrad confided to Wieser; hardly any money left at all, by then. Which reminds me of Wieser's description of Konrad's description of Konrad's last trip to the bank: This morning I went to the bank, Konrad told Wieser, they let me have another ten thousand, these will be the last ten thousand, of course, they said to me. The young teller at the counter wouldn't give me anything at all, you understand, but I went straight to the manager. The manager received me at once, most politely, of course. You know the manager's office, of course, that little cubbyhole where the air is always so bad because they never open the window, but it's only fair to remember, in this connection, Konrad is supposed to have said to Wieser, that if they opened the manager's office window the air coming in from outside would be even worse, the window being right above the parking space, you know. Well, in I went, to see the manager, those dark green metal filing cabinets, you know, Konrad said. The first thing to meet the eye, unavoidably, as you enter the manager's cubbyhole of an office, is the portrait of the bank's founder, Derflinger, hanging on the wall. Mustache with uptwisted ends, peasant face and so forth. The manager and I shake hands, says Konrad, I am invited to sit down, I sit down. On the desk in front of him the manager has my entire file, as I see immediately. Which

means that the manager and I are about to have a final, the
final, serious talk, I thought, and I was right; the manager
started to leaf through my file, then he got on the phone,
talking to somebody about the contents of my file, then he
sent for the clerk, and another clerk, and a third, a fourth,
a fifth, all having to do with my file, accounts, statements,
etc., then he phones again, then he ponders the file, phones
again, ponders over my papers again, etc. Actually the manager has all the papers relating to my account at hand, meaning all the papers accumulated through all the years I have
had dealings with the bank. As the manager leafs through
these papers I keep thinking that he may not let me draw
any money at all, there is no telling by the look on his face:
will he give me the money, won't he give me the money,
any money, he will, he won't, I keep thinking, unable to decide one way or the other. Still more papers are brought in
from time to time, men and women clerks wear themselves
out bringing in all sorts of documents connected with my
account. Finally one of the clerks is even ordered to fetch
a ladder, and to climb up the ladder in order to pull out and
bring down some papers from a drawer high up under the
ceiling of the little office. The manager urges the clerk to get
on with it, but the clerk argues that he can't climb up the
ladder any faster than he is climbing already, and later that
he can't climb down any faster than he is climbing down
already, without getting hurt, he says he doesn't want to
break his neck, to which the manager finds nothing to say,
probably restraining himself because the clerk is a good clerk,
Konrad is supposed to have said to Wieser. Then the manager noticed that through all this I had kept my coat on,
so he leaped from his chair to help me out of my coat and

hang it up on a coathook on his door, but I forestalled him
by leaping up myself, took off the coat, and hung it on
the coathook myself. It is warmer than usual in here, the
manager said, and Konrad agreed, yes, it is rather warm. It
was undoubtedly because of this that the manager was wearing only a lightweight summer suit, as Konrad had noticed
at once, finding it odd that the manager was wearing this
lightweight summer suit in the bank in the winter time, but,
as the manager said to Konrad, according to Wieser, here in
this room (he did not call it a cubbyhole, which it was) one
cannot function in winter clothes, if you dress too warmly
you catch a chill, all because of the central heating, one is
always sitting in this overheated room (not "cubbyhole") and
worries about catching cold because one is feeling much too
warm. Furthermore, it was impossible to regulate the circu-
lation of fresh air inside the whole building. Meanwhile the
documents kept piling higher on the manager's desk, Konrad is supposed to have told Wieser, until it seemed I would
lose sight of the manager altogether behind the mountain
range of documents and files between us on his desk. At the
end I could not see the manager at all, but I could still hear
what he was saying. His face was hidden from me, Konrad
told Wieser, but I could still hear his voice. Earlier Konrad
had been struck by the fact, he said, that some of the clerks did
not greet him when they entered the manager's office, among
them three out of the four women clerks who had come in,
and Konrad attributed their conduct to his being so deeply
indebted to the bank, still he felt that it was outrageous of
them to snub so conspicuously a man like himself, a client
of the bank who had kept up such excellent business relations with the bank for such a long time. Thinking it over,

however, he decided that it might not have been a deliberate snub but only carelessness, that it was unintentional, and so forth. Meanwhile the manager was telephoning, over and over again, with the teller at the counter in the outer office, with the clerks in the offices upstairs, in the so-called credit division. At long last a number of promissory notes Konrad had signed during the past year and that had come due long since, were brought into the manager's office. Konrad now understood that he was not going to get any money from the bank this time, but rather that he would be asked to pay his debts instead, beginning with these notes. Konrad was certain that his wife knew nothing about all this, according to Wieser, because he always kept their financial situation to himself, he had in fact developed a highly skilled technique for keeping secret anything relating to their so-called financial affairs. Now he feared that the catastrophic state of their financial condition would come to light and everything would come crashing down about their ears with shocking effect, Konrad told Wieser. He was thinking about this while the manager kept busying himself with Konrad's financial papers and kept the clerks running back and forth on errands connected with these papers so that Konrad began to think that it was the haste with which they were kept moving that had prevented them from greeting him in the first place. While Konrad was sitting there in the bank everything that was going on combined to give him the impression that he was its sole center and focus, everything the bank did seemed concentrated entirely on him. The manager was still telephoning for yet another document relating to my account, Konrad told Wieser, there was no end to the papers the bank held concerning me. Bank clerks all have the same faces,

Konrad said, banking people's heads were stuffed with nothing but paper money and their faces were made of nothing but paper money. By staring hard at the founder's, Derflinger's, portrait, Konrad is supposed to have told Wieser, by gluing my eyes to the founder's peasant face for considerable stretches of time, I managed to keep my naturally increasing perturbation under control. Again I thought I might after all be given some money, but this hope soon turned out to be baseless, and I resigned myself to the expectation that the manager would never again give me any money, in fact I heard him say so, although he had actually said nothing at all about money, what he did say was: How hot it is in here! and I understood him to mean that he would not give me any more money, which would have meant, Konrad said to Wieser, no, I cannot actually tell you what this would have meant, because it would have meant something too terrible to be imagined. What I suddenly heard the manager saying, actually, was that you (that is, myself) owe something above two million, most of it is owed to our bank, and if we subtract the value of your property, that still leaves a debt of at least one and a half million, the manager said. Your property is far from adequate coverage for your debts! the manager said repeatedly, Konrad claimed; he thought he heard the manager say: Your property is very far from sufficient to cover your debts! three or four or five or six times, even though the manager is supposed to have made this statement only once, I keep hearing it over and over again all the time, Konrad said to Wieser. And then the manager pronounced the following sentence, which I also keep hearing over and over again, I simply cannot get it out of my head: And as you know, we have taken steps to institute a forced auction of the lime works. Of course so admittedly painful a proceeding had been postponed for as long as possible, but it was no longer possible to put it off, it had become a matter that brooks no delay, and the expression *brooks no delay* was another that Konrad simply could not get out of his head, it kept running through his head for days and weeks on end until the day he committed the murder. For years Konrad had gone to the bank and asked for money and the bank had simply handed over the money, for years this had been a bi-weekly occurrence, a habit, Konrad would simply spend a morning going from the lime works to Sicking, to enter the bank and withdraw a lesser or larger sum, as the manager phrased it, actually the bank always let him withdraw whatever sum he asked for without the least difficulty, whether it was five thousand or ten thousand or two thousand or one thousand or five hundred, or twenty thousand and so forth. It had never occurred to the bank to refuse to let Konrad draw any sum whatsoever, the bank had always met every one of Konrad's claims on it with good grace, in fact, as the manager found he must say, rather handsomely. But the time had come when this had to end. In the circumstances, Konrad said to Wieser, I naturally decided to get up and leave instantly, to go, to get clean out of there was what I was thinking, and I did actually rise and take my coat from the hook on the door, Konrad said to Wieser, I held out my hand to the manager, and the manager, who had of course leaped up from his chair as soon as I had gotten up from mine, gave me his hand and said: Very well, you can withdraw ten thousand, we will of course let you have another ten thousand. The manager actually said "of course," Konrad is supposed to have told Wieser, *of course of course of course* I keep hearing him saying it even now, he was saying *of course,* Konrad is supposed to have said to Wieser, it was grotesque, he did it from sheer habit, according to Konrad, of course, when it would have been so much more a matter of course, Konrad said, to have given me nothing more. The manager also used the expression "oblige," "to oblige you" just like that. As I had used to withdraw the round sum of ten thousand at the beginning of the month, Konrad said to Wieser, I went, after shaking the manager's hand and saying goodbye to him, and withdrew the round sum of ten thousand, as was my habit. I slipped the money in my pocket and left the bank for the last time, I left the bank once and for all, Konrad said to Wieser. I did a little shopping, I bought shoelaces, tallow, bond paper, shirt buttons, fresh mitten wool for my wife, and went back to the lime works. The bank certainly had behaved handsomely once again, Konrad is supposed to have said to Wieser. On the way home I naturally realized the utter hopelessness of our situation. Actually, if we spend the absolute minimum, I was thinking, while I walked as far as the rock spur and back to the tavern and from the tavern to the sawmill and from the sawmill to the rock spur and behind the annex and past the annex to the lime works, we have a few weeks more, and if we spend less than that, even, we might eke out a few months on these ten thousand. If we can reduce our requirements from the minimal to something even more minimal in expenditures, it's no problem, because we are, Wieser reports Konrad saying, the most unassuming two people in the world. Of course I must get my book written in this period of grace, Konrad is supposed to have said to Wieser, but once my book is written nothing else matters, and it is just possible that the most hopeless situation is the most favorable to the writing of the book. Insofar as I was able to let this idea gain ground until it became my dominant idea, Konrad is supposed to have told Wieser, I no longer felt any uneasiness, quite the contrary, I walked whistling into my room. That evening, as I recall, Konrad is supposed to have told Wieser, she suddenly said, interrupting my reading from Kropotkin, *dance,* following it up immediately with the word *carnival dance.* She pronounces the words *carnival dance* several times in a row, I heard the words *carnival dance* several times in a row. Then she says: Do you remember? and then she pronounces the words *Venice, Parma, Florence, Nice, Paris, Deggendorf, Landshut, Schönbrunn, Mannheim, Sighartsein,* she says, and *Henndorf.* But it all goes back at least thirty years, she says. Dances, dances, she cries, again and again: You put up a lot of resistance, but I never gave up, I simply would not give up. In Paris, in Rome, remember? Let's go dancing, dancing! I said, and we went dancing, we went to all the dances. My insistence was more ruthless than your resistance. You dressed me, in Rome you put on my red dress, in Florence my blue dress, in Venice the blue dress, in Parma the white dress, the dress with the long train in Madrid, she says. Suddenly she says: the dress with the train, yes, the dress with the long train, I want to wear it, put it on me now, yes, do put it on me, put it on me! and so I put on her the dress with the train. Come, the mirror, she demands, and then: come on, my face powder compact. And she powders her face and looks in the mirror, she alternates between powdering her face and looking in the mirror. Suddenly she says: I don't see anything, I can't see a thing. Actually, Konrad said to Wieser, she couldn't see the mirror for the cloud of loose face powder she had generated. It could be a good thing that I can't see myself, she says, and then goes on covering herself with more powder. Her whole dress is covered with powder, by this time, Konrad told Wieser, and meanwhile she keeps on saying: I must put more powder on, I must cover myself with powder, from top to bottom, she says, and when the powder in the compact is all used up she says: don't we have more face powder somewhere? there's got to be more face powder! find it, find it, she says, and sure enough I find a second compact and she goes on covering her face with more powder, Konrad said to Wieser, until suddenly I can no longer see her face at all, she has completely covered her face with powder. I'm all powdered up! all powdered up! she says: all powdered up! she cries, Konrad said, and suddenly she is laughing and crying: all covered with powder, all powdered over, I've covered myself all up with powder! and she laughs and cries and laughs and cries, the same thing over and over. Then she suddenly falls silent and straightens up a bit and says: that's good. And again: that's good. And then: The play is finished. Broken off. The play is broken off, finished. Here's a scandal! Imagine, she cries out, Konrad told Wieser, we've got a scandal here, a scandal in our house, a scandal! Then, after a brief silence: that's good, she says, that's good. She is utterly exhausted, and I take off her dress, the dress with the train. You must give this dress a good shaking, she says, Konrad told Wieser, the whole dress is covered with face powder, go out into the hall and give it a good shaking out! and I do as she tells me, and shake out the dress in the hall. At eleven I tell her Good Night and go to my room, Konrad said, but in my room I find that I have left the Kropotkin in her room, so I go back to her room to fetch my Kropotkin. To my surprise I find her already fast asleep, probably from exhaustion. I feel my way to the table in the dark, and pick up the Kropotkin and go back to my own room. Reading Kropotkin relaxes me. About two A.M., the time I usually fall asleep, Konrad told Wieser, I fell asleep. To Fro: It wasn't the first time we sat together in total darkness. We'd eaten nothing for supper. I can't lift a finger to do the least thing, cut my fingernails, cut my toenails, nothing, Konrad said. Absolute passivity. I tell her: I shall now read to you from the Kropotkin, but I can't do it, or I say, I shall read the Novalis, but I can't do it. There's the depressing awareness, too, of sitting forever opposite my totally exhausted wife. Buck up, I say to myself, and read her the Kropotkin again, try; or, come on now, try the Novalis again, but I can't begin, I can't even muster the strength to pick myself up and walk to my own room. Sitting opposite her, I become more clearly cognizant of my wife's rundown, shabby state, of my own run-down, shabby state. Looking out of the window, though I can't see anything in the darkness, I know nevertheless that the weather is the cause of all this. The weather alone can drive a person like myself and a person like her crazy, on top of all our basic reasons for despair. Both of us immobile in our chairs. Till dawn we sit without a word, utterly exhausted, utterly worn out and utterly exhausted in our chairs, half awake, clutching at each other from time to time, in silence, so as not to go out of our minds from one moment to the next. The funeral of the sawmill owner: Hoeller comes to fetch me to the funeral, Konrad says to Fro, we walk together under the rock spur to the sawmill. I'd managed to dig up some black articles of clothing and to put them on, Konrad says to Fro. A pair of warm woolen socks I once bought in Mannheim for the funeral of my cousin Albert, my youngest cousin. And the warm black vest I picked up in Hamburg, and I have my black Borsalino on my head. The black woolen muffler around my neck, of course. Black shoes, bought in Venice. A man has to be careful, Hoeller is supposed to have said to Konrad, he goes to a funeral and is liable to catch his death. I've seen it many times, myself, Konrad is supposed to have told Fro; a man attends a funeral, catches a chill, and the next thing you know it's his own funeral. On our way to the rock spur, I muse about the sawmill owner and myself, and it seems to me we always got along quite well, he and I. A man who owns black clothes wears his black clothes to a funeral, I am thinking, while on the way to the sawmill. The moment you reach the house of mourning you go straight to the room where the corpse lies in state. You press the widow's or the widower's hand. You say something about what a good, dear person the departed was. Walking in procession behind the coffin everyone walks slowly, not speaking, only murmuring. Not a word is understood. Special funerals attract hundreds of people. The sawmill owner's funeral is a special funeral. Following a special funeral attended by special kinds of people and with a special kind of clergyman officiating, everyone enters a special kind of restaurant and eats a special kind of meal, I am thinking, Konrad said. A special kind of vehicle, specially decorated and drawn by specially groomed, specially decorated horses, rolls along, followed by specially concerned persons. The funeral cortege is a special arrangement, a special liturgy is pronounced at the graveside, all of it involving naturally a special expense. The day of such a funeral is a special day, I am thinking, Konrad says to Fro, as I walk toward the sawmill, toward which hundreds of people are walking now, all of them in black, Konrad says to Fro, and sometimes Hoeller is in front of me, sometimes he is behind me, because my walk is irregular, but in the end Hoeller is walking beside me again and I am thinking: the fire chief is going to make a special speech. As we reach the sawmill I can actually see that everybody is dressed specially for the occasion. Especially fine wreaths, especially white, clean clothes on the children, the especially costly-looking coffin. Finally, at the open grave, Konrad is supposed to have said to Fro, I wonder whether to keep my hat on, or not, if I take the hat off I shall catch my death of cold, if I keep it on, people will talk, so I keep my hat on. The fire chief makes an especially short speech, which at first takes me aback, Konrad says to Fro, until I remember that the fire chief and the sawmill owner were enemies, which explains the shortness of the fire chief's speech. The priest's sermon is all the longer. The depth of an open grave always shocks me afresh, Konrad is supposed to have told Fro, we do our best to be brave and put up a bold front, but the depth of those open graves frightens us every time. Did I have no differences with the sawmill owner, I am thinking, Konrad is supposed to have said to Fro, and No, I had no differences of any kind with the sawmill owner, Konrad is supposed to have decided on the way home from the funeral. Actually, Konrad says, the sawmill owner was a decent fellow, as he told Hoeller on their way back to the lime works, though afterwards he brooded for a long time over why he said this, and most of all about why he said it to Hoeller on the way home, why he said that the sawmill owner was a decent fellow, he could just as well have said a good fellow, or at least a fellow you couldn't find fault with, unobjectionable and so forth. The Konrads had planned to spend the rest of that day reading, he reading aloud to her alternately from the Kropotkin and the Novalis, as I was reading I kept on thinking about the funeral, Konrad is supposed to have said to Fro, and these thoughts were affecting my voice so that it sounded strange. Fro: a dream of Konrad's: in a sudden, not readily classifiable fit of insanity (catatonia?) Konrad had taken to painting the whole interior of the lime works black, from all the way up under the roof to all the way downward, gradually, to the ground, using a mat black varnish, several pailfuls of which he had found in the attic. He would not leave the lime works, he said to himself, until he had finished painting the entire interior with this mat black varnish, it was of the greatest importance to him to get it all painted black, everything inside the lime works, with this paint he had found in the attic. Ceilings, walls, whatever was left of the furniture, all of it was painted black inside and out, and he even painted his wife's room, then everything inside his wife's room, and finally he painted his wife black inside and out, imagine it if you can, everything in her room including her French invalid chair, simply everything as I said, and finally everything in his own room, he needed exactly seven days, Fro says, to paint the whole lime works and the whole interior and everything inside the interior black inside and out. The instant he finished, Fro says, he locked up the lime works and ran past the annex and up the rock spur, from the top of which he hurled himself down. Fro, today: Konrad lives in constant fear that the man from the bank might come knocking on his door, which is why he doesn't open the door. A man from the bank, or one of the policemen might be standing outside his front door, and so Konrad no longer leaves his room, even when his wife is ringing or knocking for help. Fro himself was admitted to the lime works only at a moment of abysmal despair. Konrad heard a knock at the front door quite often, someone knocking with intrepid stubbornness, but Konrad did not believe it was Hoeller, because Hoeller would not do such a thing. The knocking gave the impression of someone wanting to smash up the lime works. Konrad is supposed to have said: sitting in my chair I hear this knocking, and I wait from one knock to the next, the irregular intervals between knocks made it impossible for him to guess who it might be. Is it someone from the bank? someone from the police? he wonders. He stays immobile in his chair. He won't open the door. He practices self-restraint. He listens to his wife's ringing for hours, but he thinks: there's no sense in going up there. Nothing makes any sense, he thinks. To Wieser, with whom I was able to close the deal on his life insurance policy today, Konrad is supposed to have said that the immense amount of material he had collected in his head for his book was in itself enough to destroy this kind of book; the probability that such a work might be destroyed by the sheer immensity of the material, the constantly increasing immensity of the material, was a probability that kept increasing in direct ratio to the increase in the quantity of the material. Ultimately the quantity of conceptual material was likely to crush a man altogether. At first he had believed that the book was a decided possibility for him, then he believed it was decidedly impossible, and went on alternating between its possibility and its impossibility, but the intervals in which he thought it would be possible for him to write the book were growing shorter, while the intervals in which the book seemed to be a lost cause were growing longer. But he had never quite lost the sense of the possibility of starting to write it, of being able to get started, actually he believed even now (only six months ago, that is!) that he would suddenly feel able to sit down and write it all in one sitting, as he is supposed to have expressed himself to Wieser. After all it was a simple matter of sitting down and starting to write the book, only a question of a favorable constellation of circumstances that would suddenly enable him to get it all down on paper once he got started, which he could not believe would fail to come along sooner or later. Every such constellation of circumstances occurs some time at the right moment, Konrad is supposed to have said, favorable or unfavorable, it was only a question of recognizing the one right moment of such a favorable or unfavorable constellation when it came along. Basically it was simply a matter of sitting down and writing whatever it was you had to write. Once the right moment presents itself, it must be utilized, and he had merely lacked the chance, hitherto, to seize and utilize the right moment, though undoubtedly the right moment had presented itself to him quite often already, he had only to think of the favorable time in Brussels or in Mannheim or the even more favorable time in Merano or Deggendorf or Landshut, it was only that he had been unable to utilize any of them, at the right moment everything was always ready, but one failed to utilize it, most people never managed to utilize the uniquely favorable moments in life, though this was not much of a consolation to him, Konrad hoped he would not turn out to be one of their number, especially considering how important his book was, but inside every man, every brain, every head there was, he always said, the possibility of everything coming together just once, and it was this *everything just once* that he so longed to recognize and utilize, sooner or later, though he rather wished it would be in the immediate future. As for unutilized favorable constellations, times, moments, etc., he had plenty of those to show in his life, most people were made up of such so-called unutilized favorable (or unfavorable) constellations, everywhere you looked you saw nothing but unutilized constellations, favorable or unfavorable in character; besides, who could decide whether a constellation was favorable or unfavorable, since one might be favorable precisely because the other was unfavorable and vice versa, the unfavorable being favorable for one (head) and vice versa, it depended on the individual (head, to turn an unfavorable constellation into a favorable one, or turn a favorable constellation into a favorable one, or a favorable into an unfavorable, etc.). Besides, Konrad did not have much time left, he is supposed to have said as long as two years ago, for one thing I shall not live much longer, and then I live basically in constant distress, and basically there is never enough time, and so forth. On top of all that it was quite clear to him that he was already an old man, an old man who had an old head on his shoulders. And here was another consideration: a work such as this might be rendered worthless by being written down too soon, even though it had been completely written down, it might turn out to be a wholly wasted effort; or else it might be useless, absolutely worthless, if written down too late. But there was no way of fixing the exact time for writing such a book, this precisely was what was so terrible about it, the unique, exact, correct moment had to present itself of its own accord. He could so easily destroy the labor of decades by choosing the wrong moment or even by misunderstanding the right moment. Or else: what if he had to break off writing the book in mid-career, stopped cold by the sudden terrifying thought that he would not be able to complete it? Another possibility: suppose the book is made worthless by being actually completed, in writing, just as worthless as it is now because it has not been written down? It could be ruined simply by being precipitately written, or by being written in too circumspect a way, written too late, whichever. Small wonder, then, that he had let every propitious moment come and pass him by, weakened further by each missed opportunity, so that he could foresee being altogether too weak to write the book down when the moment to do so actually came. He would rather not know how many extraordinary products of the human intellect had been lost by precipitousness, how many by procrastination, how many extraordinary lives had been destroyed by such precipitousness or procrastination in the mind. Of course it was known how many had failed through carelessness or inattention or because of overcautiousness or excessive attention. He, Konrad said, had invested everything he was and everything he had in his (unwritten) book. But to say so publicly, to make a public avowal that he had indeed invested his all in the book was more than he dared, more than he could permit himself to do. For one thing, he was a megalomaniac in the most fatal sense of the term, as his wife certainly never hesitated to inform him, actually her daily pointed remarks on the subject made him cruelly aware of the fact, as cruelly as only such a cripple of a woman could persist in her unsparing criticisms, Konrad is supposed to have said to Wieser, and yet, on the other hand, he had only been feeling his way for decades hampered by the enormous timidity and fearfulness inspired by his task and increased by facing up to it, creeping in terror from one possibility of getting hurt to the next. So that if he should actually say it, just once, that he had invested all he had in his work, in the book he had entirely in his head, no one would believe him, he could not hope to be taken seriously, he would simply be making a fool of himself once again. He had, in fact, said this very thing to his wife, day after day, namely, that he had invested all of himself in his book, which he had entirely in his head, as he took good care to emphasize every time, to which she responded day after day by calling him a fool every time, he was a fool, she said, and she was his victim. Well then: so she was the cripple who had become the fool's victim, you might say that one cripple had been victimized by another, one fool fooled by another, she was a cripple of a fool while he was a fool of a cripple and so forth. The opposition, the enemy, he is supposed to have said, is always bound to be in the majority. Enemies are all there is, he is supposed to have said, because even our friends are enemies, we delude ourselves into seeing a friend by putting a mask of friendship on an enemy's face to keep the enemy out of sight, we set up the stage and let the friend enter and sit down temporarily at center stage, because we happen to need to believe in his friendship, until the time comes when we drive him away, because we are suddenly able to recognize the friend as our enemy, as just another enemy among all the other enemies that populate our stage. More enemies disguised as friends keep emerging from backstage, Konrad is supposed to have said, from every side they keep coming, out of the deepest darkness, enemies as friends, friends as enemies, all enemies, in short, and we let them down ourselves in swarms from the flyloft. The loquacity of our enemies in the guise of friends (and vice versa!) populating our stage is only our infinitely cunning, snare-setting prompter all over the stage, a stage we designed ourselves with great skill in the service of our own self-deceiving hypocrisy. The curtain goes up, our enemies (as friends and vice versa) come on stage, said Konrad, until death drops the great iron curtain, instantly crushing most of the actors. It was his own fault, no doubt about it, that he had obeyed his parents in not taking up a regular course of studies at a university, not going through with it, not completing it, as he should have, because by doing so he made himself a lifelong outsider as a scientist, though on the one hand he enjoyed the advantage of pursuing his work quite independently, but on the other hand there was the disadvantage of being completely cast upon his own resources, in utter isolation, so that he could progress only by making the most arduous efforts, having to supply the missing foundation of a so-called regular course of studies by susbtituting for it as a foundation the most extreme personal effort in the area of his unquestionably greatest talent, his gift for the natural sciences, it certainly had not been easy, but luckily for him he had never lost courage or the sense of having to take a risk where his work, that is, where natural science and therefore his work was concerned, on the contrary, the more the apparently insurmountable difficulties had increased day by day and from one so-called scientific moment to the next, he felt challenged to surmount them, and it was precisely his greatest difficulties which had spurred him on to surmount his greatest obstacles, gradually, so that he had ended up with good data and a good conscience, well able to devote himself, or as he called it, to give himself up to working on his book, which he had entitled beforehand *The Sense of Hearing*. In accordance with family tradition Konrad's parents forced him to concentrate, not on his graduate studies, a type of endeavor held in the lowest possible esteem in his parents' world, but rather and exclusively upon the enormously extensive, widely ramifying landed properties that, one had to admit in retrospect, had given life to the families who had held it for all those centuries with the marvelous economic productiveness of its natural beauties, as Konrad phrased it, though to force Konrad in this direction merely revealed the dullness of those whom a good or evil fortune has made into rich proprietors, a dullness especially manifest, as a quite deadly hereditary trait, in his own immediate family. Instead of letting him go where he wanted to go, to a university, they had fetched him home from boarding school and tried to talk him out of following his so-called megalomaniac head and into seeing instead, as they saw, the greatest natural form of happiness in not learning anything at all, and forced him instead to turn his entire attention exclusively to that in which they saw fulfillment for themselves, and therefore dared to see fulfillment for him as well, namely, to real estate and buildings, to sawmills, storage cellars, lime works, rental properties, fisheries, to wood and stone and to the lower and the higher kinds of cattle. But Konrad's total lack of interest in his family property, in property as such, had manifested itself unmistakably in his youth, it was there for anyone to see, no one in his immediate circle could have been blind to his native and ever increasing indifference to property, which in fact had resulted in the Konrads' having lost virtually everything they had ever owned (as Konrad said a year ago). His parents knew that he was interested only in his scientific studies, and not at all in their property, and with what enthusiasm he regarded the study of natural science, which they had not permitted him to pursue, how passionately he could have devoted himself to so pure a disinterested pursuit of scientific learning, had they only permitted it, but they in turn held such pursuits in the deepest contempt, they loathed his intellectual aspirations with all the omnipotence of their traditions, and they would in the end have crushed him totally with the weight of their centuries on the property where they forced him to stay, had they not suddenly died, relatively young in years, Konrad said, one right after the other. After their death it was too late for him to take up an academic course of study, but he felt free and able to develop freely and had made up for lost time in an amazingly short span of years. Despite everything that had stood in his way, in fact, Konrad had in a relatively few years reached the point where he had his book all complete in his head, he is supposed to have told Wieser, regardless of all the obstacles put in his way, and in defiance of the most hateful kind of obstacles, he had been able to generate his book unaided in the back of his head, as it were. With him it was always the same sequence, Konrad said to Wieser, hearing came first, then he saw, then he could begin to think, no matter what was involved. He had to begin by hearing, which enabled him to see, which in turn enabled him to think. He had tried to make this characteristic clearer to his wife day

after day, but in vain. But he did think every day that it was
a good thing he had started so early in the day on the Urbanchich exercises, in the early twilight before dawn, and in fact
often even before the twilight, it was for both of them the
time of greatest receptivity and best judgment, two faculties
that tended to wane toward noon, to experience a certain
resurgence after the midday meal, reaching a high point
around five o'clock in the afternoon, and then they slowly
declined, though registering a sporadic flicker of life between
about eight and nine in the evening, until complete exhaustion set in by about midnight. He would tell his wife over
and over again that a scientist had to arm himself for such
a task as his book with the greatest secrecy but also with the
utmost ruthlessness, of course she listened to him, but on this
point in particular she resisted him with all her might.
Apart from this one point he had learned to eschew all statements of principle on the book decades ago, for as long as
the book was still suspended in air, as he is supposed to have
expressed it, as long as he had not yet brought the book into
safe harbor by writing it down. To Wieser, Konrad is also
supposed to have said that he did his best, pacing the floor
in his room for hours. But instead of thinking about my
book, and how to write it, as I go pacing the floor, I fall to
counting my footsteps instead until I am about to go mad.
Instead of thinking about my book, the most important thing
of all, I keep digressing to irrelevancies. Several times in the
course of this floor-pacing the notion had popped into his
head to go down and chop wood with Hoeller; pacing the
floor, he is supposed to have told Wieser, I think about going
down to Hoeller and chopping wood with Hoeller for a
whole hour until I realize that it makes no sense to go down

and chop wood with Hoeller, but still I keep casting about for some distraction from my work instead of doing my utmost to concentrate on the book as I should. You can't concentrate on the main thing while at the same time digressing to irrelevancies without doing damage, the greatest possible damage! to the main thing, Konrad is supposed to have exclaimed in conversation with Wieser. But even though he knew this, he nevertheless kept on incessantly thinking about his book and simultaneously about something completely irrelevant, such as thinking at noon about what they would both have for supper, thinking in the evening about what they would have for breakfast, thinking at breakfast about what to have for lunch, what to order Hoeller to pick up at the tavern, etc. Wieser says that Konrad told him how, suddenly, in the midst of thinking about his book, he would suddenly think about his Paris apartment, his apartment in Mannheim, their house in Bolzano, any number of things quite unrelated to the book, he would take a peek, as it were, into his apartment in Paris at a time when he should be concentrating one hundred percent on his book, Konrad is supposed to have told Wieser; all sorts of unrelated images would intrude upon the image I have of my book, pop into it and destroy it for me, shatter the clear image I have of my book into thousands upon thousands of unrelated images, imaginary human faces, etc. etc. There was always something to prevent him from writing his book, in Paris and London it was the huge extent of the city, in Berlin, it was the superficiality, in Vienna it was the feeblemindedness of the people, in Munich, the foehn blowing down from the Alps, no matter what it was, the mountains, the sea, the spring, the summer, the coldest of winters, the rainiest of all summers, then again family quarrels, the catastrophic nature of politics, or finally and always his own wife, there was always something that made it impossible for him to write. They had moved to so many places, entirely for the sake of the as yet unwritten book, and they had left so many places, precipitately, for the sake of the unwritten book, they had left Paris post-haste, London post-haste, Mannheim post-haste, Vienna post-haste, not knowing in the morning that by that evening they would have their trunks packed and broken off all their ties to the city in which they had been living for weeks, for months, usually in the belief that it was to be for always, and yet by that evening they would have found a distant city to move to for life, only to go through the same process of settling down for good only to suddenly pack up and leave, Konrad actually said: leave head over heels, Wieser recalls. For instance, Wieser says, Konrad told him that from the moment Hoeller's nephew, that shady character, a criminal through and through, had moved in with Hoeller at the annex, Konrad had been able to think of nothing else but this nephew for weeks, even though he should have been concentrating one hundred percent on his book, while incessantly pacing the floor in his room and then in his wife's room, criss-crossing the room in every direction, thinking hard about the book, which he simply had to start writing, but at the same time thinking with the greatest intensity about Hoeller's nephew, who had appeared so abruptly out of the dark and who struck Konrad as a weird criminal type, fascinated by the question of what this nephew of Hoeller's meant by living in the annex, what he wanted there, and meanwhile Konrad's book suffered from neglect, suffered irreparably from the withdrawal of Konrad's attention. Over and over Konrad asked himself: How old is Hoeller's nephew, anyway? meanwhile neglecting the work on his book, and: What kind of clothes is he wearing? and: What color is his hair, anyway? and: Isn't the fellow rather weird? and: He has long legs and a powerful torso and gigantic hands, the largest hands I've ever seen, he kept thinking, meanwhile neglecting his book. On one occasion Konrad is supposed to have confided the following thoughts to Wieser: Pacing the floor in my room, I keep thinking that Hoeller's nephew must be planning to do me in because he thinks that I have money, he doesn't know that I have no money at all, he naturally believes that I am well off, there is a type of habitual criminal, after all, Konrad thought while pacing the floor, that isn't sick at all but is simply a malignant character, and one must be on one's guard against them. Konrad heard the two men laughing together, all the way from the annex, he kept hearing Hoeller and his nephew laughing, and he naturally asked himself: What is the meaning of this laughter? Isn't there something weird about it? It was possible that the two of them were conspiring against him, Konrad thought, but he promptly shook off any such ideas as absurd and managed to suppress them; for days he was troubled by the thought that he was sabotaging his book by letting his mind dwell on Hoeller's nephew and Hoeller himself, on their relationship to each other, or, if not sabotaging his book exactly, he was certainly lessening any chance of writing his book. He also knew that it was morbid to brood about not being able to write his book, about never getting it written at all, it was morbid to the point of becoming a disease, Konrad is supposed to have told Wieser. Nevertheless he must have heard aright, because when he was standing outside the annex at one A.M. (!) he heard the two of them, Hoeller and his nephew, laughing again inside the annex, even though it was pitch dark inside, and yet I hear the two of them laughing, how strange, Konrad is supposed to have said. It wasn't loud laughter, exactly, nor was it suppressed laughter, either, it was just a weird kind of laughter. Thinking that the two of them, Hoeller and his nephew, were laughing in the middle of the night inside the darkness of that annex, Konrad had felt so irritated the rest of the night that he simply could not get back to sleep at all, Konrad is supposed to have said, instead he had to get out of bed and pace the floor, constantly thinking about those two in the annex, occasionally looking out of the window in the direction of the annex to see if the lights were back on, by any chance, but he saw no light, yet the two of them did laugh together, or could he possibly have been mistaken? and as he kept asking himself this question it was growing light outside. Lately I wear myself out brooding over the most absurd notions, all of them pretexts for not writing, for not facing the fact that I am simply unable to write my book, Konrad is supposed to have told Wieser, if only I could write, if I could have written my book, everything would be different, I'd be feeling all relieved inside, meaning that I could be indifference personified, I could let myself be old and indifferent, cool, what could be more desirable? Konrad is supposed to have said to Wieser. But the last time he spoke to Wieser, Konrad is supposed to have confided the following to him: At about half past two in the morning he had gone down once more to the annex, absent-mindedly slipping into a jacket too light for the season, bareheaded, in his bedroom slippers, imagine! and stationed himself under the an-

nex windows to eavesdrop. At first he heard nothing and he
was freezing, but the excitement of eavesdropping saved
him from catching cold, he thought, because a body fully
tensed up in an act of supreme attention would not take a
chill, and Konrad's head and body had been tensed to their
utmost in the act of eavesdropping, pressing himself to the
wall of the annex under the windows; it was not curiosity
that drove him back to the annex to eavesdrop, it was fear,
real fear, and an enormous, soothing mistrustfulness toward
this nephew of Hoeller's who was suddenly playing so dominant a role in the lime works area, this stranger who had
slipped into the annex behind Konrad's back, probably seek-
ing a refuge from the long arm of the law, Konrad would
of course be the first to grant a refuge to any fugitive from
the law, Konrad is supposed to have said to Wieser, it went
without saying that he would have protected, hidden, rescued
from the fangs of the law, any man threatened by the law,
his sympathies were entirely on the side of all fugitives from
the law, the law pursued chiefly the innocent, the most innocent, Konrad is supposed to have said, the law persecuted the
poorest of the poor, anyone who was being hunted down by
the police had to be given shelter in every way, and when
Konrad said in every way he meant exactly that, he meant
by every available means, because he was acquainted with
the law's way with people, he had himself been raped by the
law a number of times, he is supposed to have said, the law
raped the individual and therefore the individual had to be
protected from the law; however, Hoeller's nephew fright-
ened him, and anyway Konrad had a feeling that Hoeller's
nephew was by no means helpless and entitled to protection,
but that he was a public menace, not by nature or anything

he couldn't help but out of deliberate viciousness; anyway,
to get back to his story, Konrad suddenly heard the two of
them laughing again, Hoeller and his nephew were in there
laughing, Konrad could hear them even through the double
storm windows, they must have been sitting on the corner
bench in the kitchen, Konrad is supposed to have told Wieser,
sitting there in the pitch dark and apparently talking about
something to do with him, Konrad, one thing in particular,
always the same thing, and from time to time they would
laugh about it; what led Konrad to the conclusion and then
to the conviction that they were talking about him was the
nature of their conversation, though he admitted that he could
not understand a single word they said, despite the fact that
he could hear everything, but it did seem to him that he
heard them pronouncing the name *Konrad* several times, alternately *Konrad* and the *Konrad woman* was what he heard,
he thought, so that evidently the subject of their conversation
was himself and his wife, as he soon clearly understood;
other words he thought he distinguished were *lime works,
annex,* and finally the word *cash box,* after which the two
of them laughed again, it was three o'clock by this time, and
the two of them had suddenly risen, Konrad heard them
walking from the kitchen to the entry which meant, Konrad
thought, that they were about to come out of the annex, so
he made tracks away from there, he actually ran back to the
lime works and as quickly as he could up to his room, not
without first shooting all the bolts and locking all the locks,
every last one. Once in his room, still breathless from running, he is supposed to have listened intently, for any sounds
from Hoeller and his nephew, but he didn't hear a thing,
looking out of the window he could see nothing but the

darkness so that by the time Konrad was in bed at last he is supposed to have asked himself whether his weird experience, or what seemed to be a weird experience that he had just barely survived, was in fact a real experience, because it was after all possible that I only imagined all that I believed I saw and heard while pressed against the annex wall, eavesdropping; thinking that he might merely have imagined the whole thing, Konrad finally fell asleep, and when he woke up early that morning his first thought was that Hoeller and his nephew might have been fast asleep all night long, after going to bed as early as six or seven in the evening, and that he merely imagined all the weird things he remembered, he said. He told Wieser that he told his wife the whole story of his nighttime experience in every minute detail, and she commented that he was clearly the victim of overwork, that he had so drained himself of energy by overdoing the Urbanchich exercises that experiences such as he had just recounted from the night before could be the natural result of his weakened condition, as long as he understood that these were imaginary experiences, not realities, the Konrad woman is supposed to have said to her husband; you are suffering from delusions, she said, nothing more than delusions. Instead of sticking to his writing, to writing his book, he let his mind wander off in every conceivable direction, distracting himself in ways that bordered on the absurd, such as for instance the idea of walking out of the lime works to chop wood with Hoeller, going into the timber forest with Hoeller, lumbering, carpentry at the annex, tying brooms, anything. Every second day, in fact, Konrad said to Wieser, he would actually dress warmly, in work clothes, as Hoeller recalls, and leave the lime works wearing ankle warmers, a

woolen cap, and his long leather pants, of course, planning
to join the loggers in the forest, walking briskly away from
the house but after passing the thicket he turned right back,
recognizing the absurdity of what he was doing and saying
to himself: I've got to get back to my work, my book, back
to my desk, back to making sense. But no sooner had he
started back to doing the sensible thing, i.e., back to his
work, to his desk, to the stack of papers piled on his desk in
preparation for writing, he began to be plagued by doubts
whether he was doing the right thing after all in not going
to join the loggers in the forest, in not doing something irra-
tional, in fact, instead of making an effort for the hundredth
or thousandth time to tackle the work on his desk, the same
doomed effort, his doubts becoming stronger as he reentered
the lime works and back in his room the closer he approached
his desk where his work awaited him, the less he felt like
writing; however, at this point he dressed himself properly
for the day ahead indoors; then he lay down on his bed to
brood, trying not to despair but not succeeding, so he got
up again, paced the floor, and waited for his wife to ring.
When she rings I shall go to her room, and she will ask me
if I have made any progress with my writing, and I shall
say: No, as I always do, simply by not answering the question, Konrad is supposed to have said to Wieser, remarking
that the proverbial sentence: *No answer is also an answer,*
certainly applied to what went on between the two of them
day after day to an extraordinary degree. All the proverbial
truths, in fact, he said to Wieser, had come to roost for him
and his wife in the lime works, as a clear if heartbreaking
expression of their daily truth, reality, and hardship. Lately
he tended to say to his wife, again and again: I'm going to

the woods, to join the woodcutters, I'm going with Hoeller
to the woods, to do some logging. He once did go daily to
the lumbermen in the woods, but he had not done this for
years now. He never realized until just a while ago that he
had long ceased to take his walks of inspection into the forest.
I am not going to the sawmill any more, I am not going to
the tavern any more, I won't go to see Fro, I won't go to see
Wieser any more, I won't go again to see the works inspector,
the forestry commissioner, he is supposed to have said to his
wife over and over and in the way he merely listed all the
people and things he would no longer see or attend to, there
was so much bitter reproach against his wife that he could
spare himself reproaching her with all the other things he
might mention. The book and you are killing me between
you, he is supposed to have said to her repeatedly toward the
end. He often wondered, for instance, whether it might not
help if he attended to his lapsed correspondence, even though
it was not really the way out of his more and more frightening
predicament, it was years since he had written a letter or a
card to anyone, there was a huge pile of unanswered correspondence from every corner of the world on top of the
bureau in his room, the drawers too were stuffed full of unanswered letters, so many people had written to him from
time to time, with a persistence impossible to understand because, surely, a man who did not answer his mail was clearly
serving notice that he had no desire to stay in touch with the
correspondent, and Konrad had long since ceased to answer
hundreds of thousands of letters and cards, but his correspondents would not leave him in peace, Konrad is supposed to
have told Wieser, they kept on writing, it was only after years
of not hearing from him in reply that these innumerable

correspondents, largely people I detest from the bottom of my heart, Konrad is supposed to have said, finally desisted from writing to him; to be perfectly frank, he is supposed to have said, I haven't been receiving any mail for years now, my wife still gets mail, the most insignificant kind of mail you can imagine, embarrassing letters from former servants, for instance, who write partly out of loyalty, partly because they hope to be remembered in her will, but also because it is customary, has been customary for centuries, they write to recall themselves to her memory, possibly one or another even writes to her out of pity, Konrad is alleged to have told Wieser, my wife differs from me, I despise being pitied, I hate it in fact, while she accepts pity as a kind of medicine, even in its lowest form, the rudimentary greeting on a post-card, despite his having tried for years to dissuade her from answering all these letters and cards, it was far too much trouble for her considering the strain she was undergoing for the book's sake, but she insisted on answering all her mail, meaning that she made him answer it for her, because as you know, my dear Wieser, my wife is in no shape to write letters or postcards, in the first place she can't see, and she can't hold a pen or pencil steadily enough to write with it, just taking one in hand makes her extremely jittery, her entire body begins to tremble with resistance against the act of writing, so that he had to answer all her mail in her name, all she did was sign the letters, he had to mail the letters and the cards too, which meant taking them to the post office, or at least making sure that Hoeller took them to the village, not to mention the fact that these mailings cost a lot of money, when they certainly had no money to waste on such nonsense as letters and cards addressed to a lot of totally useless people whom he estimated to number in their hundreds still, and yet, Konrad is supposed to have said to Wieser, from time to time I wonder whether I myself shouldn't go back to answering all the unanswered letters and cards on my bureau, give a sign of life to one or another of my correspondents, some of whom must have been thinking that I died years ago, because if a man like myself isn't heard from for any length of time and doesn't reply to his mail, to two or three letters in a row, people are likely to assume that he is dead, though if I died they would probably hear about it, so from time to time it occurs to me that it might be advisable, though I can't say why, to sit down and answer all those letters and cards, get back in touch with all those people from whom he hadn't heard a thing, actually, in a long time, because of his own failure to continue the correspondence, to find out what had happened to all of them, at least; a sudden curiosity would seize him like a fever and he would actually sit down at his desk to reopen his correspondence with all the people who must be feeling rebuffed by him because he had dropped the correspondence without giving any reason, but even in the act of arranging his stationery and filling his pen with ink he would suddenly think how idiotic of him to write letters all of a sudden when he could use the time and the same effort to write his book, the time he would be wasting trying to think up answers that were no longer awaited, to letters from forgotten correspondents, could be put to so much better use in writing his book, and so he would give up the idea of reviving a correspondence interrupted now for three or four years, and he would remove the stationery from his desk and bring back the bond paper for his manuscript and arrange it in front of him on the desk. But as soon as he had the stack of paper for the manuscript back in place, i.e., when he had restored the ideal conditions for working on the book, he became incapable of setting to work writing it, he would sit there for a time, a long time, staring at the stack of fresh paper, until it was clear to him that, once more, he could not begin to write, whereupon he would move the stationery back in place on the desk, and so it went for hours, the stationery alternating with the manuscript paper in front of him on his desk, the business of manuscript paper forward, manuscript paper back, stationery forward, stationery back, was enough in itself to make writing impossible, whether to write the manuscript or to reopen the correspondence, so he did neither, but instead took to pacing the floor of his room every which way, thinking alternately about the book and the interrupted correspondence, thinking what an immense number of letters I would have to write, and thinking alternately, how immensely difficult it was to start writing the book, and then he would think: I shan't write any letters, or, I won't write the book, I shall write neither the letters nor the book, and he would think: in every one of these letters I would have to start by thanking them, always the same formula of thanks, one letter like the other and basically every one of these letters is nothing more than a demand, demands for money or other demands, vulgar demands, outrageous demands, on the one hand these people always want money, on the other hand they want affection, recommendations, he thought, so he really couldn't answer all these letters, since he had neither money nor any affection to give, in fact he couldn't care less about these people. All of these letter and card writers were angling for some advantage, to get something or other out of him. Basically there's something underhanded about all

of them, all these letters and cards without exception are
dictated by some veiled or hidden or even shamelessly un-
disguised infamous motive. To the attic with the whole pile!
he would think, off to the attic with them at once! and instantly begin to make a single pile of all those letters and
cards, hundreds of thousands of them, a man could be suffocated by the mere smell of so many hundreds of thousands
of letters in one heap, Konrad is supposed to have said to
Wieser; while embarked on this he realized of course that he
was doing something to distract himself from writing the
book, something new, because piling the letters in one heap
and then carrying them gradually up to the attic was a brand
new thing to do, compared with the two, three dozen kinds
of things he had done for years, over and over, to distract himself from writing the book, things like sweeping up, wiping
up, pulling nails from the walls, shining shoes, washing socks,
etc., chores that had begun long since to nauseate him, all of
his disgusting maneuverings to distract himself from what he
should be doing nauseated him, so he grabbed an armful of
letters, Wieser says, and dragged it up to the attic, and invariably, as always, banged his head against the great wooden
beam over the door to the attic, running his head against it
with such force, Konrad is supposed to have told Wieser, that
I thought I had cracked my skull, but actually the pain let up
fairly soon and the wound, though bleeding profusely, was
quite superficial; so he went on dragging armfuls of letters
and cards up to the attic, thinking all the while: this whole
correspondence has been a big mistake, all correspondence is
a mistake! At the end, after the last of the letters and cards
had been dragged up to the attic, he collapsed with exhaustion, on the bed in his room, naturally too weak by this time,

supposedly, to give the least thought to his book, in a state of exhaustion too profound even for him to feel the usual irritation, the profound irritation he has felt for years, at the fact that everything on his desk is now arranged perfectly so that he could begin at once to write his book, as he explained to Wieser: precisely because I can see clearly that I can begin to write at any moment, that everything is arranged and in perfect order for starting to write, everything is pointing toward this moment of readiness to write, the very awareness that everything is pushing me in that direction naturally makes it impossible for me to start writing. Every time it occurs to him that the very sight of his desk with everything on it prepared and ready, so that he can begin to write his book, is just what makes it impossible for him to begin writing, the thought that this is so becomes unbearable, so he gets up and drinks a glass of water. He immediately follows this up with a second glass of water swallowed in one long gulp, though in the midst of this gulp he is already thinking whether he isn't going to catch a terrible cold from drinking the ice-cold water down so fast, because it's a fact that drinking a glass of icy water too fast one is bound to catch cold, which he always lived in fear of doing, but, on the other hand he had never actually caught cold that way. Just one week before he shot his wife, however, he did say that it suddenly came to him that he had actually caught cold by drinking down a glass of cold water too quickly. According to Wieser: Konrad suddenly found himself unable to speak, he tried to speak but couldn't. To calm himself down Konrad left the kitchen where he had just taken a quick drink of water and went back to his own room where he lay down, but quickly got up again, in constant terror that this as he hoped only momentary loss of his voice might possibly incapacitate him for carrying on with the Urbanchich method and put a sudden stop to his further experimental studies, causing him to lose his grip not only on the Urbanchich method but on his book itself. He made several attempts to speak, but in vain. You can imagine my wife's pretended horror, her open relief, her secret joy at my sudden speechlessness, Konrad is supposed to have told Wieser, when I confronted her with the fact that I had lost my voice. But just as suddenly as his voice had disappeared, it came back and he could talk again; I remember exactly how it happened, Konrad said to Wieser, all at once I said *naturally,* I heard myself saying the word *naturally,* and it occurred to me that my sudden loss of voice probably was linked in some way to my eye trouble, I remember thinking that now I shall be losing my voice alternately with losing my eyesight, from this day on the fading of my voice will alternate with the fading of my vision. Yet, although he believed that now he could speak again, meaning that he could speak again quite normally, he ought to hasten upstairs to continue the experimental work using the Urbanchich method, with his wife, he nevertheless did not leap up in his usual impulsive way but stayed abed, Wieser says, thinking, as he told Wieser: now the both of us are badly in need of help, to such a degree that help becomes almost impossible to give. From here on out nothing but inadequacy and infirmity was in the cards for them both. His wife deserved a better fate than a man like himself, Konrad thought, as he said to Wieser, not me, not me, not me, he said to himself over and over again. And yet a woman as greatly in need of help as his wife, more dependent on help than anyone, and who deserved to have found the most helpful man in the world, had nevertheless turned herself over unconditionally to Konrad, because by the time they married she had long since been sick and crippled, Konrad told Wieser, her disease began to manifest itself years before they married, it had in fact broken out suddenly with all its terrible ramifications before the actual marriage ceremony took place; Konrad had in fact married her knowing full well that she was already gravely diseased and crippled, he actually knew then, he said to Wieser, that her crippling disease was incurable. Konrad did not really understand why he had chosen to marry a sick, crippled woman, whose crippling disease would in all probability, as he insists he knew perfectly well at the time, worsen from year to year; actually, he married her precisely because of her crippling disease which would make her completely dependent on him, that was it, he said to himself: I am marrying a woman who will be totally dependent on me, a woman who needs me, needs me absolutely, he reflected at the time, a woman who cannot exist without me, or at least thinks she cannot exist without me, but who in turn will be available to me unconditionally for my purposes, i.e., for my scientific research, a woman I can use in any way I need to use her, a woman I shall even be free to abuse, misuse, if necessary, as Konrad explained to Wieser, if the exigencies of my scientific circumstances demand it. But to get back to his room where Konrad was gradually getting used to the idea, and resigned to the fact of his recurrent eye trouble, as previously mentioned, as well as to his having to suffer a temporary loss of his voice from time to time, because it was becoming clear to him as he lay on his bed thinking about it that the momentary loss of his voice had not been caused by his rapid drinking down of that glass of icy water, as he had at first believed though not for long and only because the cold water seemed the most obvious immediate cause of his sudden mutism, but that actually the sudden loss of his voice was as mysterious as his eye trouble, both were equally inexplicable organic weaknesses arising from within, from inside his head, that is, in which, as he is supposed to have said to Wieser, quite a few other infirmities, even more disastrous ones than the two under consideration, were at this moment busily hatching out, no doubt about it: in no time at all his head was certain to breed him a lot of organic infirmities, cessations of organic functions, which were quite likely, in the circumstances, to have lethal effects quite soon. Konrad could not believe in his chances of living more than a couple of years more, he is supposed to have said just eight days before he shot his wife dead. Well, on the day he completely lost his voice for the first time he lay on his bed for hours, he is supposed to have said, occasionally wondering why she (his wife) didn't ring for him, what could be the reason she did not ring? but actually he was only thinking how not to tell her that his temporary loss of vision was not all, that he would be suffering from a recurrent loss of voice as well, because he did not want to tell her about his new trouble, not out of consideration for her feelings, but in order to avoid giving her a pretext for urging him to drop the Urbanchich exercises and generally weakening his position in the area of the work to be done. So-called spasms, he is supposed to have said to Wieser, meaning that he alternately could not see or speak, occasionally both vision and voice might fail him simultaneously, for a few moments, and of course he might find himself unable to see or speak for lengthy periods of time, or unable either to see or speak for lengthy stretches, but what matters the most, he said, is that I can hear, after all, and

I do hear extraordinarily well, although I must say that I would not be surprised to find myself suddenly also unable to hear, but it was precisely his uninterrupted work with the Urbanchich method, his incessant experimentation with everything related to the hearing that would prevent any sudden weakening or any sudden loss of hearing, though on the other hand, he is supposed to have said to Wieser, it was of course possible that it was just such an incessant application of the Urbanchich method, incessant experimentation with the hearing that might in fact cause a sudden failure of hearing, a sudden cessation of the hearing function, naturally a man could cause his hearing to cease by making inordinate demands on it; in fact, Wieser says he wonders whether Konrad might not have actually suffered a hearing failure the night he did his wife in; that Konrad suffered a lessening of his auditory capacity for the first time that particular night was a genuine possibility, and the more he thought about it the more firmly Wieser believed that Konrad must have suffered a seizure of auditory failure on the night of the murder. To Fro, whom I finally managed to sell his policy, Konrad is supposed to have said that his, Konrad's, great mistake was to have kept on waiting for an even more favorable moment, the most favorable moment possible to serve as a point of departure for writing his book, because he had always clung to the belief that the ideal, even the most ideal constellation of circumstances for enabling him to write his book was just around the corner, but in waiting for this moment he had lost more and more time or, as Konrad expressed it, the most valuable time, so that at last he was forced to admit to himself that he had now reached the end of his forces (!), that for two or even three decades he had waited in vain for the ideal

moment in which to begin writing his book, and just before
the disaster (this is what Fro calls the murder of Mrs. Konrad by her husband) Konrad is supposed to have said to Fro
that he realized there was no such thing as an ideal, not to
mention a most ideal moment in which to write such a work
as his, because there simply could be no such ideal moment,
or most ideal moment, or point of time whatever for any
undertaking or cause of any kind. Like thousands of others
before him, Konrad said, he too had fallen victim to a mad
dream of one day suddenly bringing his great labor to fruition
by writing it all down in one consistent outpouring, all trig-
gered by the optimal point in time, the unique moment for
perfect concentration on writing it. And now he would never
be able to write it, neither in the prison at Stein nor in the
mental institution at Niedernhardt; Konrad's book, like Konrad himself, was a lost cause (Wieser), an immense life work,
as one must assume (says Fro, doing a sudden complete
about-face) totally wiped out. Here was a failure, owing to a
chronic deferment, of the realization of a concept that was
basically all there, wholly and flawlessly extant in his (Konrad's) head, as the book was, a perfect, fantastic, scientific
work extant in his brain though unrealized either for lack of
courage, of the necessary decisiveness, and finally the failure
of intellectual audacity; it was certainly most depressing to
think that such a work had remained unrealized on paper
where it would have been of great benefit to others, to the
world of science, to all posterity. Konrad had certainly not
been lacking in the necessary ruthlessness, even or perhaps
especially toward himself, for the execution of his tremendous
task, during those decades that had dragged on at such humiliating length, as he is supposed to have phrased it himself,

though on the other hand they had passed at a terrifying clip, but he had lacked what was perhaps the most important quality of all: fearlessness in the face of realization, of concretization, fearlessness, simply, when it came to turning his head over, suddenly, from one moment to the next, ruthlessly flipping it over to drop everything inside his head onto the paper, all in one motion.

GARGOYLES

One morning a doctor and his son set out on daily rounds through the grim, mountainous Austrian countryside. They observe the colorful characters they encounter—from an innkeeper whose wife has been murdered to a crippled musical prodigy kept in a cage—coping with physical misery, madness, and the brutality of the austere landscape. The parade of human grotesques culminates in a hundred-page monologue, a relentlessly flowing cascade of words that is classic Bernhard.

Fiction/Literature/978-1-4000-7755-7

THE LOSER

The Loser centers on a fictional relationship between piano virtuoso Glenn Gould and two of his fellow students who feel compelled to renounce their musical ambitions in the face of Gould's incomparable genius. One commits suicide, while the other—the obsessive, witty, and self-mocking narrator—has retreated into obscurity. Written in one remarkable unbroken paragraph, *The Loser* is a brilliant meditation on success, failure, genius, and fame.

Fiction/Literature/978-1-4000-7754-0

FROST

Visceral, raw, singular, and unforgettable, *Frost* is the story of a friendship between a young man beginning his medical career and a painter in his final days. A young man has accepted an unusual assignment, to travel to a miserable mining town in the middle of nowhere in order to clinically—and secretly—observe and report on his mentor's reclusive brother, the painter Strauch. Carefully disguising himself, he befriends the aging artist and attempts to carry out his mission, only to find himself caught up in his subject's madness.

Fiction/Literature/978-1-4000-3351-5

WITTGENSTEIN'S NEPHEW

It is 1967. In separate wings of a Viennese hospital, two men lie bedridden. The narrator, named Thomas Bernhard, is stricken with a lung ailment; his friend Paul, nephew of the celebrated philosopher Ludwig Wittgenstein, is suffering from one of his periodic bouts of madness. As their once-casual friendship quickens, these two eccentric men begin to discover in each other a possible antidote to their feelings of hopelessness and mortality—a spiritual symmetry forged by their shared passion for music, strange sense of humor, disgust for bourgeois Vienna, and great fear in the face of death. Part memoir, part fiction, *Wittgenstein's Nephew* is both a meditation on the artist's struggle to maintain a solid foothold in a world gone incomprehensibly askew, and a stunning—if not haunting—eulogy to real-life friendship.

Fiction/Literature/978-1-4000-7756-4

CORRECTION

The scientist Roithamer has dedicated the last six years of his life to "the Cone," an edifice of mathematically exact construction that he has erected in the center of his family's estate in honor of his beloved sister. Not long after its completion, he takes his own life. As an unnamed friend pieces together the puzzle of his breakdown, what emerges is the story of a genius ceaselessly compelled to correct and refine his perceptions until the only logical conclusion is the negation of his own soul. Considered by many critics to be Bernhard's masterpiece, *Correction* is a cunningly crafted meditation on the tension between the desire for perfection and the knowledge that it is unattainable.

Fiction/Literature/978-1-4000-7760-1

VINTAGE INTERNATIONAL
Available at your local bookstore, or visit
www.randomhouse.com

Meet with Interesting People
Enjoy Stimulating Conversation
Discover Wonderful Books

Visit ReadingGroupCenter.com where you'll find great reading choices—award winners, bestsellers, beloved classics, and many more—and extensive resources for reading groups such as:

Author Chats
Exciting contests offer reading groups the chance to win one-on-one phone conversations with Vintage and Anchor Books authors.

Extensive Discussion Guides
Guides for over 450 titles as well as non–title specific discussion questions by category for fiction, nonfiction, memoir, poetry, and mystery.

Personal Advice and Ideas
Reading groups nationwide share ideas, suggestions, helpful tips, and anecdotal information. Participate in the discussion and share your group's experiences.

Behind the Book Features
Specially designed pages which can include photographs, videos, original essays, notes from the author and editor, and book-related information.

Reading Planner
Plan ahead by browsing upcoming titles, finding author event schedules, and more.

Special for Spanish-language reading groups
www.grupodelectura.com
A dedicated Spanish-language content area complete with recommended titles from Vintage Español.

A selection of some favorite reading group titles from our list

Atonement by Ian McEwan

Balzac and the Little Chinese Seamstress by Dai Sijie

The Blind Assassin by Margaret Atwood

The Devil in the White City by Erik Larson

Empire Falls by Richard Russo

The English Patient by Michael Ondaatje

A Heartbreaking Work of Staggering Genius by Dave Eggers

The House of Sand and Fog by Andre Dubus III

A Lesson Before Dying by Ernest J. Gaines

Lolita by Vladimir Nabokov

Memoirs of a Geisha by Arthur Golden

Midnight in the Garden of Good and Evil by John Berendt

Midwives by Chris Bohjalian

Push by Sapphire

The Reader by Bernhard Schlink

Snow by Orhan Pamuk

An Unquiet Mind by Kay Redfield Jamison

Waiting by Ha Jin

A Year in Provence by Peter Mayle

Printed in the United States
by Baker & Taylor Publisher Services